BREEDA LOONEY
STEPS FORTH

BREEDA LOONEY STEPS FORTH

Oliver Sands

DEGREVILO PUBLISHING

Cataloguing in Publication details are available from the National Library of Australia www.trove.nla.gov.au

Creator: Sands, Oliver
Title: Breeda Looney Steps Forth / Oliver Sands

ISBN: 978-0-6487448-1-8 (paperback)
ISBN: 978-0-6487448-0-1 (ebook)

Editing: Bernadette Kearns
Cover design: Jack Smyth

Set in Times New Roman 12 pt

Disclaimer: This is a work of fiction. The characters contained within its pages are wholly imaginary. Any resemblance to actual persons, living or dead, is entirely coincidental. The village of Carrickross and the town of Dunry, although both loosely based on real places, have been re-imagined to suit the convenience of the story. The opinions expressed are those of the characters and should not be confused with the author's own.

For more information on the author and his books visit
www.OliverSandsAuthor.com

For Ged

CHAPTER 1

The acidic stench of cow dung coaxed Breeda Looney back to her senses. She cracked open her eyes to find her fingers splayed against the tarmac and the contents of her handbag spewed around her on the sunlit road. Her dry-cleaned red dress – ready for this evening – lay crumpled in a heap on the ground beside her. Breeda shook her head, but a fog clung on: the blackness was paying her a visit. A low groan left her lips. It was the afternoon of her thirty-seventh birthday and Breeda was on her hands and knees in the middle of the street. She just hoped to God that Aunt Nora wasn't witnessing everything with a silent scowl from the pavement.

The blackness had been visiting Breeda more often since her Mam died last month. In the past weeks Breeda had found herself slumped at the kitchen table, minutes gone and tea cold, or on the hallway floor, the print of rug on her cheek. Until now there'd always been some warning sign, a rising din of white noise in her addled brain. But today had been different. Today it had sideswiped her – and it had bloody well done so in the middle of Main Street.

Ignoring the sting of gravel in her palms, Breeda turned her head gingerly towards the persistent chugging noise to her right. An ancient Massey Ferguson sat inches from her body, its thick tyres caked in a mixture of manure and straw. From a high perch above her, a bulbous-nosed old farmer was craning his neck to peer down at the obstruction in his path. Breeda struggled herself back onto her feet, wiped her sore hands on her jeans, and nodded an awkward apology to the farmer.

She reached for her dry-cleaning, and as she bent stiffly to stuff the spilled contents back into her handbag, she spotted her bottle of Diazepam wedged under the tractor's front tyre. She grabbed the bottle and buried it in her jacket pocket, its very touch an instant salve. Over on the far side of the road a group of tourists queueing to board a coach watched on with concerned bemusement, and as Breeda reached the pavement her cheeks flared with mortification. The state of her. She must look like the village drunk. She dug up a sheepish smile for the tourists – *Clumsy Breeda!* – and then stood back into the shadow of a shop front, willing them to look away.

With her bag clutched tightly against herself, Breeda waited for her short, jagged breaths to settle. Across the road the over-bright shop fronts of Carrickross village – all pinks and yellows and cornflower blues – glared back at her in a blast of late May sunshine. Two seagulls overhead, guts full from the trawler down at the pier, lost interest in her and followed an ice cream in the sticky grip of a chubby child. Breeda closed her eyes against the world, inhaled a deep lungful of briny North Atlantic air, and blew out slowly through her cheeks. The sparking in her synapses was at last fizzling its way back into the dark recesses of her skull.

She turned her back to the road and looked at the shop window in front of her. For a startling moment she didn't recognize the woman reflected back. Her face was puffy and there was a sunken tiredness to her grey-green eyes. Breeda thought of the creeping earliness of each evening's wine bottle recently and the regular clatter of the recycling bin. The few shifts she did at the wine shop each week came with a generous staff discount which definitely wasn't helping matters. A serious detox was long overdue. She forced a gap-toothed smile at herself, then brushed a hand through her shoulder-length waves of thick black hair. As she turned from the shop window, the briefest movement behind the glass caught Breeda's eye. Myra Finch, Aunt Nora's neighbor, was staring out from behind the counter of The Treasure Chest. The old lady had her arms folded and a face on her like a smacked arse.

'Hiya Myra!'

Breeda waved in through the window but received only a tight little nod in response before Myra turned curtly to the shelf behind her to finger her display of Donegal tweeds. For the second time in two minutes Breeda groaned to herself.

Myra would be on the phone within the minute, no doubt provoking a tight-lipped conniption in Aunt Nora. They'd be offering their thanks-be-to-Gods that at least Margaret Looney was no longer alive to see her daughter's public descent into lunacy. Breeda thought of tomorrow's lunch at the golf club which Nora had insisted on putting in her diary – *twelve sharp!* – and felt a little knot of dread in her stomach pulse and echo. As Breeda pictured her aunt – a tweed two-piece beneath the world's most perfect blow-dry – her late mother's words arose from within, chiding her:

She's been good to us, love. More than you know.

Breeda sighed. The woman was hard going, and tomorrow's lunch would likely involve a lecture on Breeda's many shortcomings, served with a side of hand-wringing, and a generous dollop of Catholic guilt. In the background the bells of Saint Colmcille's chimed three times and Breeda glanced at her watch. Her best friend Oona had insisted on dragging her out later for birthday drinks – her first evening out since they'd laid her mother to rest – and Breeda wasn't going to let thoughts of Nora Cullen spoil things. She turned her back on Myra's gift shop and set off in the direction of the supermarket.

The seasons seemed to have changed overnight, the last clawing chill of the long winter now banished from the streets of Carrickross. A hanging basket cascading with an embarrassment of new flowers taunted Breeda with its effortless beauty as she walked under it, and she stopped on the pavement to rummage in her bag for her shopping list. Excited out-of-towners bustled past her towards the beach, lugging windbreakers and cool boxes under their arms. Already-pink kids scuttled after their parents, their virgin buckets and spades clipping Breeda's legs. The keen tourists and busy locals weaved around her, like currents skirting a stubborn rock. Breeda recognized some of the families from last year; the babies now toddling, the children rangier, the parents paunchier. It seemed like the world was moving on, everyone growing, going places, living life. Everyone but Breeda. She frowned at her shopping list, pretending to read it, and felt her throat rise and fall. A familiar heaviness tugged at her heart, and with it came a sense

4

that somewhere out there a better version of her life stood waiting: one where she might just feel content and complete. Breeda exhaled slowly. She was a thirty-seven-year-old cat lady who worked a few shifts in the local wine shop. She would never climb Everest. She would never have a hospital wing named after her. Breeda Looney was simply destined for a small life. She closed her eyes and tried to convince herself that she was OK with that. But deep down she knew she couldn't go on, not like this. She thought once more of the seasonal change blowing through the streets and wondered if there might be some spare change left over for her, something to sweep through her humdrum life and fix those unfixable parts deep within her.

Up ahead a movement pulled at Breeda's attention. A young man in biker boots and a leather jacket was crouching down to look through the buckets of flowers on display outside the florists. There was something oddly familiar about him, and she watched him discreetly over the top of her shopping list. He wasn't from Carrickcross, that was for sure, and although Breeda wasn't the sort to stand staring gormlessly at randoms in the street, she found herself unable to look away from this stranger. She bit distractedly at her bottom lip, a growing frustration at not being able to place him. She wondered who he was buying the flowers for – maybe his Mum, maybe a girlfriend, maybe even a boyfriend. She continued to observe him, intrigued, as he selected a bunch of dahlias from a bucket, stems dripping as he picked them up, happy with his choice. And just then he looked over. His eyes met hers, and both he and Breeda stood frozen for an awkward moment. A hint of confusion clung to his face, as if he, too, recognized her. The dry-cleaning slid over Breeda's arm, and she grappled for it before the dress hit the ground. When she looked up again the stranger had gone, a few drops of water on the pavement the only proof that she hadn't imagined him.

She stood for a moment, lost in her own thoughts, her head still woolly from the blackness. And then a desolate little laugh came up from within.

You're a buck eejit, Breeda Looney!

She shook her head and shoved the shopping list back into her bag. So desperate for a bit of intrigue in her boring-as-batshit life that she'd grope around for meaning where it didn't exist. She didn't know the guy – he probably just looked like someone off the TV. She tutted, then glanced over at the sliding doors of Flynn's supermarket, and thought of the muzak and florescent strip lights inside. Her groceries could wait. What she needed now was a dirty big G&T and a long soak in the bath before her night out with Oona. She adjusted the bag on her shoulder, held her dry cleaning aloft, and turned for home. Nothing was going to scupper her birthday drinks.

CHAPTER 2

Nora Cullen stood back from the clothesline, placed her hands on her hips and fumed at the carnage flapping in front of her. The pristine white tablecloth which she had hung on the line not two hours before was no longer pristine. She leaned in to inspect the bird shit now spattered in a long muddy streak across the white linen, then closed her eyes and sighed through gritted teeth.

Really. Was it too much to ask...?

She pulled the pegs and tablecloth off the line and flung the angry bundle into the laundry basket at her feet. She hadn't time for this. The annual church fete was in less than forty-eight hours and she simply could not use a soiled tablecloth on her bookstall. She sucked on her cheek for a moment, toying with the idea of strategic book placement to mask the droppings. But there was a risk that Father McFadden – a man who read widely – would pick up a random book and discover it. And then what would the man think of her! She snatched the basket up off the lawn and huffed towards the back door.

It wasn't just the bird shit putting her in foul humor. The phone call from Myra had caught her unawares. Nora slammed the door on her trusty old Zanussi, cranked the button to a pre-soak setting, and then stood looking out the back window, hoping the slow gurgle of water might soothe her frayed nerves.

She could still hear Myra's voice down the line, the barely concealed pleasure in her words, as she relayed that afternoon's fiasco on Main Street. Nora's fingers found the small silver crucifix which hung permanently around her neck, and she rubbed at it distractedly as she peered out towards the old cherry blossom up the back of the garden. Breeda was a liability, and as her only living relative it was up to Nora to do something about her. The girl lacked discipline, she needed order, she was crying out for a guiding light to shepherd her back onto the straight and narrow. Nora mouthed the words over the soft rumble of the washing machine. *A guiding light.* Yes, she liked the sound of that.

Nora thought of the promise she'd made to her dying sister as she'd sat smoothing the pale skin on her frail hand not long ago. She remembered the gentle wave of relief that had washed over Margaret's face as Nora had solemnly promised that of course she'd keep an eye on her only child. An image of Breeda came lurching unbidden to her mind now. Nora sighed. She had tried to love her niece over the years, and sometimes there were indeed little embers of affection that would glow briefly in her chest. But there'd always been a push-pull in her heart – since Breeda was a young girl – an emotional balancing act which saw the scales tip in the favour of aversion and disdain. Nora would never admit to her dislike of her niece, of course. After all, it wasn't the girl's fault that she was the spit of her father. But Nora had made a vow to her sister: a promise was a promise, and Nora Cullen was true to her word.

She crossed her black and white tiled hallway, and by the time she reached the top of the stairs a solution had come to her. Breeda Looney was too long in the tooth to be living such a shambles of a life. Nora brushed a piece of fluff from her tweed skirt and leaned her shoulder against the door frame of the spare room. The room itself was plain and unfussy, small and dark, but with everything that was needed. The single bed was perfectly fine, albeit with the odd stray spring, there was a spacious old armoire for clothes, and a nice picture of Saint Brigid hung centrally on the far wall. Nora adjusted the large crucifix hanging over the bed head, and as she did so Myra Finch's words rang in her ear once more.

Crawling around like a drunk.
A public embarrassment.
What would her mother say?
The girl has no shame.

Nora turned to the small window overlooking the back garden and drummed her fingers on the windowsill. She tutted to herself. It seemed like only yesterday that she'd spent ages pushing that cantankerous lawn mower up and down the garden. And now look! It was as if the grass had shot up three inches overnight. A woman of Nora Cullen's standing simply had better things to do. She needed to be out there, helping the community, leading by example, not struggling a rusty old lawn mower up and down in the heat. That was a young person's job. The more she thought about it the more it made perfect sense. It would be a win-win.

Nora exited the spare bedroom, her decision made. She'd tell the girl over lunch tomorrow.

CHAPTER 3

Thin clouds scudded over the bay and moved swiftly up the ragged patchwork of fields leading from the village to a cluster of cottages on Bayview Rise. The whitewashed walls of Number One stood blinding in the late-afternoon sun, and upstairs, in the steamy bathroom, Breeda lay motionless beneath a spread of dying bubbles. A niggling little disquiet had been nibbling at the corner of her mind since she'd walked home from Main Street, an image of the weirdly familiar stranger in his biker boots hooking onto her consciousness. Try as she might, she hadn't been able to shake it. To make matters worse, her neighbor had spent the last twenty minutes stomping around on the adjoining roof. Every time he dropped his hammer Breeda tensed, half expecting it to smash through her ceiling and land in the bath. She glared at a discolored piece of grout near the taps and waited for the racket to start up again.

Her neighbor, Finbarr Feeley, was one of those country men of an indeterminate age, somewhere between thirty-five and fifty, Breeda guessed. It was probably the big beard that hid his age – a dense, dark brown bush halfway down his broad chest. Finbarr had moved into the attached house just over five years ago, and aside from his constant tinkering on his bloody roof he'd always been a decent neighbor. To a degree he was a man from a bygone era, always addressing Breeda and her mother as *Miss Looney* and *Mrs Looney*, respectively. From the time he'd moved in he'd regularly left the Looneys a box of fresh eggs from his hens on their kitchen windowsill. And whenever he took his lawn mower out, he always made sure to go over their garden too. In those early days Margaret had attempted to give him a few quid for his trouble, but he'd always insisted sure she could sort him out next time, and of course that had never happened. Breeda had come back from the shops one afternoon — a few days after Margaret had died — to find a dozen eggs on the windowsill and the lawn neatly mowed. She'd sat at the kitchen table and bawled her eyes out, unsure why she was in such a state, but aware of a bittersweet relief that at least some small acts of kindness would continue in this cruel world, even with her poor mother no longer alive to witness them.

Above Breeda's head the blasted hammering kicked off again, and she stood quickly, abandoning the bath, and cursing as sudsy water sloshed onto the floorboards. She pulled on her dressing gown, nudged open the window, then attacked her scalp vigorously with a towel.

Downstairs the letterbox clattered – better late than never – and Breeda exited the damp air of the bathroom. On the hallway floor, inside the frosted glass of the front door, sat two envelopes. She squatted down and touched her finger softly to them, keenly aware, all of a sudden, that here she was – for the first time in her life – an orphan on her birthday. A little tightness came to her chest as she realised there'd be no more birthday cards from her mother. Breeda walked slowly back along the hallway with the envelopes, and as she entered the kitchen Ginger stretched and looked up from her sunny spot on the floor. Breeda ripped open the first envelope, noticing the perfectly-squared stamp, and the tiny birdlike handwriting, precise and unmistakable. Aunt Nora.

Happy Birthday to Breeda. From Aunt Nora.

Breeda shook her head and laughed to herself. There was no fear that anyone would ever accuse Nora Cullen of being overly effusive. The woman had probably sprinkled the envelope with holy water from Lourdes, before slotting it deftly into the mailbox, and then striding off to save the community. How different her mother had been from her aunt – 'chalk and cheese' was the expression that came to mind – but Margaret and Nora had been tight, too, over the years. Breeda had plenty of childhood memories of the two sisters talking in hushed tones, clamming up when young Breeda entered the room.

She walked to the kitchen sink and tilted the second envelope towards the window. The large spidery scrawl was smudged in places but was just as distinct as Aunt Nora's. She could tell it was from George Sheridan, her manager at the wine shop. As Breeda ripped open the envelope she could picture her boss in the stockroom out the back of Cork!, his tongue sticking out and the fat fingers of his left hand doing their best not to smudge the ink. He was a good man, George Sheridan. When Margaret Looney had got sick, Breeda had packed in her project management role at Digitron and moved back home to look after her. It had been George Sheridan who'd suggested she do a few weekly shifts at the wine shop to keep things ticking over. Breeda had begrudgingly accepted at the time, wary of being pulled away from her mother's care. But in hindsight it had been a godsend. As she'd watched her mother slowly thin and fade, the few hours of distraction each week in the wine shop had kept Breeda relatively sane.

She looked out the kitchen window and her eyes found the trawlers tied up on the stone pier down below. As she watched the boats bobbing in the glinting water, she bit at her bottom lip. It had been ages since Breeda had last checked her bank account balance – she was scared to look, if truth be told, and she knew she couldn't delay a return to proper work for much longer. A few shifts in the local wine shop wasn't going to cut it. She thought of the daily emails she received – the job alerts full of business speak she used to be fluent in. She sighed and leaned forward on the kitchen counter. In her heart she knew what she wanted to do for a living, and it definitely didn't involve a return to corporate life with its spreadsheets, status reports, and hours in airless meeting rooms.

Breeda had discussed it with her mother once – her real dream. It was only a modest fantasy, but what Breeda Looney dreamt of was to one day run her own guesthouse. She turned to survey the kitchen and looked at the long, gnarly table in the middle of the room – her own sad chair sitting alone at the end – and imagined it laden with local produce, pots of tea, and homemade breads and jams. She imagined the people who'd stay in the three upstairs rooms, sitting around this very table and sharing their stories, the house alive for once with bustle and newness. Breeda would relish being the host, advising the cyclists on their tour of the Wild Atlantic Way about the secret coves and unspoilt beaches. Or maybe, like her own mother, her guests would be artists, drawn by the ever-changing light, the dramatic skies and the expansive clarity. It seemed like only yesterday Margaret Looney herself had whittled away her afternoons sitting out the back with her easel, meditative and lost in the moment, her oils and watercolors soothing her senses. But then the headaches had started. And then the shadowy X-rays had been passed around consultants, and in a matter of days Breeda had packed up her room in the flat down in Galway to move back in with her mother, and Margaret's slow decline had begun its fateful course.

Ginger bumped the back of Breeda's calves and miaowed up silently.

'Well, hello there, missy. Are you hungry?'

Breeda bent to scratch the cat under the chin and poured some pellets into the yellow bowl by the back door. She stood for a second and watched the cat wolfing down the food. Recently Breeda had begun to have morbid thoughts, the type involving tripping and bashing her skull on the sharp corner of the kitchen table, or maybe having a massive stroke. In either scenario, she'd end up lying paralyzed for days on the cold kitchen floor, the ravenous cat circling her solitary body, nudging her limbs like a shark at sunset. The cat turned, as if reading Breeda's mind, and regarded her coolly.

'Ah, Ginge. You wouldn't eat your poor Mammy, would you?'

The cat held her gaze a moment longer, then turned back to the remaining kibble.

'What's that, Ginge? A wee G&T while I get ready for my night out with Oona?'

Breeda's hand found the bottle of Tanqueray on the shelf above the fridge. She turned up the radio, grabbed a glass full of ice and a bottle of tonic and headed upstairs to get ready.

A few minutes later, with a half glass of gin gently coursing through her veins, Breeda loosened the belt on her dressing gown and sat herself at her mother's dressing table. She touched her fingers delicately to Margaret's old perfume bottles and face creams, careful not to disturb them. She picked up the hairbrush and smiled sadly as her index finger traced the bristles. As she ran the brush through her still-damp hair she remembered how Margaret had used it countless times on young Breeda's scalp: one thousand tangles tugged and tamed, while Breeda had stood in her flameproof nightie, practising French imperatives in front of the fire. She knew she'd been spending too much time in this room recently, like a doe-eyed dog awaiting his master's return. The old cast iron bed still stood covered in the patchwork quilt that Margaret herself had stitched. On the rug, beige slippers still peeped out from under the bed. The wardrobe remained stuffed full of her mother's clothes, and a dusty hatbox sat half-hidden atop it. Christ, if Aunt Nora walked in and saw the place untouched, she'd have hysterics. She'd banish Breeda to the back step, snap on the marigolds, and have the bed stripped and wardrobe emptied before the kettle had even boiled. Breeda had been finding excuses not to do it, her heart still bruised, her head not able. It had only been four weeks after all. She would get around to it, soon.

Right, Bree. Focus.

From the top drawer she lifted the jewelry box and took out her mother's pearl earrings. She put them on and turned her face left and right, remembering the first time she'd seen Margaret wearing them. She'd looked like a movie star. Breeda looked at her own reflection again, the grey-green eyes, the gap between her two front teeth. She was her father's daughter, that was for sure, more Looney than Cullen.

On the tall chest of drawers near the bedroom door stood a range of framed photographs; Margaret and Breeda down at the pier; Margaret and Nora in London in the mid-seventies; Nora, Margaret and Breeda out for dinner on Breeda's twenty-first. Other random ones too – bad hair and big shoulders – but not one pixel of Malachy Looney among them.

Her father had died shortly after Breeda had turned twelve years old. He'd drowned, a twilight swim with one too many drinks in him. A freak current, and just like that – gone. Breeda had quickly learned not to mention her father, not to remember Malachy Looney out loud, or ever to ask anything about the man. Twelve years old and overnight she'd become fluent in the language of avoidance. Warning frowns from Aunt Nora, her mother retiring to her bedroom early, a house heaving under a heavy and loaded silence. Breeda had muddled along, not knowing any better. She had just accepted it – this was how adults dealt with death and loss, behind closed doors, at opposite ends of the house.

Every shred of evidence of her father had vanished, any memories too painful for Margaret and too likely to send her off to a dark place. Whatever Breeda's own needs had been – to understand, to process, to learn the language of mourning – had been held under water and starved of oxygen, until those needs lay silent and still.

Breeda turned on the stool and took another generous swig of gin. On the far wall hung a cluster of Margaret's oil paintings and watercolors. Canvases and boards – some framed, some not – of local landscapes and seascapes, flowers and birds. Breeda leaned forward for a closer look at the slashes and daubs. As her gaze travelled over the pictures, she found her eyes drawn to the bottom left corner and the one piece not painted by Margaret.

It had been their wedding present from Aunt Nora – something bequeathed to her from an ancient Bishop up in Dublin who'd been fond of her. An oil painting of a man wading into the sea at Rosses Point in Sligo, all greys and greens, teals and turquoises. Breeda regarded it, attempting an air of detachment, but she found she could never shake the eerie symmetry with her father's last moments. The man in the painting looked out at her from the brushstrokes, chest-deep in the rolling expanse of wild water. Breeda swirled the cool drink in her hand. It was an odd choice of subject for a wedding present. But Aunt Nora had always prided herself on being an adept collector. It was a Jack Butler Yeats, worth a pretty penny, Nora had enthused. And Margaret had loved it, so Breeda, too, had learned to love it over the years. It was a rare constant in their lives, always around, as far back as Breeda could remember.

The ice-cube in her glass cracked. Breeda turned back to the dressing table. As she closed the jewelry box her eye fixed on Margaret's engagement ring. She had taken it off her mother's thinning finger just after Christmas. But now as Breeda held it up she realised that she had never actually tried it on herself. She squeezed it over her knuckle, still swollen from the bath, and turned it this way and that in the early evening light. Beside her, on the dressing table, her phone beeped into life.

Your taxi will be arriving shortly.

'Shit! Shit! Shit!'

Breeda downed the remaining gin and ran to her room, yanking her good red dress out of its plastic cocoon.

CHAPTER 4

Heeley's Bar was wedged that evening. It was as if the temperate May day had flicked a switch in the brains of the locals, and everyone was in a celebratory mood. Summer – or as good as it got in this small corner of Europe – had arrived. Further around from the busy main barroom was a quieter cozy nook and a couple of snugs. Framed posters of old arts festivals hung on the dark paneled walls and watched over Breeda as she sat at a tall table, waiting on Oona to return from the loo.

Amid the amiable din of tipsy chatter, with the sparkling wine working its magic on her, Breeda realised just how much she needed this night out. When she thought of home she could now see there was a cloying scent of death still lingering on in the nooks and crannies of the empty house. She shuffled herself into a more upright position on her stool and stole a sly glance at the Heineken mirror tilted at an angle above the bar. She swept a loose strand of hair behind her ear, then dribbled the remains of the prosecco bottle into their two glasses. It was good to be out, doing what normal people do.

'Same again, Breeda?' Tom the Yank was looking at her with his eyebrows raised, as he lifted some steaming pint glasses from the dishwasher tray. Breeda pretended to consider it.

'Ah, I suppose we could have another one. Go on then, Tom.'

As the barman shoveled some ice into a fresh bucket, Oona's trademark hooting laugh came through from the main bar. Breeda turned to see her friend steadily making her way back from the ladies, squeezing between the thirsty hoards waiting to be served. Oona Mahon was an inspiration. As well as being Breeda's best friend, Oona was a wife to Dougie, a mother to Connor and Eva, and a sought-after couples counsellor. She could achieve more in an hour than Breeda could muster in a week. As Breeda watched her blonde friend appear back around the corner she felt her bones relax and her spirit soften, safe in the world once more. Oona slid onto the bar stool beside her and topped up their glasses from the fresh bottle.

'A toast to you, Miss Looney. An old soul and a true friend. Here's to having you back in the world, kiddo.'

'Cheers, Oona.' Breeda chinked her glass against her friend's. 'I meant to say it earlier, but thanks for dragging me out. I needed this.'

Breeda took a generous sip from her glass, but noticed that Oona had barely wet her lips, and was now looking decidedly distracted. Oona set her glass down and directed her pale blue eyes to her hands on the table. She took a deep breath, then looked back up at Breeda.

'The gobshite's here.'

Breeda managed to swallow her sparkling wine, then put her glass down, and turned slowly to look over her right shoulder, through the gap, into the main bar behind.

'You've got to be kidding me.'

Brian O'Dowd was stood there, holding court with a few of the lads from five-a-side. Breeda and Brian had been dating for a few months in the lead up to Margaret Looney's death. Or – as Oona once corrected her – Breeda and Brian had shared a weekly curry every Thursday night, followed by an uncomfortable go at it in the back of his Ford Fiesta. The guy had vanished from Breeda's life a week before her mother died. Word on the street was that he'd gone to the States on business. Not one word to Breeda though. Not even a text.

'Bree, do you want to leave? The restaurant's booked for eight o'clock. We could see if they can squeeze us in a little early?'

Breeda looked back at Oona. If truth be told she did want to leave, but there was no way that waste of skin was going to chase her out of her own local. It was her first night out in a month. She picked up a beermat and proceeded to tear at its ages.

'I'm absolutely fine here, Oona,' said Breeda, keeping her eyes on the coaster. 'Seriously, I'm fine.'

'As in Fucked up, Insecure, Neurotic and Emotional?'

Breeda flicked a torn piece of the beer mat at Oona. 'You're not at work now, love. Take the evening off.'

'Fair enough. But don't waste a second thought on that fool. There's plenty more fish in the sea.'

Breeda took a hefty swig of bubbles from her glass, feeling an urgent need to be drunk. She stared at the shredded coaster in front of her and tried to ignore the tightness in her chest. How could she explain it to Oona? After all, she was happily-ever-aftering with Dougie, and had two great kids and a fulfilling life. Hooked up and settled down, Oona was just like everyone else in this whole damn village. She had purpose. She helped people. She changed lives. It had recently dawned on Breeda that without her mother to care for her life had lost its meaning. She was rudderless, each featureless day a carbon copy of the one that had gone before. And worse were the nights. Breeda would often find herself waking in a cold panic and giving her mind over to a turmoil of worries. Hateful as it was to admit to herself, the loneliness was slowly dragging her down. She knew she was drowning. And the worst part was she didn't know how to stop herself. She watched a drop of condensation run down the side of her glass. There was a world out there which scared her shitless; a new frontier of instant judgements, swipes left, dick pics and fakery. And she wanted no part of it. She was prepared for a life devoid of caresses. She would get used to the meals for one with the cat pressed against her thigh on the sofa. She'd make do with the radio constantly on to drown out the silence permeating her every day. Breeda felt the numbing effect of the alcohol and she leaned forward to top up her glass. She glanced discreetly back over her right shoulder, but Brian was gone.

'Howya Breeda. Hello Oona.'

Breeda's stomach spasmed. Brian O'Dowd was looking down at her, all loose tie and permanent stubble. A tang of stale cigarette smoke slithered up Breeda's nostrils as he stood smiling shamelessly at her, oblivious to the daggers Oona was shooting his way.

'Brian.' Breeda forced a tight smile in his direction. 'You're back?'

'Yeah. I was over in the States. They're training me up for a new role. Exciting times ahead …'

As he whittled on about his hopes for an upcoming promotion, Breeda felt her eyes glaze over. She nodded her head, a dashboard dog on a potholed road, and wondered to herself what she'd ever seen in this clueless man-child. To think that it was only a couple of months ago she'd been planning to ask him to move in with her after her mother died. Margaret Looney had never liked him — the woman had sense. Breeda glanced at his hands and remembered those fat fingers and their clumsy gropes. She tried not to picture his heavy wet tongue and its insistent explorations of her face and body. Her gut churned as the memories came back. And now, as his voice droned on, it occurred to Breeda that the arrogant feck hadn't even asked after her mother. Did he even know she'd died? Breeda's eyes settled on the little patch of exposed neck between his shadowy band of stubble and a sprout of chest hair. She wondered how it would feel to deliver a swift punch to his voice box and then watch him clutch, wild-eyed, at his broken throat. But instead she nodded, then looked at her own hand as it tightened slightly on her wineglass.

'Breeda?'

'Hmm?'

'Did we lose you?' Brian was waving his hand in front of her face. When Breeda looked up she saw that a well-dressed brunette had appeared at Brian's side with two drinks. She was smiling at Breeda and Oona with perfect teeth and now held one of the drinks towards Brian. Breeda knew it was a JD and Coke. One cube of ice. Just how he liked it.

'Thanks, Alex.' Brian took a slug of his drink. 'Let me introduce you. This is Breeda and Oona,' then turning back to the brunette. 'And this is Alex. From the Boston office. She's come over to check up on us, isn't that right?' Brian winked at his colleague.

'Nice to meet you both. And it's so good to be here. I've been trying to get over to Ireland for ages to do a little digging into the old family tree …'

Alex from the Boston office held herself confidently and spoke cordially. Already Breeda could sense Oona warming to her. She was one of those alphas that other women would want to please. Breeda fidgeted on her stool and realised she was holding in her stomach.

'It's nice to meet you, Alex. We hope Brian's looking after you.'

'So far, so good!'

Brian reached past Breeda to hang his jacket on a hook beside Oona's handbag. 'So, what's with the bubbles? What are we celebrating?'

'It's Breeda's birthday, Brian,' said Oona, throwing him the filthiest of looks. Breeda took a long sip from her glass and stared at some chipped paint on the skirting board.

'Ah Bree. Many happy returns. You should have said.'

Brian's heavy hand touched her awkwardly on the shoulder, a needy mongrel deserving a pat. He signaled to the barman for another bottle of bubbles — 'the good stuff' — making sure that his colleague heard him. Breeda wanted to check her watch, but Alex-from-the-Boston-office was smiling at her as she tilted the glasses for Brian to fill.

'Well, I think this deserves a toast.' That confident voice, that perfect smile.

Brian turned to his colleague, a flash of admiration in his eyes.

'Yeah, good idea. A toast – to Breeda!'

'To Breeda!'

As Breeda lifted her glass, she felt a draft come through from the side door. She glanced up at the mirror above the bar to her right to see the reflection of none other than Myra Finch shrugging off her jacket in the doorway, and intently regarding the merry foursome clinking champagne flutes before her. Breeda kept her eye on the mirror as she sipped her drink, savoring the act of observing Myra for a change. The old woman was looking Breeda up and down, no doubt making a mental note of the impropriety of a red dress and high heels so soon after a death in the family. She'd be chomping at the bit to tell all to Nora. But something suddenly changed in the woman's expression, and she raised a hand to her chest. As Breeda turned to face Myra, a rare and natural lull fell across the loud bar, and when Myra spoke it was at a moment so spectacularly timed that she couldn't *not* be heard.

'Oh, Dear Lord, in Heaven. Breeda and Brian are engaged!'

She gripped the arm of a baffled stranger heading out the door. 'Did you hear? Breeda's getting married!'

People in the main bar turned to listen. Breeda opened her mouth, but found no words, and closed it again. Sweat needled the back of her neck and she turned to Brian, but he was shaking his head in confused laughter and was whispering something to Alex-from-the-Boston-office.

'Did you hear the news?' Myra continued across the packed barroom, 'Breeda and Brian are engaged!'

Breeda watched, horrified, as Myra came towards her with a bony hand thrust out possessively. A crowd of faces now peered around the partition wall at her, and necks craned over the main bar to get a better view. Nearby someone emitted a panicked laugh. It took Breeda a moment to realise it was herself. Around her the tall walls of the tight space stretched upwards and the air took on a sudden staleness. Breeda wanted to run, but Myra had a vice-like grip on her, and was now tilting Breeda's hand, splashing champagne onto her dress, as she leaned in for a better view of the ring. Breeda's mother's engagement ring.

'Myra, we're not —'

'Oh Breeda! I'm thrilled for you.' Myra was on a roll. 'Folks, with all due respect to Breeda here–', turning to Breeda, 'Your Aunt Nora and I always said you were fit for the knacker's yard. *"Good for glue!"* No offence.'

The crowd of onlookers laughed in good-natured agreement. Breeda felt her face burn the same color as her dress. Her eyes prickled as she stole a glance towards the door, desperate to escape.

'Myra, please. You've got it wrong—' Breeda tried again, but her throat was tight, her words muffled by the rising din of the pub.

Someone shouted from the far end of the bar, 'Speak up, Bree!' Someone else yelled, 'Speech! Speech!'

Breeda cleared her throat, and tried again, but it was Brian's voice she heard. He had a hand raised and had turned to face the excited crowd. Someone from the main bar whistled, and a few lads started a rhythmic chant of 'Bri-an, Bri-an, Bri-an.' Breeda looked at the skirting board again. She pulled frantically at the damned ring, but it wouldn't budge.

'Well, folks. There seems to have been a bit of a misunderstanding.'

He was struggling not to laugh. Breeda stared down at the splotches on her dress and tried to force a grin onto her own face, but her mouth felt on the point of collapse. Why hadn't she just stayed home?

'Yes, I'm sorry to say, but Breeda and myself are nothing more than friends. *Absolutely* nothing more.' A murmur of disappointment rolled through the bar. 'But if any woman is ever lucky enough to tie me down, then you'll all be the first to hear about it.'

At this he gave Alex-from-the-Boston-office a squeeze on the shoulder, and the bar erupted in a cheer. The young woman slapped his hand away, but she did it playfully enough, and when Breeda looked up she could see that Alex-from-the-Boston-office was the sort of woman who'd never settle for a Thursday night curry and a fumble in the back of a Ford Fiesta.

Breeda risked a glance towards the crowd. One hundred faces beamed benevolently at Brian O'Dowd and his glamorous colleague. But when anyone met her own eye they looked slightly panicked, the smiles hanging for a split second, before they dropped their gaze. They were embarrassed for her; a sad, broken woman, trussed up like a Christmas turkey, a fool to be pitied. The entire village, unable to look her in the eye.

And just like that Breeda knew what she had to do.

'Breeda, what in heavens are you playing at?'

Myra Finch was glaring at her with a furrowed brow of bewildered disappointment. The old woman was shaking her head and looking Breeda up and down, no doubt already embellishing a version of events for Nora Cullen about her delusional joke of a niece.

'Bree, let's go.'

Oona was gathering up their bags and jackets, a good friend in rescue mode. Breeda stood, wobbled. The tightness in her chest was now crushing its way up towards her skull. She needed to move. She needed to be alone. There wasn't much time — the roaring numbness was on its way.

'I'll just pop to the loo, Oona. Give me a sec.'

Breeda swallowed down the guilt of the lie. She hoped Oona could forgive her in time, but there was no other way. Breeda smiled at Oona for a fleeting moment and tried to capture her best friend's pale gaze and the smattering of freckles across the bridge of her nose. One final look. Oona deserved better than this. She deserved a proper goodbye.

Breeda set off for the ladies in the direction which avoided the main bar. And when she reached them she kept walking until she came to a small corner door. She exited out onto a cobbled side street, just as her shoulders began to shake and the tears began to trip down her cheeks. She would take the back streets. She wanted no witnesses for what she now must do.

CHAPTER 5

A crescent moon scythed through the thickening rain clouds and struggled to illuminate the deserted stone pier. The trawlers had gone out and now low waves lapped and chopped at the stone structure, empty pallets and discarded bits of rope peppering its length. Breeda stood in her bare feet. From her hand she dropped her shoes onto a thick coil of greenish rope as the wind picked up around her. Soft drops of cold rain had started to fleck her bare shoulders. She hugged herself against the chill and walked distractedly towards the end of the pier. She looked upwards and wished more than anything for a storm to rise up and smash everything to pieces.

Since leaving the pub the white noise in the back of Breeda's skull had become louder and more insistent. Her brain felt clamped, her thoughts scrambled, and as she stood at the edge of the pier, she shut her eyes and tried to breathe life into it. For once Breeda was hungry for the blackness, keen to surrender herself fully to it. Her nails dug deep into the flesh of her upper arms as the noise continued to swarm and churn, raging and thundering through her tormented synapses. She shifted the weight from her heels to her toes, her toes to her heels, and rocked rhythmically in the rain. Across the bay, Muckish mountain stood cold and impassive, and

29

she watched a trail of mist streaming slowly down its side. The anxiety and panic and dread which shadowed Breeda — and which had been choking her with an increasingly tight grip since her mother's passing — had now completely drained her. Well, it was welcome tonight. It could do its worst. Because Breeda Looney had no fight left.

Out of nowhere, Myra Finch's words reared up and twisted in her gut, demanding to be heard once more:

Fit for the knacker's yard.

The old woman was right. Nobody in this godforsaken hole was going to miss Breeda. In the murky depths of the black water below her, faces merged and swam before her. Those same people from the pub, witnessing her mortification, unable to look her in the eye.

Breeda shut her eyes against the elements and swallowed down the shame of it all. She could only imagine how fiercely disappointed her poor mother would be, looking down on her tonight. As Breeda stood there, lost and broken, she felt an urgency take hold of her mind. Her memory lurched back through the years, searching for a time when she hadn't hidden behind her own four walls pretending that everything was perfectly fine; to a time when she didn't sit on the sidelines while slowly dying from the inside out. She searched her battered brain, because if that Breeda ever existed, then there might just be a glimmer of hope, a breadcrumb to lead her back, to keep her in this world.

She held her breath and stood motionless in the biting wind, waiting. But she knew no trace of hope was coming. Instead a bitter taste of bile arose from her stomach and Breeda forced it back down. She opened her weary eyes. Beyond the pier the cold night stretched out in front of her, unpeopled and colorless. The sea air filled her nostrils, the shadowy darkness of the water continued its rhythmic swell, and for the second time that day, Breeda's thoughts turned to her father.

She imagined Malachy Looney's bones, brittle and bleached, and long ago picked off their flesh by countless fish, resting in a watery grave somewhere on the far side of the country. What would her father have thought of her, this awkward lump of a woman? Would he have been able to muster up some semblance of pride in his daughter? Would he have held her, and shushed her, and told her everything would be alright? She felt the engagement ring press into her upper arm, the one thing she had to connect Maggie and Mal, her Mam and Dad. Were they reunited now in some far-off realm? Content and fixed and forever young? She pressed the ring to her lips and allowed herself to believe that yes, yes they were.

Below her the water continued its surge and suck. Breeda watched, entranced. Just a few moments of struggle, she thought, and then utter, permanent peace. She stared up at the blackened sky, as if seeking permission from above. There was no other way. Looking down at the water again she felt fresh tears escape and mix with the spitting rain. As the finality of her decision settled over her, the chaos in her brain seemed to give up its fight, and she stood like a lone survivor in the deathly quiet eye of a storm. Breeda made the sign of the cross on her forehead one last time, then closed her eyes, and stepped forward.

CHAPTER 6

Nora wound down the window and wriggled her bottom on the cramped backseat of the car. A smell of damp dog hung in the air and she leaned towards the window – ignoring the light rain falling on her face – to inhale some cool night air. It was one of those impractical two-door cars, and now she regretted not getting out when she'd had the chance a moment ago. She struggled her hips a couple of inches into the air and extracted a naked Barbie from the gap between the seats. The doll's blond hair was matted and at some stage a child had applied clumsy lipstick with a red felt tip. Nora tossed the disheveled Barbie onto the passenger seat in front of her, and then turned her attention to the life-size replica banging Breeda's front door.

The lanky-limbed blonde shrink seemed to have a penchant for knocking on peoples' doors at an ungodly hour. Only twenty minutes earlier, Nora had awoken to a racket at her own front door and had opened it to find Oona Mahon and her browbeaten husband stood on her doorstep. No doubt they'd woken up the whole of Nora's street, and now Nora sighed and pulled her dressing gown tighter across herself. She'd have to conjure up something plausible for the neighbors tomorrow. She touched a hand delicately to the rollers in her hair. *Control the narrative* – isn't that what they called it these days?

Nora squinted at her little wristwatch and then looked back at the front of Number One, Bayview Rise. All the curtains were drawn, and no hint of light seeped out from within. It was nearly midnight on a Thursday and Breeda Looney was obviously still out gallivanting somewhere. Nora couldn't fathom why they were making such a fuss. The girl would turn up when she was good and ready. She dug out her mobile from her bag, ignored the two missed calls from Myra, and scrolled to Breeda's number. As she pressed it against her ear she heard it ring out and click through to voicemail.

The husband was turning back to the car with a hangdog expression, and now, as he remembered Nora in the backseat, he attempted a friendly grimace in her direction. She'd noticed he'd been slowly retracing his steps, edging closer to the car, obviously keen to get to his bed. Now he stood equidistant between the house and the car, absentmindedly kicking the scuffed toe of his boot into the wet gravel driveway. He checked his watch discreetly but said nothing. It was clear who ruled the roost in that household.

And now next door's light had come on. Nora peered through the drizzle to see the front door open and the Feeley man come out in a dressing gown and wellies. He came to stand with an umbrella over the blonde shrink and both of them were staring at the front of the house as if that alone could make Breeda appear from thin air. Nora cocked an ear to try to catch their words but could only hear a low mumble. The Feeley man's excitable black Labrador had escaped from the open front door and bounded about their legs. At least someone was enjoying being out at this unholy hour. The blonde said something to the farmer, and then turned moodily towards the car.

At last, thought Nora.

The digital clock on the dashboard flicked over to 00:00. If she got to bed in the next twenty minutes she might still manage seven hours sleep. Not ideal. And she'd make sure to let Breeda know about it during their lunch at the golf club. As the Mahon couple climbed back into their messy car, Nora cast a glance back at the house. She'd already noticed a large patch of mildew on the driveway near the front door, and now she could see that the ridge of tiles on the roof needed to be re-pointed. It was a decent sized house, too big for Breeda. Nora thought of the uninterrupted views of the sea and the mountains from her late sister's bedroom window. And then she found herself wondering how much the house would fetch in the current market.

That house had been a much-needed fresh start for Margaret and young Breeda all those years ago. A fresh start that Nora had bent over backwards to provide for them both. A fresh start built on a secret that Breeda must never find out. Nora wound up her window. She would take her secret to the grave, even if it killed her.

The bedraggled blonde turned and rubbed an overfamiliar hand on Nora's knee.

'Don't worry, Nora. I'm sure she'll turn up shortly. You know Breeda.'

The Mahon woman turned back to click in her seatbelt, and Nora smoothed her dressing gown back over her now-damp knee. She shuffled in the cramped seat again, comfort eluding her, and tried to console herself with thoughts of her awaiting bed. As the car slowly reversed back along the driveway, the headlights caught the mizzle and wavered over the front of the deserted house. The car reached the cattle grid with a jolt, and the sudden violence startled Nora as her hand came to her heart. And as the reversing car continued to swing around onto the road, the headlights abandoned the front of the house and Nora couldn't help but remember the promise she'd made to her dying sister. She found herself mouthing the start of a silent Hail Mary as she rubbed at the little crucifix at her neck.

CHAPTER 7

Breeda sat in darkness on the middle stair and waited until the sound of the car had faded, just leaving behind the insistent thrum of the rain outside. Her hand plucked at a tuft of carpet on the stair. She couldn't face anyone. Oona would have turned on all the lights, and her pale blue eyes would have drilled into Breeda and made her talk about things she didn't want to talk about – didn't *know* how to talk about. A phone call and an apology in the morning would smooth things over. But for now Breeda listened to the rain on the roof, and rubbed distractedly at the raw skin on her bare ring finger. What on earth must Mad Paddy Byrne think of her?

She thought back to the stone pier. The man must have been watching her from the shadows, must have read her thoughts. Breeda hadn't heard him stepping up behind her, but he'd grabbed her by the shoulders as she'd stepped forward to meet the sea. Her heart had jumped in her chest, before she'd turned and broken down in his arms, choking and snottering over the poor man's tatty jacket. He'd made her put that same jacket on as he'd walked her home, respecting her silence, and allowing her to calm her breathing. Mad Paddy Byrne of no fixed abode: a man on the outskirts of society who would do odd jobs for a hot meal. He had saved her life.

At Breeda's front door he'd searched her face for some sign — an unspoken pact — that she'd not do anything stupid. She'd nodded, and as he'd turned to walk off into the night she had watched his retreating back and swallowed down her shame. Here was someone dealt a bad hand in life, someone with something to complain about.

So now Breeda sat halfway up the staircase, a towel wrapped around her damp hair, and a red-raw finger from where she'd just yanked off the engagement ring. Around her, the central heating pipes murmured lowly and the house began to gently creak and tick. She closed her eyes and pretended the noise was her mother, pottering around, fit and nimble once more, making tea for two and a comforting plate of toast slathered in butter.

God, what would her poor departed mother be thinking of her now.

Breeda wiped her nose, then stood abruptly, abandoning the awkward thought on the stairs. She headed to the kitchen and stood in the yellow glow of the fridge door.

Wine. She needed wine.

She reached past her mother's half-empty jar of bitter marmalade on the top shelf — she couldn't bring herself to throw it out, not yet — and grabbed the full bottle of pinot gris, something from a new range that Mister Sheridan had given her to sample. She poked around the jumble of contents in the shit drawer, unable to remember the last time she'd needed a corkscrew. Digging one out from under the mezzaluna, she started to twist it into the bottle. She caught her reflection in the kitchen window, noticed the haggard face staring back at her, and found herself wondering how life had brought her to this point.

It had been two years since she'd packed up her life down in Galway, with its bustling bars, the swans on the Corrib, and the little flat above the music shop she shared with Padraic the gym instructor from Mayo (who pissed like a horse at two in the morning and let the toilet seat clatter after too many pints), and Jenny the nurse from Waterford (who screamed the house down in moments of passion and regularly clogged up the shower with long tangles of red hair). Two years since Breeda had received the frightened phone call from her mother while sitting in her cubicle at Digitron, immediately resigning from her mid-level I.T. management role. Two years since she'd jammed ten years of life into a borrowed van and handed over the lease on the flat to Padraic and Jenny, racing home to hold her mother's hand. And two years since Breeda had pulled on the handbrake outside the house on Bayview Rise and felt a renewed sense of purpose settle over her as she decided her mother's welfare was to be her new project: Margaret Looney would want for nothing until she took her final breath.

The corkscrew turned slowly in her hand and Breeda bit distractedly at her bottom lip. It was two years since she'd pulled on that handbrake, and now she was clueless as to what to do next. Her mother was gone and Breeda was adrift, each passing day frittered away, a waste. Wasted. She looked at the opened wine bottle in her hand and felt her taste buds unfurl and moisten. To hell with tomorrow and the unfed cat and the bleary-eyed shuffle for painkillers. Breeda needed this. She *deserved* it, after the shambles of a day she'd just had. A few glasses to bring on sweet oblivion and quieten the constant criticisms in her wired brain. She reached for a wine glass, but her hand paused. There was a sudden sourness on her tongue, and she could guess what it was. Breeda glanced at her reflection again and had to drop her eyes. It was the familiar distaste for what she was about to do, but stronger than usual. She gripped the neck of the bottle and exhaled slowly. Here she was again, about to numb herself out and going nowhere fast. Sure, wasn't she the queen of procrastination. She was suddenly sick of herself. Sick to her back teeth.

Breeda flipped the bottle before she could stop herself, turning her face as the expensive wine glugged down the plughole. She let the empty bottle roll in the sink and scanned the kitchen — her eyes wide — an urgent need for something to quell the tremble in her hands and the buzz in her brain. She needed something to give her even just a whiff of forward momentum. And just then she knew. She headed for the stairs — she would put if off no longer.

The bed was first. It was the easy place to start, and Breeda whipped off the flat and fitted sheets. She jostled the pillows out of their cases, shaking them roughly, working the restless twitch out of her arms. She balled the linens into a pile outside the bedroom door, then turned her attention to the queen-sized mattress. Her mother's body had left subtle contours along the thin blue and white stripes running down its length. Breeda stopped for a moment and began to trace her fingers slowly down the ghostly furrows, her memory filling with images of Margaret's pale and bony body, as it wasted by the day. But she caught herself – her mood beginning a downward shift – and she gripped the fabric handles on the side of the mattress. Yanking it towards herself, she struggled it up onto its side, and let it slam down again, a fresh side facing upward. She wiped her brow with the back of her hand, then turned towards the chest of drawers. This felt good.

She worked hard for the next few hours, sorting and boxing, polishing and sweeping, until she turned to face her mother's wardrobe which stood solemn but expectant like a man awaiting the firing squad. This was going to be the toughest thing to do – maybe that's why she'd left it to last. This was where she'd need to focus and be ruthless; one pile for charity, one for the bin, only one or two mementos for herself. She creaked the door open and started to work through the mix of wooden and plastic hangers. Almost instantly her pace began to slow as the contents revealed themselves and snagged forgotten memories. Her fingers danced over frocks she hadn't seen since her teenage years. She held swathes of silk and bunches of cotton to her face and inhaled deeply, allowing the subtle scent of Estee Lauder to take her back to evenings shelling peas at the kitchen table, or bringing Margaret an afternoon cuppa while she sat with her paintbrush, squinting across the bay. Breeda smiled at the memories, a welcome distraction from this evening's gobshitery at the pub and the pier. She slid a few dresses off their hangers and folded them neatly into the bag destined for the charity clothing bin.

And then, behind a heavy black dress, she saw it: her mother's yellow coat from Portobello Market. Breeda quickly slid it off its wooden hanger and slipped into it, the lining cool and sheer against her bare arms. She did up the chunky brown buttons, cinched the belt, and stood regarding herself in the floor-length mirror. She laughed at the width of the lapels, and turned to the left and then the right, smiling at the state of herself, her pale blue towel still turbaned on her head, and looking at odds against the bright sunflower hue of the coat.

Breeda grabbed the framed photo from the dresser; the small black and white picture of the Cullen sisters in their heyday. It was the one of Margaret and Nora, thick as thieves, carefree and young, and with infinite possibilities stretching out ahead of them. It had been Nora who'd got a job in London one summer – '74 or '75 – as a temp in an insurance company. It was to be for a month or two at the most, better than being on the dole back in Ireland, and she had pleaded with Margaret to come over to the big smoke for a visit. And so here they were, in Soho, Margaret in her new coat – this very coat – looking every inch the movie star.

Breeda leaned closer into the picture and examined her mother's face, creased with laughter on that sunny London afternoon. Hadn't she met a young London Irish fella during that visit? Hadn't she been wearing this very coat when they'd met? Breeda touched a fingertip to the glass in front of her mother's face and stroked the wool of the jacket in her other hand. She imagined a radio frequency opening between them, faint and staticky, a stolen moment across the years. What would Breeda say to this young, happy woman in front of her? Would she tell her to watch out for a cocky young man named Mal Looney, and that she should turn on her heel, cos he wouldn't live long enough to grow old with her? Of course she wouldn't. They'd found love. And who was Breeda Looney to give advice anyway.

The sound of Sweeney's cockerel from up the hill brought Breeda back to the present moment.

Shit.

The morning had crept up on her. It was not yet five, but the first ribbons of muddy grey dawn were raking the sky outside. If she left now she could get to the charity bins and be back before anyone was up and about. The thought of even one concerned face or sympathetic touch to the shoulder made her shudder. She'd give it a few days before fully venturing out in public with her brave face. Let them laugh at her behind her back, they'd get bored soon enough. But for now, she couldn't face anyone.

With the innards of the wardrobe now empty, Breeda reached for the ancient cardboard hatbox which sat on top of it. She struggled everything down to the front door in one go and then quietly stuffed it all into the boot of her car. She'd be there and back within the hour. No problem. She closed the boot softly – not wanting to waken Finbarr – and sat into the driver's seat. Taking a firm grip of the steering wheel she looked defiantly ahead.

Today was a new day. A fresh start. Everything was going to go Breeda Looney's way.

She turned on the engine, nodded to no one in particular, and set off.

CHAPTER 8

The coast road was empty that morning. The tide was fully out, and the sea lay calm and flat, its layers of grey merging insipidly with an underwhelming horizon. Out in the distance a trawler gave up its diesel fumes to the sky, and Breeda flicked on her wipers as the first fat raindrops of the day met her windscreen.

In the hotel car park in the village there was a charity clothing bin, but she figured there might be someone about even at this time on a rainy Friday morning – some triathlete in training, or an insomniac dogwalker she'd know. It would simply be less risky to head the few miles up the road beyond Carrickross to the big supermarket car park on the way to Letterkenny.

The world turned over and continued to sleep as Breeda pressed on, her wipers screechy and juddery on the glass. The combination of yesterday evening's drama and the sleepless night were beginning to catch up with her now, and Breeda found her mind sneakily trying to return to last night's humiliation in Heeley's bar and latch on to the memory of the villagers unable to meet the eye of broken and banjaxed Breeda Looney. She slapped herself once across the face, as much to keep herself in the here-and-now as to stop herself from falling asleep at the wheel. In the rear-view mirror her grey-green eyes looked back, bloodshot with exhaustion. She'd drop off the clothes, then get straight home to her bed where she'd turn off her phone and sleep for Ireland. Around the next bend the blue and yellow supermarket sign shone like a beacon and Breeda exhaled slowly.

The only evidence of life in the empty car park was the distant beeping of a reversing forklift moving palettes. The rain had momentarily eased off, and Breeda popped the boot and lugged out the black bags of clothes and the hat box.

She pulled open the metal flap on the top of the clothing bin, and peered into the blackness, questioning its worthiness to receive her mother's garments. From the top of the first bag she carefully removed a cream cable-knit sweater, something Margaret had worn regularly for sunset walks on the beach. As Breeda held it up to the opening she paused, aware that this was her last touch, her last chance to change her mind. She closed her eyes and opened her fingers, and it was swallowed, gone for good. She picked up another item and released it into the belly of the bin, easier this time, a goodbye by stealth. In the distance, the heavens flashed, and seconds later a low grumble echoed over the bleak car park. Breeda glanced at the sky, and then picked up the bag, and started shaking the jumble of clothes into the bin.

A couple of minutes later, as the rain arrived proper, she balled up the three empty bags and flung them back into the car. The ancient hatbox on the pavement was already peppered in dark splotches and its sodden mottled walls looked saddened at the chewing gum and fag butts on the kerb beside it. As she wondered for the first time if the hat inside it would fit through the slot, a cold fat raindrop found its way down Breeda's neck, and she cursed herself for wearing her mother's good coat - the wool would get ruined. She pulled the coat tighter around herself and flipped the lid off the box. Inside a pale blue pillbox hat sat cozy in a nest of tissue paper. It took a bit of persuading, but she managed to shuffle the hat in through the flap without too much crushing. She was getting properly wet now, the rain splashing her shins, the dampness working its way into her gym shoes. Her thoughts turned to her dry warm bed and she grabbed the empty hatbox from the pavement. She felt it stick, the slick tarmac not wanting to give up its new friend. The base gave way, the walls unable to retain their integrity, and she cursed and chucked the broken piece of wet flapping cardboard into the car.

In the remains of the broken box on the ground, a lone sheet of tissue paper was being drummed by raindrops onto the soggy base. Breeda glanced around but there was no-one about. Someone else could pick it up. She hopped back into the dry cocoon of the car, started the engine, and flicked on the heater. Job done.

She sat for a moment, then got out again, the rain lashing her face, stronger and colder than a minute ago.

'Damn it, damn it, damn it.'

Peeling the wet sheet of tissue from the box, Breeda balled it into her pocket, then reached her numb fingers towards the soaked cardboard base on the ground. She stopped, mid-bend, noticing something pale, something a lighter shade than the color of the box. Shielding her eyes from the rain, she squinted in the gloom. It was an envelope. She stooped, the hem of her mother's coat now touching the rain-slicked ground. Her eyes scanned the black ink on the front of the envelope, already patterned by the rain. Breeda picked it up, and stood, angling herself towards the artificial overhead light above the trolley bay. The envelope was addressed to her. It was addressed to Breeda, but at her old address in Dunry, a place she left at the age of twelve. In the top right corner was a stamp and a faded, illegible postmark. There was nothing written on the flip side, but the thing had been opened.

Breeda looked off towards the shop, as if the back-lit poster in the window announcing this week's specials would bring some clarity to the situation. She looked at the envelope again and pulled out the contents with her clammy fingers. It was a birthday card. A picture of two pink balloons looked up at her from the front, a one and an eight in thick orange print. She flipped open the card, and bent over it, trying to shield it from the pelting rain. Inside were some scrawled words, the handwriting tugging at the recesses of her memory.

Dearest Darling Bree, Happy birthday.
It's hard to believe you are now a proper adult.
I wish I could be there with you, but you know how things are. Maybe someday I'll be able to buy you your first grown-up drink. How nice would that be, you and me having a proper natter down the local!
I hope you've been getting on OK. Write back if you can. Good girl.
Lots of love. Dad x

Breeda flipped the card over, then back again, and re-read it twice more. She leaned her back against the car and let the rain soak through the wool of her coat, making it heavy, tempting her downward. Her eyes read the words once more, the scrawls now jumbled and dancing on the card. Her eyes narrowed and searched the puddles in front of her.

She felt herself slide further down the outside of the driver's door, and as her backside came to rest on the wet pavement, the earth began to shift beneath her.

This didn't make sense.

It wasn't possible.

He died when she was twelve.

Breeda pulled her knees up towards her chest, and closed her eyes, trying to ignore the icy shakes which had crept up and seized her body. The rain plastered her hair to her skull, and rivulets of cold water blagged their way through her collar and down onto her back and chest. Inside her head the white noise was back, her brain muddled, her thoughts rendered useless.

She leaned to her right and punched the ground, again and again, harder and harder still. The pain in her left knuckles became her singular point of focus. But no sense came to her. She watched her blood cloud a small puddle of rainwater and felt her shoulders heave against the tightness of the coat. She sat back against the car once more, beyond exhausted, and gulped the wet air, raising her face to the sky and letting the rain meet her confusion of tears. There just had to be an explanation for this.

And suddenly she knew what she had to do. Only one person could make sense of it all. Aunt Nora.

CHAPTER 9

Nora Cullen's two-storey townhouse sat back from the road, in the middle of a row of five similar houses. The neighbors had filled their modest front gardens with bursts of color - climbing rosebushes, window displays and hanging baskets of pansies and peonies. But Nora's stood apart. A simple pathway of plain brickwork cut between two squares of maintenance-free gravel. Two grey pots holding shoulder-height olive trees stood guard on either side of the steps which lead up to the black front door. A polished brass knocker caught the mid-morning sun.

Across the street, Breeda sat in her car and frowned at her aunt's house. She fiddled with the radio and found the nine o'clock news, but then flicked it off again. She attempted a half-hearted stretch in the tight confines of the car but felt the exhaustion from her night without sleep suck her body back into the seat. At least she'd had the good sense to change into dry clothes before coming here. But now she rubbed distractedly at her sore knuckles. What she really needed at this moment was a new brain, one with an ability to think coherently. She looked back over at the house, silent and brooding, and thought of Nora inside. Her aunt would no doubt be sitting in her rollers in the kitchen out back, having her poached egg 'just so', with a slice of buttered wholegrain. She'd be tutting her way through the opinion page of the Irish Times and listening to the radio on low in the background. Nora Cullen did not take well to unexpected guests.

A movement caught Breeda's eye – a window blind in the neighboring house being opened.

Myra Finch.

The bloody busybody was looking straight at Breeda, and for a split second the two women froze, Myra's hand holding the cord of the blind, Breeda's body in mid-slink down her seat. Breeda felt her face flush, and she grappled for the car door and got out, hoping to appear as if she'd just pulled up and had not been sitting there like a fool for twenty minutes. Myra disappeared back into the shadows of her living room, no doubt lurking and watching from a safe distance.

Breeda grabbed her leather shoulder bag off the seat and strode purposefully across the road and in through Nora's gate. She rapped the brass knocker twice – louder than she'd meant to – and winced as the noise assaulted her tired brain. The street was quiet for a Friday morning, and Breeda cocked her ear to the door, part of her dreading hearing any sign of life inside. Another few seconds and she could turn around, drive home, pop a sleeping pill, and crawl into the welcoming warmth of her bed.

As she stepped back down onto the brick pathway, she could feel Myra Finch's eyes on her, and she imagined how delicious it would feel to turn and give the old biddy the finger. But instead she kept her eyes on Nora's door, and held her chin high, doing her best to channel some nonchalance.

Footsteps echoed up the hallway, and Breeda stood up straight, shoulders back. She looked down at the tote, slung over her shoulder, its wide mouth gaping, the birthday card in its envelope wedged in amongst the jumble of contents. It looked so innocuous, so silly in the daylight, a million miles away from the murk and madness of the car park a few hours earlier. She wanted to bolt, to take her foolishness and scarper. But it was too late. She could hear Nora's hand sliding the chain. Without knowing why, Breeda pulled the birthday card out of the envelope and put it in her back pocket. She stuffed the envelope back down deep into her bag and hid it with a balled-up scarf. When she looked back up again, she found the door open, and Aunt Nora regarding her coolly.

The good room, like the olive trees out front, was perfectly symmetrical. Two beige sofas faced each other across a glass coffee table, upon which sat a perfectly-angled collection of books on Vatican artefacts and topiary. Breeda sat perched at the end of one of the sofas, her ankles crossed and her bag at her feet. Across the room Nora stood at the fireplace with her back to the mantelpiece, her fingers drumming lightly on the tweed skirt of her two-piece suit. Her grey hair was recently out of its rollers and below it her blue-grey eyes regarded her niece unblinkingly. She was most definitely put out at her unexpected visitor.

'So, should I even bother to ask?'

Nora sucked on her cheek and nodded to her niece's skinned knuckles. Breeda hesitated; this wasn't going to be easy.

'I tripped. On my driveway …'

Breeda looked up from her bruised hand but her aunt had already turned to face the large mirror over the mantelpiece, tutting her disapproval while she wrangled an invisible wisp of hair back into place.

'Honestly, Breeda. A drunk woman is never attractive. But at your age? You need to wise yourself up.' Nora tilted her head in the mirror, then smoothed down her tweed jacket. 'Your friend Oona Mahon dragged me out of bed on a wild goose chase last night, while you were no doubt three sheets to the wind, doing God only knows what.'

Breeda dropped her gaze to her chipped fingernails and fidgeted as she remembered last night's missed calls on her phone. Later on she'd no doubt be slamming around her own kitchen, coming up with countless smart retorts in her head, and firing off a volley of them at Nora. She hadn't come here for a lecture. She'd come for answers, something to clear up this riddle so she could get home to her bed. The wave of tiredness rolled over Breeda once more and she sighed deeply.

'Sorry, am I boring you, Breeda?'

Breeda adjusted her bum on the hard sofa and felt the birthday card poking into her from her back pocket.

'Sorry, no. It's not that Aunt Nora. But there was a reason for me coming here …'

Nora turned to look at her.

'Well, I assumed there was a reason for you turning up unannounced. Lunch isn't for another three hours, Breeda. If you don't mind, do spit it out. I'm due over at Saint Colmcille's to help set up tomorrow's fete. I'm helping Father McFadden with the bookstall. And if you don't mind me saying so, it would do *you* no harm to volunteer a few hours … only if you've time, of course.'

Breeda ignored the undisguised sarcasm. She held out the birthday card, face down.

'Aunt Nora, have you seen this before?'

Nora squinted, and groped for the pair of glasses hanging around her neck.

'Show me …' She took the card and flipped it over.

Breeda watched her face closely, unsure what she was expecting to see. Nora studied the front of the card, then opened it and read it slowly. Her face remained devoid of expression. As Breeda looked on, she remembered that Nora played Bridge every Tuesday at the community center.

At last the little blue-grey eyes, slightly rheumy, looked up over the bifocals and locked onto Breeda's.

'What is this?'

'I found it. In amongst Mam's stuff …'

Nora looked back at the card in her hands and turned it over again.

'Was there an envelope with it?'

Those cool eyes again, regarding her steadily. Breeda struggled to hold her gaze, the gravitational pull towards her open bag almost too strong. Was the envelope poking out from beneath the balled-up scarf? She kept her eyes on her aunt.

'No. Just the card.' Breeda had a desperate urge to swallow but resisted.

Nora mulled this over for a moment, then came and sat down beside Breeda on the sofa. She continued to look at the card in her hands, and when she next spoke her voice was mellow, and tinged with sadness.

'The thing is Breeda – and we've never talked about this – but your mother had a hard time of it when you were younger.'

Nora clasped her hands together, and Breeda could see the thin blue veins through the papery skin.

'You'll remember your father being away, of course. He had to go where the work took him. Well, back in the day it was laboring work in London, that's where his contacts were. Your Mam would take it hard sometimes, him being away so much. I think for whatever reason it brought stuff up, rejection, and whatnot.'

Breeda sat stock still, afraid of breaking the spell and losing this unexpected and rare moment of candor from Nora.

'Anyway, the lower her mood went, the less time he'd want to spend at home. He couldn't really deal with it. Men weren't equipped in those days ...'

Breeda turned to look at her aunt and noticed the lines around her downturned eyes. She wondered where all this was going.

'Remember the times she went into hospital?'

Breeda did remember. Margaret had had *women's issues*, as they'd called them back then. Something to do with her pelvic floor. Breeda recalled Margaret disappearing off to her room for hours at a time and remembered being given strict instructions by Nora about the need for absolute quiet in the house. On those evenings Breeda would grill a small plate of fish fingers and sit with her homework in front of the muted TV. And now, as she sat on Nora's sofa, more memories came to the surface. Her tenth birthday, when Margaret had had to go for a lie down and their long-planned day trip to Funtasia never happened. That afternoon, Breeda had been standing by the living room window, bored out of her brains, when she'd quietly asked Auntie Nora if they might go to Funtasia some other day. Nora had snapped at her, causing young Breeda to jump. She'd told her in an angry whisper that it was her own birth that had caused her poor mother's condition in the first place, and that Breeda should just shut her spoilt little mouth. Young Breeda had gone and sat quietly on the edge of her bed that afternoon, stewing for the rest of the day in a confused shame.

'I do remember, yes, of course.'

'Yes. Well, in all honesty those episodes weren't strictly of a gynecological nature …'

Nora paused and raised an eyebrow at Breeda.

'What do you mean?'

Nora sighed.

'Your dear mother sometimes found the world a little … overwhelming. There were a couple of times when things just got a bit too much for her …'

The grandfather clock in the hall tocked loudly in the stillness of the house.

'Do you mean …?' Breeda's voice trailed off, her lips not ready for the words.

'Yes. The worst episode was just before your father died. She struggled – some very black days indeed …'

'How …?' Breeda's voice sounded dry and reedy, and the word hung in the still air.

'Pills.' Nora said, matter-of-factly, before standing and walking back over to the fireplace.

'You see, Breeda, we all cope with life's challenges in different ways. After Mal died it all took a strange

54

turn. Your mother was in a dark place. I walked in on her talking to him once – this was months after he died – blathering away to an empty chair. When she saw me she went silent. Would never admit it or talk about it. This …,' Nora held up the card now, 'This was just your mother's way of coping. Oh, it wasn't a one-off,' she turned to face Breeda, 'I found others over the years too. I even caught her writing a Valentine's Day card to herself one year – from him! I stood at her bedroom door and watched her sign it at her dressing table. She barely held it together. But then, thank goodness, not long after we moved over here, she discovered painting. She seemed able to slowly work through things. The episodes occurred less often. It grounded her. Art therapy, I suppose they'd call it these days …'

Nora turned back towards the mantelpiece and left Breeda to sit with the news, to absorb the fact that her poor mother had been so depressed that it had brought her to the brink. But her aunt's words jarred. This woman Nora was describing sounded more like a stranger, not Breeda's Mam. Not her mother who made the world's best Irish stew, and who could identify every wildflower on the Northwest coastline on their brisk weekend walks. Could Breeda have been so blind to her torment, so unaware of what was going on within the same four walls? An image came to her now, of walking into the kitchen back in Dunry. It would have been around the time of Mal's death. Nora and Margaret had been sat at the big table, talking in hushed tones, stopping when Breeda walked in. And her mother had tried, but failed, to appear chipper behind her bloodshot eyes. Breeda had hated the two sisters for it at the time, for locking her out. But hadn't they just been trying to protect her at the end of the day?

A ripping noise came from over at the fireplace. Breeda tried to stand, but her body froze. She watched from the sofa, stunned, as Nora prodded the pieces of the birthday card with her poker.

'So, let's leave the past in the past. Let your poor mother rest in peace, shall we?'

Nora hung up the poker, wiped her hands on each other, and turned back towards Breeda.

'Now. About yesterday …'

Breeda wanted to grab the smoking pieces from the grate, but she continued to sit in shocked silence. That was *her* card.

'Yes, no need to play dumb. I heard. Sure, half the village witnessed it …'

'What do you mean?'

Nora walked over to the window now and surveyed the street.

'Crawling around on your hands and knees in broad daylight? In the middle of Main Street! I mean, have you no shame at all, Breeda? Are you the village drunk now?' Nora smoothed her net curtains with the back of her fingers. 'I don't know what to say. And your poor mother not long in the grave. Is it a cry for help? Is it?'

Breeda's left leg had started the smallest of tremors. For a fleeting second she considered telling her aunt all about the blackness and the power it held over her. But something told Breeda to keep it to herself. Instead she rubbed her face. She needed her bed, to let her poor head settle. She focused on a picture of the Sistine Chapel on the front of the coffee table book.

'I think you should move in here.' Nora had turned from the window to face her.

'What?' Breeda did look up now.

'Well, why not?' Nora was back at the fireplace again, standing tall with her hands behind her back.

'I've been thinking about it. I could do with the help – this place is getting too big for me on my own. And the house you're in is too big for you – with your mother gone.' Nora blessed herself and continued. 'I've got the spare room lying empty. And anyway, I promised your mother I'd keep an eye on you.' She paused for a moment and nodded at Breeda's skinned knuckles. 'And God only knows you need someone to keep an eye on you, Breeda …'

Breeda looked up at the ceiling and pictured the poky dark box room above it. She thought of the creaky bed and the fusty chenille bedspread, the framed picture of Saint Brigid, and the scary crucifix hanging over the bed head. There was no way in hell she'd have Nora guilt-trip her into moving in here. Breeda was perfectly happy in her own home, and she'd be damned if she'd let Nora scupper her dreams of running her own guest house one day.

Nora was at the living room door now, one foot in the hallway, and was checking her watch again. Breeda looked at her aunt's birdlike neck, and imagined twisting it, snapping it, crushing it.

'Anyway, we'll talk more in a day or two. There's no point in delaying the inevitable. Right then. Off you go.'

Then Breeda was on her feet. She cast a quick glance at the torn birthday card which had started to blacken and contort in the greedy flame, but Nora's hand was on her shoulder now, ushering her away.

'Oh, and I think we'll skip lunch at the golf club later, hmm?' She nodded at Breeda's skinned knuckles. 'Maybe some other time when you're a bit more … presentable.'

Outside the front door, Nora gave her niece a bright cheerio, using a different voice to the one she'd used indoors. When Breeda turned to close the gate, she saw that Myra Finch had chosen that moment to come out to fuss with her window displays. The two elderly women were leaning into each other and watching her cross the road.

Breeda climbed into the car and noticed a shake in her hand. She struggled the key into the ignition and forced herself to exhale slowly. One day soon she would stand up to Nora. She was sick of being spoken to like a delinquent teenager. Soon, she promised herself. Soon.

As Breeda indicated and pulled out onto the quiet street, she glanced at her rear-view mirror and felt a chill run down her spine. Nora was watching her with the queerest of expressions.

CHAPTER 10

She didn't mean to stare at his arse. He had just taken off his tracksuit pants to reveal a pair of black shorts and muscular legs with a shadow of dark hair which grew thicker as it approached his glutes. Breeda watched him through the glass wall separating the fitness studio from the cafe, as he squatted and rolled out his yoga mat. She'd recognized him straight away as the guy who'd bought the flowers yesterday on Main Street. Breeda sucked noisily for the green remnants of kale and spinach gloop at the bottom of her glass and wondered once again who this oddly familiar stranger was. She sat, transfixed, with her rolled-up yoga mat nestling between her thighs. Across the cafe table, Oona sat frowning into her phone, her face still flushed from downward-dogging.

'Dammit. Dougie's running late. He's doing the electrics for the house in Riley's Hill.'

'Hmmmm…?' Breeda continued to suck.

'Actually, I think he said the new owner is from your old neck of the woods … they come from Dunry originally. I doubt you'd know them. You left when you were a kid, hey?' Oona looked off into the middle distance. 'He did tell me the name. It's a bit weird. Anyway …' Her voice trailed off, suddenly distracted, and she jabbed a message back to Dougie.

Breeda continued to watch the stranger. He stood and stretched his hands over his head, bending to the left and then to the right. He turned around and caught her looking. She sat up quickly and whacked her knee on the underside of the table.

'Bugger!'

Green smoothie dribbled down Breeda's chin. She rocked back and forth and rubbed her kneecap. Oona turned her phone face down on the table and sat back in her chair.

'You know, I think you do owe me a proper apology, Bree.'

Breeda looked up from her knee. 'I know, I really–

'I don't think you do know. We were up the walls with worry last night. You could have at least sent us a text, just to tell us you were OK.'

Breeda looked at Oona and saw the dark circles under her friend's eyes. She deserved better. Breeda held her palms up, embarrassed by the drama she'd caused.

'I know. You're dead right. It's just …'

Oona reached forward and took her hands.

'It's just that your head fills with too much noise sometimes, and you can't control it or make sense of it, so how could you expect someone like me to make sense of it …? I am good at listening, Bree. It's kinda what I do for a living, remember?'

Breeda did remember. She had visited Oona's practice once. There were two identical armchairs, sitting across from each other, slightly angled so as not to appear confrontational. A three-seater settee sat under an abstract print, and Breeda had wondered about the rowing couples and families her friend must have guided out of stuckness over the years. Oona worked three days a week, and Breeda marveled at her ability to switch off – she never took her clients' work home to her and Dougie's personal life.

'You look tired, Bree. Trouble sleeping again?'

'Hmm. Something like that. Listen, Oona, there's something I need to talk to you about.'

'Well, walk downstairs with me. Dougie's giving me a lift before he goes up to Riley's Hill, and I don't want to make him any more late than he already is.'

Breeda's chair scraped on the floor as she stood. She glanced into the studio again, but the guy was lying on his mat now, down the far end of the room, his eyes closed and his focus inward.

Oona was waiting at the top of the stairs, her rolled-up yoga mat under her arm.

'Bree? Chop, chop!'

Down on the street, Oona looked up and down for Dougie's car, and then leaned her bum against the windowsill of Cheeses Christ. She closed her eyes and turned her face to the early afternoon sun.

'Well, I'm all ears.'

When Breeda sat down beside her and stayed silent, Oona cracked her eyes open, and looked at her.

'What's up, Bree?'

Breeda gently rubbed the bruising on her hand, trying to find the words.

'I think I'm cracking up, Oona …' She shook her head. 'It's like I'm in some parallel universe, where everything's just a wee bit skewiff …'

'Ah, Bree. I can't imagine how hard all this must be. But he's an dipshit in the extreme. I wouldn't waste—'

'Oona, this isn't about Brian O'Dowd.'

Oona closed her mouth and waited.

'Well – long story short – it would appear that yours truly here had a depressive mother who wrote letters to herself from her dead husband.

'What?'

'Yup. She'd chat to his ghost, write herself Valentine's cards.'

'Sweet Jesus.'

'And there's more.'

'Go on …'

Breeda paused, fascinated by the absurdity of what she was about to say, allowing herself an indulgent moment to lap up the drama.

'I found an eighteenth birthday card he wrote to me. I found it in amongst Mam's old stuff, at five o'clock this morning.'

'Feck me. Is it any wonder you look wrecked.'

'Ah, thanks Oona. You're a pal.'

'Sorry.'

Oona stood, her brow creased, and looked past Breeda to a display of pickle jars and cheese boards in the window behind her. She nibbled on a piece of loose skin by her thumbnail.

'But didn't your Dad …'

'Yep. When I was twelve …'

'Jesus. So your Mam was still writing letters and stuff from him, six years after he died?'

Breeda made a non-committal noise.

Oona sat back on the windowsill and rested her chin onto the end of her rolled-up yoga mat. Both women stared vacantly into the middle distance.

'This is the thing though. Nora said it's a hoax – said it was just another one of Mam's moments of madness. But … I dunno, I'm being daft …'

Breeda kicked the wall of the fromagerie with the back of her heel.

'It's just … it's started me thinking, and I can't get it out of my head now. I mean, what if it was from him? What if my Dad was alive and well, kicking around somewhere … thinking I hated him cos I never wrote back. Imagine …'

Both women breathed out slowly. A small cloud dragged itself across the sun and sent a thin blanket of shadow diagonally over the street. Breeda pulled up the zip on her hoody.

'But why would Nora lie to you?'

'I dunno. No reason. As I said, I'm just being daft. It's just …' Breeda remembered her aunt's face in the rear-view mirror.

'Do you have it - the card?'

'No. Nora tore it up. Told me to leave the past in the past.'

'No way!'

'I know, right?'

The afternoon sun reappeared, and the two friends turned their faces towards it again.

'What do you remember about him?'

'My Da? God, what do I remember about my Da? His comb! He always carried a comb in his shirt pocket. He had a great head of hair, jet black. And the smell of tobacco. He'd always be rolling from his little pouch. And Mam would give out to him for smoking by the back door and stinking up the house. She'd shoo him outside. And he loved the horses too. Loved the racing on the telly.'

Breeda could remember other things too. The screaming matches in the kitchen, the slammed doors and the smashed plates, but now wasn't the time.

'Well, you know what they say …?'

'What do they say, Oona?'

'That things come in threes. Last night in the pub you had Myra Finch publicly embarrass you over a mistaken engagement to fuckwit-extraordinare, Brian O'Dowd. This morning you've discovered your mother's a ghost-whisperer who writes psychic letters to your dead dad. What generous slice of headwreck is next on the menu for Breeda Looney?'

'Ah, thanks!' Breeda laughed and pushed her friend on the shoulder.

Across the street a car horn tooted. Dougie had double-parked and was beckoning Oona over. Behind him a large tourist coach braked with a pneumatic hiss and waited. Oona gave him an impatient wave.

'Frig it. Bree, I have to go, or this one will be late for the Riley's Hill woman'.

'It's fine, love. You go. We'll talk later.'

'Listen, my advice, for what it's worth … if your dad is out there somewhere a day or two won't make any difference. You need a plan.'

'Respond, don't react.' said Breeda, mimicking her.

Oona gave a throaty laugh as she hugged Breeda, then turned for the car. She stopped halfway across the road and shouted back to her friend.

'You know what, Bree? What doesn't kill you makes you stronger!'

'I know, right?' Breeda had started to laugh. It felt bloody marvellous to give in to the lunacy for a moment.

She watched Oona walk around to the other side of the car, still shaking her head, and step her long legs into the passenger seat. Oona was asking Dougie something and got back out of the car. She was mouthing something to Breeda, but an old tractor was now trundling the other way and belching black fumes in its wake. The coach behind Dougie sounded his horn, and Breeda could see Dougie shouting at Oona to get back in. But Oona was standing with her hands cupped around her mouth and was trying again. Breeda could make out the words 'Rileys Hill', and she stepped to the edge of the pavement, the sharp stench of slurry hanging on the air as the tractor moved on.

'The new owner – up on Riley's Hill – she's Sneddon. Dervil Sneddon!'

Oona waved a conciliatory hand back at the bus driver, and sat back in the car, shouting at Dougie to calm down. She had barely slammed the door when they screeched off up the road, to leave Breeda walking backwards in a daze. Her thighs met the windowsill of Cheeses Christ, and she sat back down, dumbstruck.

CHAPTER 11

Breeda remembered exactly the day it had all
started to go wrong. It had been a blustery
Tuesday morning at school, twenty-five years
ago, and double physics had just finished. Religious
education was up next and poor old arthritic Sister
Jacinta always took ages to hobble up the stairs with her
cane. Up until that normal September morning in 1989,
young Dervil Sneddon had always been perfectly civil to
Breeda Looney. The Sneddon family were quite well-off
by Dunry standards. They had a big house on the other
side of town, they took a foreign holiday every summer,
and Breeda had heard that Dervil had not just a TV, but
also her very own video player in her bedroom. Apart
from a slightly affected accent, Dervil was just another
well-behaved girl who mostly flew under the radar.

Dervil's twelfth birthday was that coming Saturday,
and there was to be a party followed by a sleepover at
her house. That morning, as they'd waited on Sister
Jacinta to arrive, Dervil stood at her desk and riffled
through a stack of flowery invitations which she'd
extracted with a flourish from her leather satchel. The
din in the room subsided momentarily, then increased to
an excited murmur, as girls elbowed each other, and last-
minute homework was discarded. Dervil glided
benevolently between the desks, handing out the

personalized invitations, and as Breeda Looney sat waiting on hers she thought of her fusty sleeping bag back home, and whether she'd need to air it on the line before Saturday. Breeda turned to see Mindy Chen receive her invitation, which meant everyone was invited. Mindy was the Chinese girl whose family had only moved to town last year. They ran the takeaway down by the bookies, but Margaret Looney wouldn't have Chinese food in the house as it was full of E numbers or MSG or something. Breeda peeked to her left at Sharon Doran's card, as someone behind her said they'd bring their *Dirty Dancing* video, while someone else said they'd bring along a Ouija board, but was being told that was too babyish, but sure bring it anyway. Dervil had returned to her desk now, just behind Breeda. Everyone else had been given an invitation, and Dervil sat back down with her hands crossed and her eyes forward. Breeda smiled at her, knowing she was just teasing, and would roll her eyes and flick Breeda's invitation at her. But Dervil's eyes had taken on a vacant coolness. She looked through Breeda, as the door opened, and Sister Jacinta stood there stomping her cane with a big red face from the exertion of the stairs.

'Girls! Settle down. Breeda Looney face forward. Page 53 of your textbooks.'

That day, when the class had finished, Breeda took her time to pack her books away, and let the room empty around her. She wasn't aware of it at the time, but this was to be the start of a long and steady retreat into herself. During lunch she had hidden in a corner of the library where she tried to lose herself in a book but struggled to stay focused on the words in front of her.

When she went to that afternoon's classes, she forced herself to sit up straight, and tried her best to look as if everything was normal, to rise above her churning hurt. But a few of the other girls had noticed that she hadn't been invited to the party, and soon word had spread. In that way that girls form alliances, Breeda Looney quickly started to become a bit of a pariah. No-one wanted guilt by association, especially prior to the Sneddon sleepover.

That weekend Breeda stayed indoors and tried to distract herself in TV show after TV show. A sense of unease had hummed persistently in the back of her brain, and she sat cross-legged inches from the cathode ray tube, flicking through the handful of channels and trying to lose herself amongst the pixels on the rounded screen. She would just push it down and ignore it. Besides, her Mam had her own health concerns, and her Dad was laboring over in London. So young Breeda had kept her own company that weekend, mostly passing the time in her room, observing the outside world from behind the thin net curtains.

The belief that she was in some way faulty, that she was somehow guilty of wronging Dervil, started to slowly solidify and take hold, and she muddled on like a child with a pebble lodged under her sock. The following week her classmates seemed only too happy to overlook the defective girl in their midst, to actively ostracize her, and let her watch on from the shameful shadows on the periphery of the school yard.

By the middle of October low, heavy clouds seemed to hang daily over the town, trapping in a permanent state of mizzle. When the other schoolgirls ate their packed lunches inside, and chatted in huddles in the long marble corridors, Breeda would retreat to a sheltered spot behind the tuck shop, where she would stand in her tartan school skirt, the wool damp and heavy with the rain. She would count down the minutes until the bell would ring, when she could once again pretend she had some sense of purpose until it was time to go home.

And so it was, behind the tuck shop, as she half-heartedly nibbled on a salad sandwich, that she first encountered Father Green.

'Now there's a girl with the weight of the world on her shoulders.'

Breeda had jumped, startled, and dropped the sandwich on the wet ground. She looked up to see a young man, around thirty, with wavy dark hair in a black cassock. He was holding a huge black umbrella and smiling like a long-lost pal.

'Oh dear'. He looked at the damp bread, its contents spilled at Breeda's feet.

Breeda's chin had begun to tremble. She dropped her gaze to the ground and felt the mortifying threat of tears. She kept her eyes on his feet. Black socks under black sandals. But it was suddenly all too much for her, the unexpected relief at being noticed, at being seen, by someone – anyone. The tears brimmed and spilled, and she hated her shoulders for giving into their shudders. She hated her face for the pitiful contortions into which it was now shaping itself. Unable to keep up the facade, she allowed herself to crumble.

He had come to her side, his arm around her, as she buried her face in his shoulder and wept silently. That rainy afternoon he'd held his umbrella over Breeda in the playground and said nothing more than, 'Of course, of course,' as she sobbed and whimpered. When Breeda blew her nose noisily into his handkerchief he had laughed freely, and then she found that she was laughing too.

'And with whom am I enjoying a laugh on this lovely soft day?'

'Breeda. Breeda Looney, Father.'

He held out his hand and she shook it three times.

'Well, Breeda Looney, I'm guessing the bell is about to ring and you have a class to get to?'

'Yes, Father …'

'Father Green.'

'Yes, Father Green.'

His name was Peter Green and he was a chaplain from the monastery up the road. He was standing in for Sister Jacinta, who'd had a nasty fall, and he would be around for a few weeks while the nun recuperated. He was to take the Religious Education classes and would also be around to give any pastoral guidance, if and when it was sought.

He stood back and inhaled sharply as he looked up at the low blanket of grey overhead.

'I reckon it's going to last for a few days at least,' he had said. 'What do you reckon, Breeda Looney?'

She lifted her face to the sky and felt the fine mist.

'I reckon so too, Father.'

He turned with the umbrella and sauntered off towards the double doors at the side of the building.

'Come on then …'

She scurried after him and they reached the building as the bell began to ring. He held the door for her.

'Are you going to be alright, Breeda?'

She looked past him into the echoing corridor, where groups of girls were swarming off to their next classes.

'Mmmmm.' She had to get to Geography at one of the prefabs.

He said nothing, and she looked back at him. He was mulling something over.

'Listen, I have a proposal for you, Breeda. While I'm here I've been allocated Sister Jacinta's office on the third floor – God in Heaven only knows how the poor woman managed those stairs all these years. Anyway. I could do with a little help with some paperwork – just filing, filling envelopes, that sort of thing. A few days work. If you were free during your lunch breaks would you have any interest in sparing me a few minutes here and there? You'd be doing me a huge favour …'

He shook his umbrella, stomped his feet, and followed her inside.

Breeda didn't need to turn around to see the rain-slicked yard, the lonely corners of the veranda, or the sad spot behind the tuck shop.

'I could manage a few minutes, here and there, yes Father.'

'Grand. We'll start tomorrow lunchtime. See you then.'

And with that he walked off down the middle of the corridor, his black cassock parting the tartan skirts, some heads turning to take in this male stranger in their midst. Breeda looked after him, and for the first time in a long while the toxic fog in her mind began to slowly lift.

The next day, at midday, as the girls poured out of English Lit. Breeda held back, took her lunch box from her locker, and then strolled casually along the corridor to the back staircase near the Principal's office. She glanced over her shoulder and then headed up the stairs. She walked slowly, her hand trailing the glossy wall beneath the handrail. The noise from the girls below died away as she climbed, and by the time she stepped onto the third floor all was whisper-quiet.

'Come in, come in, Breeda.'

The door was ajar, and he'd heard her approaching. Father Green was standing at a large mahogany desk under a high diamond-paned window which overlooked the gardens. Outside a light rain was falling, and Breeda thought about the sad spot behind the tuck shop. She stepped in and closed the door behind her. The smell of books and furniture polish filled her nose. She hadn't been in this room before. She instantly liked it.

Father Green was wearing a pair of glasses with thick black frames. Breeda thought he looked a bit like Elvis Costello from her Dad's vinyl. He took them off and gestured for Breeda to take a seat on the other side of the desk. Her eyes flicked over the various stacks of papers and pages sprawled on top. He laughed.

'A bit of a mess, isn't it?'

Breeda smiled but didn't know what to say. She felt self-conscious, suddenly aware that she was alone in a room with a strange man. He stood up and walked over to the door, as if reading her mind, and opened it a few inches. Then he picked up a tall pile of printed papers and brought them over to Breeda's side of the desk.

'These ...' he dropped them in front of her, 'are what I'd like your help with. I need you to take the names and addresses from each letter, write them on an envelope, then put the letter inside. Nothing too difficult. You good with that?'

Breeda leafed through the first few pages. All of them seemed to have been hand-typed.

'Sure. Could I borrow a pen please?'

He rifled around in Sister Jacinta's top drawer until he found a biro.

'Here you go. I'm a leftie myself, so if I go near a pen it smears everywhere. Not a great skill for addressing envelopes ...'

He'd sat now and slurped noisily from a chipped Arsenal mug.

'Sorry.'

Breeda smiled at him and got on with the job at hand. For the next forty minutes they sat in a comfortable silence. He didn't pry and she was relieved – she didn't want him asking why she'd been crying the day before. So that lunchtime she worked steadily through a wedge of letters from the top of the pile. She'd nibbled on her cheese and pickle sandwiches, careful not to drop any crumbs onto the paperwork, and bit her lip every time he slurped from his chipped mug of tea.

The next day as Breeda climbed the back staircase she took the stairs two at a time. She had slept well the night before, and for the first time in ages felt halfway alright. Her feet grew faster on the stairs and she arrived at the office out of breath. She knocked and entered and sat at the desk. On the windowsill she spied a second mug, a teapot and a plate of shortbread fingers. Father Green was watching her over the top of his glasses.

'Well, we need to keep our strength up, don't we? Doing God's work, and all ...'

He filled their two mugs from the pot. Breeda's had a picture of Lourdes on it. She was a little peeved her mug wasn't chipped too.

'Here, I'll let you do your own milk.' He handed her a small carton, and then playfully shook the plate of shortbreads in front of her.

'Thanks, Father.'

'You're welcome, Breeda. All OK?'

Ah, here it comes, she thought. A piece of shortbread fell onto her top page and she scooted it off with her hand. She kept her eyes down on her page. 'Mm-hmm.'

She could sense him looking at her for a moment, considering his next move, then thinking better of it. He grabbed the nearest pile of paperwork and started sorting it into various folders. After a minute, a silence had returned to the room and Breeda slipped off her shoes. The room was quiet but for the tick from his wristwatch.

As her pen formed the curves and angles of parishioners' names on the envelopes she sat and wondered how it would be to open her heart to him. To take a risk and see if this stranger across from her could help her make sense of everything happening at school and at home. How would it be to pull the stopper from the bottle and lose control of its contents?

She suddenly realised there was no sound from his side of the desk, and she could tell he was looking at her again. He must have been reading her mind. She kept her eyes down, kept her pen moving. She knew he was opening his mouth to say something. She couldn't do this. She wanted to, but she wasn't ready, didn't know how. She grabbed the bundle from her lap and stood quickly, jamming her feet back into her shoes.

'I better go, Father. I've just remembered I have to get all the way over to the prefabs for science.' She clicked the pen away and was at the door with her bag over her shoulder before she dared look his way. He sat looking back at her, a little baffled.

'Right so, Breeda. I'll see you tomorrow?'

She nodded back.

'By the way - I'm not here on Friday. I have to take the lads down to a quarter final match in Dublin. It's an all-day thing.'

He seemed to lose himself for a moment, as he sat back and turned to look out the window, cracking his knuckles out in front of him. 'It could be ours this year.'

'OK, Father. Sure, I'll see you tomorrow.'

'See you, Breeda.'

Breeda left the door ajar behind her and trailed her fingertips slowly along the wall. She pictured him sitting there on the other side of this wall. A good man, ready and willing to help her. He'd be able to listen. Wasn't he trained to be? She felt a slight queasiness in her stomach, picturing his face when she told him about how she was bumbling through her crappy life. But here was her chance. As she stepped onto the first stair she promised herself – tomorrow. That was the deal. *Tomorrow*.

The next day Father Green was looking in Sister Jacinta's stationery cupboard for some folders when a walking cane had come clattering out onto the floor. He'd picked it up, hunched himself slightly, and then huffed and puffed past Breeda as she'd tried not to choke on a biscuit. His crunched-up face was Sister Jacinta to a T.

'Stop, Father!' Breeda had tears streaming down her cheeks. 'I can't breathe.'

She had set him off too now, and he couldn't stay in character through his own laughter. He leaned the stick against the desk. Breeda didn't want him to stop.

'God forgive me,' he said, collecting himself. 'I reckon I'm going straight to hell, Breeda.' He suddenly looked slightly abashed, and threw a glance towards the door, open a few inches as usual.

'Well, three Hail Marys, two Our Fathers and a packet of Jammy Dodgers on Monday should save your soul, Father,' Breeda replied *sotto voce*. She marveled at her newfound playfulness, this unexpected cheekiness in her own voice. It felt good.

'I think we might both be going to hell, with that attitude, Miss Looney. Here …' he slapped another bunch of papers in front of her. 'Let's see how you get on with these …'

Breeda had just dunked her chocolate digestive into her Lourdes mug when a sharp rap came to the door. Father Green got up to answer it, but not before Breeda saw Mrs Shields, the school secretary, peering in at her through the gap. The woman had a queer look on her face, something Breeda didn't recognize. As Father Green reached the door, momentarily blocking the secretary's view, Breeda crammed the biscuit into her mouth and slipped her shoes back on.

Outside, in the corridor, a murmur of voices had started up. Father Green opened the door.

'Ah, Mrs… Shields! And to what do I owe the pleasure?'

'Father Green. Is everything alright?'

'Oh fine, fine. I'm getting a bit of assistance from Breeda here.'

Father Green stepped to the side.

'Breeda. Alright?' There was a strange tightness in Mrs Shield's voice, and when Breeda looked up from her letters she noticed a deep furrow in her forehead.

'Yes, thank you, Miss Shields.'

The secretary stepped back from the door now and beckoned the chaplain toward her. She nodded up the corridor.

'Father, when you get an opportunity there are quite a few *other* pupils who would appreciate a moment of your time …'

Father Green followed Mrs Shield's gaze and appeared momentarily bewildered.

'Of course, of course …' He took a moment to gather himself. 'No problem. Hello ladies. Is it a hand with your homework you're after? Who's first? Come in, come in …'

Breeda turned her eyes back to the paperwork in front of her, then glanced up as Father Green walked in with Sharon Doran. Breeda looked up to find that Mrs Shields was still watching her. Lisa Maguire was craning her neck from the corridor, having a good gawp too. Breeda felt a shock of heat rise up through her face. She heard her name and turned back to the desk.

'Sorry, Father?'

'I was just saying that will do for today, Breeda. You can run along now. Thanks for your help. And don't forget I'm not here tomorrow. See you next week?'

Mrs Shields had turned her focus back to Father Green now. Breeda sensed a wordless accusation flying through the air towards him. She stole a glance at the man. The confusion had ebbed from his face now, and something else was settling onto it. Breeda realised he was hurt. He was looking back at Mrs Shields, his eyes suddenly sad and his brow heavy. He had taken his seat and was holding out a weary hand for Sharon Doran's book. Breeda wanted to run to him and hug him.

'Let's go, Breeda.' Mrs Shields clicked her fingers and stood with an arm outheld to shepherd the young girl away. Breeda stepped into the corridor and was hit by the withering looks of contempt from the line of waiting girls. Anne-Marie Carlin was stood there with her jaw set and her arms folded, subtly shaking her head as Breeda slinked past. Lisa Maguire looked Breeda up and down and mouthed the word slut just out of earshot of Mrs Shields. Titters and tuts found their target and Breeda's eyes blurred as she walked past them and slumped down the staircase after Mrs Shields. She watched the woman's shoulders as they descended the stairs in front of her. She felt a sudden urge to shake them, to spin this woman around and slap her face. To shout at her with spittle flying that she'd done nothing wrong – that poor Father Green had done nothing wrong. But instead she followed in Mrs Shields' wake, a pointed silence between them. A confusion of shame weighed heavier and burned hotter with each step Breeda took. There was something filthy about her. Filthy and broken. When they got to the Principal's office the secretary turned.

'Breeda. I don't want you going up there again. You'll have plenty of opportunity to ask Father Green any questions in class.'

Breeda stood there like a fool, still trying to work out what she'd done wrong.

'Do you hear me, Breeda?'

Breeda forced herself to look up at the secretary, the glasses too big for her face, the little bleached moustache fooling no one.

'Yes, Miss.'

Mrs Shields opened her mouth to say something else, then thought better of it.

'You'd better get to your next class.' She disappeared back into her office and faded behind the opaque glass door.

Behind her Breeda heard a rustle and turned. Leaning against the wall was Dervil Sneddon. She was pouring the crumbs from a bag of Tayto cheese and onion into her mouth. She scrumpled up the crisp packet and then slowly licked her fingers, all the while keeping her cool gaze on Breeda. A smirk played victorious across her face. She dropped the crisp packet at Breeda's feet, then turned and walked off, her blonde ponytail dancing behind her.

CHAPTER 12

You couldn't get a nicer welcome than a freshly-baked cake, that's what Margaret Looney used to say. Breeda looked down at the still-warm carrot cake in her basket and allowed a satisfied smile to play over her face as she pedaled on. She had wrapped it neatly in a fresh red and white gingham cloth, a thoughtful little 'welcome to the neighborhood' gift for Dervil Sneddon. And Oona had been right, of course. Breeda should just put the whole Mal Looney conundrum out of her mind, for a day or two. Better to let it percolate, to sleep on it, and devise a sensible plan. Besides, something told Breeda that she'd need to tread carefully around Aunt Nora.

An hour or so of baking had been a welcome distraction from the previous twenty-four hours. And now it was good to be out on her bike. It was a mild afternoon, and the sun warmed Breeda's back as she cycled down Main Street and then hung a left past the butchers. An old donkey raised his head and watched Breeda dolefully from his frayed piece of tethered rope, as her tyres hummed past. The village slowly retreated behind her, and as the roadside became less tamed, Breeda could make out glimpses of hawkbit and bindweed, buttercups and asters. Or were they chamomile? Her mother would have known. She pushed on along the quiet road and looked once more at the gingham peace offering for Dervil in her basket. Breeda Looney was big enough to let bygones be bygones.

After a few minutes the sound of a motor pulled at Breeda's attention. The road had narrowed and on either side fat hedgerows loomed over her, casting shadows which flickered as she pedaled on. Breeda pulled over to the side of the single lane and steadied herself with a foot on the ground. A motorbike roared around the corner. She spotted the guy before he spotted her; a cliché in black leathers and reflective helmet. He hit his brakes up ahead of her – slowing him marginally – but he was still bombing along as he passed her. Breeda glowered at whoever it was behind the visor as she turned to look at his retreating figure.

Dickhead.

She pushed on, and a moment later came to the crossroads. Up ahead stood Riley's Hill, and the new home of Dervil Sneddon. Breeda found her pace slowing. The lack of a good night's sleep was catching up with her now, and the heat of the day was more than she was used to. Her legs had started to feel heavy and her head was hot under her cycling helmet. But she knew there was something else; a temptation to slow down further, to turn the bike around, no harm done. After all, who would know? But she forced herself on, until she stopped beside an old yew tree at the foot of the driveway up to the house.

A damp strand of hair had licked itself to Breeda's forehead, and she blew at it in vain as she walked her bike over the cattle-grid and up the steep driveway. Bits of loose gravel crunched underfoot, and she tried not to think of the sweat beads running down her back and sticking her white blouse to her. She glanced up at the house. Everyone in Carrickross knew this place. The guy who'd built it had lost his job in the crash, and every bank had quickly pulled up its drawbridge, cutting off his finance before the house was completed. It had been a dead weight around the poor man's neck, a fading 'For Sale' sign stuck in the ground by the yew tree for close to six years. The symmetrical facade was wide and unfinished, the windows draped with net curtains which gave nothing away. Wires stuck out from holes in the wall where lights were to be fitted near the double-width front door. Breeda could imagine the echoey hard-to-heat rooms inside. Dull sample colors had been painted in patches beside the windows and Breeda could tell already that it was going to be an ugly home, all concrete and driveway and shitty shades of grey. Dervil would have picked it up for a song. To the side of the house a shiny black Range Rover sat regarding her, a guard dog waiting for the kill signal. Breeda looked down to her pannier and frowned at the little carrot cake. She rested the bike against the wall, grabbed the cake, and knocked briskly on the door. It was all going to be fine. Dervil would be delighted to see a blast from the past and to have an old friend in her new town. After all, weren't they a pair of grown-ups, for goodness sake.

Breeda cocked an ear and heard footsteps – a pair of heels – coming down the hallway. She felt a sharp clench in her bowels, took a step back, and prepared her best smile.

And then, there she was. Those same brown eyes under a haughty brow, blonde hair tied back in a no-

nonsense ponytail, the beginnings of a smile which never fully bloomed or reached the eyes. Dervil Sneddon. Breeda looked up at the woman towering over her, a warrior in a leopard print kaftan. Neither woman spoke at first, and Dervil's expression seemed to be one of mild bemusement.

'It's Breeda, isn't it? How are you?'

The voice was cool – deeper and plumier than at school – but strangely accented now too. With perfect timing a bead of sweat ran down Breeda's forehead from under her cycling helmet and hung at the end of her nose. Breeda did her best to ignore it and tried not to think of the state she must look.

'Dervil!' A forced jollity. 'I brought you a cake, a little welcome. I heard you'd moved to town. Small world, hey?'

The proffered cake merely elicited a tightening of the smile, and the slightest raising of the eyebrows.

'Breeda, that is so sweet. But to be honest, I don't really *do* cake.' At this, her eyes flicked towards Breeda's waist.

'Oh, right. No problem. I just thought …'

The blonde seemed to momentarily lose interest, and her gaze drifted past Breeda, and to the view in the distance behind her. A fresh trickle of sweat ran down Breeda's neck and into her blouse. She bit at her bottom lip and dropped her gaze to Dervil's feet, where a perfect pedi poked out from a pair of open toe strappy stiletto heels. Breeda would kill to be anywhere else but at this front door right now.

'Was there anything else, Breeda? It's just that I'm a little busy.'

The cool gaze was fixed back on the unexpected sweaty interruption.

'Um–'

'Well, I must get on. Oh, and Breeda, I don't do popping in. OK?'

'Em, OK. Sorry. But Dervil, I just—'

The door closed firmly on Breeda's face. She blinked, stumbled back a step, then stared at the knocker on the front door. Part of her half-expected Dervil to fling open the door, shout 'Gotcha!' and pull her into a joker's embrace. But the stiletto heels continued their echoey clack down the hallway until Breeda could hear them no more. Breeda turned her back slowly to the door and hugged the cake close to herself. She gazed off towards the village, her body in a state of shock, her mind doubting what had just occurred. The gravel crunched pitiably underfoot as she guided her bike carefully down the steep driveway. Once again Breeda felt the bitter sting of being a twelve-year-old loser. And as she fought to keep the tremor from her lower lip she realised, with no lack of dread, that there still existed unfinished business between Dervil Sneddon and Breeda Looney.

CHAPTER 13

'She what?'

'Yep. She looked at the cake and grimaced. I wanted to deck the bitch.'

Breeda had the phone cradled to her neck. She slammed the kitchen drawer and stabbed at the carrot cake with a fork. She could still picture Dervil's face, all condescension and tight ponytail as Breeda had stood like an idiot on the doorstep only an hour ago.

Breeda scooped more cake into her face.

'Yeah, get this Oona. She doesn't "do cake"', Breeda air-quoted from the kitchen sink. 'Like, can you believe it? Stuck-up madam with her stuck-up accent - what is it anyway? Is she Australian now? I reckon the Botox has leaked into her brain.'

Breeda shoveled another hefty forkful of cake into her mouth.

'Christ, Bree. That really surprises me. Dougie told me she was absolutely lovely when he was up working on the house. But you know what? Well done you for trying …'

Bless Oona. She'd find a positive in a lump of shite.

Breeda nodded through another mouthful of cake. She had tried. She had attempted to build a bridge. But good old Dervil hadn't changed one iota, even after twenty-five years. Breeda looked out the window down towards the pier. Already the shock at her run-in with Dervil had begun to harden into something spiky – an anger with herself for being such a sap. She took another mouthful of cake – it tasted bloody good – too good to waste on the likes of Dervil Sneddon.

'But Bree, here's the thing. Why does she actually dislike you so much?'

Breeda raised the fork to her mouth, then slowly returned it to the dish. It was a good question, alright.

Oona continued. 'I mean something must have happened, back in the day …'

Breeda put the dish on the countertop and sighed down the phone.

'That's the weird thing, Oona. I was harmless at school. You know me, I wouldn't say boo to a goose. She just seemed to turn on me one day in class. Decided I wasn't invited to her birthday party, and then it all went downhill from there. But I never did anything to annoy her.'

A non-committal noise came down the phone from Oona, a sly encouragement for her friend to engage in more self-reflection. A memory clambered up from Breeda's vault now - a difficult one that she'd never choose to revisit. A difficult one because it involved poor old Father Green.

The day that Breeda had been escorted out of Father Green's office by Mrs Shields, the tongues had wagged like never before. Breeda had spent a free class hiding in a toilet cubicle, but it had been impossible not to overhear the cruel words that flew about each time the girls entered the bathroom. She could handle the lies they spread about her – her name was mud, after all. But Father Green…? Their self-righteous hatred stunned Breeda into a kind of paralysis that afternoon. And in French class the next day, Dervil had oh-so-cleverly even started referring to Father Green as *Père Vert*. The vicious moniker had instantly taken off, and the man's tainted status was sealed. There were barbs about Breeda too, of course. Even an innocent discussion on French food had Dervil tripping over herself to comment on how Brie was smelly, and it spread easily. The sniggers had rippled through the class, but the teacher was oblivious – or as Breeda suspected – willfully ignorant.

And there was worse to come. Father Green was to be transferred – that was how things were done in those days – and had naively come over to the Looney house to say his goodbyes to Breeda. Breeda had been staring out her bedroom window – devoid of friends, and homework finished – when she'd caught sight of him coming down the road. He'd rested his bike against the front wall and had been walking up the front path when Breeda's mother had flung open the door. Breeda had listened from her bedroom as Margaret launched hysterically at the poor man. All 'how dare you show your face here' and 'you should be locked up!' He'd tried to calm her, saying he'd just come to say goodbye, and to thank Breeda for all her hard work. Breeda had struggled to hear his exact words, but she could grasp the defeat in his voice. Back at her window, she watched him close the gate behind himself, and rest his hand on the handlebars of his rickety old bike. He looked broken, his shoulders slumped, his face collapsed and hanging with defeat. He must have sensed something at that moment, for he turned and looked up towards her. For a reason, that to this day Breeda could never fathom, she stepped back from the window. Maybe she felt the weight of guilt that everyone else should have been feeling at that time. She stood rigid behind the curtain, her eyes tightly closed, and held her breath. And suddenly she did feel ashamed. She could snap out of it and do the right thing – run down the stairs, out past her protesting mother, and catch up with him. She could tell him it was all OK, and sure aren't people awful, and keep in touch Father, and don't let them get you down. But when she did finally open her eyes, he was already disappearing around the corner, his black socks in his black sandals, pedaling him away from this hell hole.

Back in Breeda's kitchen, Ginger bumped into her calves, hoping for a scrap of whatever was in the abandoned cake dish. Breeda blew her nose into a tissue and looked up at the clock. The cradled phone was beginning to seize up her neck.

'Jesus, Oona. Look at the time. I've a cat that needs feeding, and I think I need to get to bed myself. I'm cream-crackered. Chat tomorrow?'

'Alright so. Have a good sleep, my crazy friend.'

'Thanks, love. Night night.'

Breeda hung up and spooned a tin of cat food into Ginger's bowl, then rested her bum against the countertop. The cycling had left her with a satisfying ache in her glutes and thighs. A good night's sleep was on the cards.

She grabbed the shiraz from the window sill and emptied the remains into her favourite wine glass.

Turning her back to the window, she took a generous sip. Carrot cake and red wine: the supper of champions.

Her eyes felt tired, and her gaze drifted slowly around the kitchen. She sucked half-heartedly at a small piece of chopped carrot still stuck between her teeth. What a headwreck the past twenty-four hours had been. The blackness on Main Street, Myra's mix-up in the pub, the stupid business down at the pier (her face reddened at the thoughts of Mad Paddy Byrne), the birthday card, Nora, Dervil. She found herself shaking her head at the whole madness. It was like she was off kilter with the universe, two steps too far to the left.

The envelope which had managed to avoid Nora's fireplace that morning was poking out from behind an overripe banana in the fruit bowl. Breeda picked it out and turned it over in her hands. Was her poor mother really that loopy that she'd have written a birthday card to Breeda pretending she was a dead man? Sitting at the table she took another sip of wine and stared vacantly at the banana in the fruit bowl. Breeda pictured how Nora had been that morning. There'd been a kind of wariness about her. She held up the envelope to her nose and inhaled deeply. Then she stroked it gently against her cheek, hoping her senses could bring forth the truth of the matter. The paper was bone dry now, the only evidence of this morning's rain in the car park a subtle warping. The writing, if anything, seemed even more faint than before, and the postmark over the stamp was illegible. Breeda looked at the top corner of the envelope again, squinting closer in the twilight gloom of the kitchen. She stood quickly. The chair clattered behind her, and she lunged for the light switch on the wall.

How had she missed it?

The little red stamp, so obvious now that she'd spotted it. The side profile of Queen Elizabeth II. The envelope hadn't been posted in Ireland. Breeda sat back down at the table and stared blankly at the envelope. There had to be a simple explanation. It could have been posted in Northern Ireland. But Breeda knew her mother had been paranoid about setting foot across the border, even if it was only up the road; Margaret had been terrified of being in the wrong place at the wrong time. The blood swooshed in Breeda's temple as she searched for some logic. And Margaret definitely hadn't been back over to England since they'd moved to Donegal. Breeda reached for her phone and scrolled to her Aunt's name. Nora would know what to say. She'd tut and sigh at Breeda's silliness, make sense of it, and tell her that she was being ridiculous. Breeda noticed a tremor in her hand. Her finger wavered over the dial button. Then she slowly placed the phone back on the table. Her mother hadn't written that birthday card. Nora was lying to her.

Breeda skulled the wine and thought back to Nora that morning, ripping up the card and casting it in the fire, a cold and mask-like quality about her face. A chill ran over Breeda's body and she stared at the envelope again. She grabbed her laptop from the kitchen counter and sat it down on the table beside the envelope. The browser waited patiently. She hovered her fingers over the search bar while her teeth played with her bottom lip.

The Dunry Examiner, that was it.

She typed the words into the search bar, then stopped. It still wasn't too late. There was still time to stop the whole thing – to pretend she'd never found the card – and put her trust in Nora. She still had the opportunity to sweep the whole silly episode away into the dark recesses of her mind. The cursor blinked expectantly, but the envelope drew Breeda's eyes back, and she ran her fingers softly over the faded handwriting.

Her poor father could be out there somewhere, believing that his own daughter wanted nothing to do with him, not bothering to write to him even once over the years. Her foot jiggled on the floor.

It mightn't be too late.

She allowed the briefest little flutter of excitement to travel up into her chest where it danced and tapped at her heart.

He might still be alive.

She took a deep breath and hit the *Enter* key.

CHAPTER 14

A staircase loomed up in front of Breeda. It looked familiar, yet alien, each step covered in a slick and shiny tar-like black. She stepped her left foot onto the first stair and felt a warm squelch as her bare skin sank into the sticky darkness. Something up ahead called to her, but the space was dark and gave nothing away. She forced her right foot onto the next stair, and gripped the banister, slowly climbing, each stair sucking and unwilling to surrender. She knew this place, but not like this. The voice again, called her. Breeda felt movement on her ankles and looked down to the darkness underfoot. A writhing mass of brown and pink worms was spilling down from the upper stairs and slopping onto her feet. She looked behind her, but the lower stairs had vanished now, leaving a nothingness in her wake. She turned her focus to the top stair and pushed on. When she reached the landing, she saw a low light from under a door. The door opened silently at her touch and she knew where she was. The crucifix on the wall. The single bed with the fusty bedspread. This was Nora's spare room. Breeda lay on the bed, the springs creaking under her weight, and looked up at the crucifix hanging above her head.

Someone was watching her from the doorway. She turned her head, but the stranger's face was hidden in the gloom. It was a man. Someone she knew but couldn't recognize. He took a step towards her now and she tried to lift her head, but her body was heavy and pulled her down onto the mattress. She stared at him, the face constantly changing, the features washing in and out to form a thousand permutations. For a split second his face seemed to settle and become Mal Looney. But just as quickly the eyes changed, then the shape of the chin, and Breeda found herself looking at Brian. He swaggered towards her and sat on the side of the bed, stroking her hair. He smelled of curry and cigarettes and had a cold sore on his lower lip. He leaned in to kiss Breeda, and she struggled her face away, left then right, her head like a dead weight on the pillow. He took her chin in his hands now, and when she looked at him again, he was no longer Brian. A pair of green eyes smiled down at her. She knew this man, yet she didn't. But she felt safe nonetheless, sensed goodness in him.

The stranger climbed onto the bed and Breeda guided his body onto hers. She felt his weight rest on her, and she gently eased her legs apart, letting the man settle into the warm shape she created. Her hands trailed smoothly down his back, and cupped his arse cheeks, her fingertips playing with the thinness of his yoga shorts. A slow and rhythmic thrusting had started up between them, a wordless dance that Breeda was hungry for. She felt his hardness push against her, enter into her, and she gripped his shoulders as she gave herself to him. The bedsprings creaked, and the whole bed shifted under the crucifix. She could hear a noise from next door – Nora, stirring from her sleep. Slippered feet shuffled in the next room. Nora was coming. Breeda raised her feet high in the air and used the back of each foot to drive the man even deeper into her. She needed this. Their speed increased. She could hear Nora's door.

Nearly there, nearly there.

Breeda looked back at the man's face, but the features were starting to swim again. It didn't matter. She pushed against him, their rhythm perfect. Nora's footsteps were at the door. But she didn't care. Breeda had arrived. She arched her back and …

Breeda woke up, fierce waves of pleasure pulsing through her core. Her skin was damp, her breathing heavy, and as she lay there in her own bed she gave herself over to it. But even fully awake, something continued to thrust at her groin. She grappled for the lamp switch. Ginger sat at the hot space between her legs, rhythmically kneading her with two front paws. Ecstatic purrs resonated in the air.

'Get off!'

Breeda pulled her legs up and shoved the cat off the bed with her heel.

'Fuck. Fuck, fuck.'

She watched the cat's retreating bum, its tail in the air, a study in indifference.

'Sorry, Ginge!'

Breeda shook her head and sat cringing in a shameful confusion for a moment, realising that her sex life had just reached a new low. She exhaled slowly, swung her legs gingerly over the side of the bed and squinted at the clock. It was nearly midnight. She'd make herself a hot milk and hopefully get back to sleep. As she pattered down to the kitchen, she tried to remember the various elements of the dream, but already they were darting from her consciousness. Breeda poured some milk into the saucepan and tipped a little bit into Ginger's bowl. The cat looked at her afresh, its unglamorous eviction from the bed already water under the bridge. Breeda ran a hand gently down Ginger's spine as the cat lapped happily at the milk.

'If only humans could be as forgiving, hey Ginge?'

Breeda unlocked the back door to let in some night air. It was still and cool and welcome on her clammy skin, and she stepped out into the back garden. The stone pier down below was deserted, the trawlers out again for their nightly catch, and Breeda remembered her silliness down there last night and felt a lump in her throat.

In the background she could hear the faintest trace of music. She walked slowly along the back of her house, trailing her fingers along the whitewashed wall, to where it joined with the Feeley house. A warm orange glow was coming from Finbarr's kitchen window. Breeda stood back in the shadows and looked in at her neighbor as he played a haunting slow air on his fiddle. The lit fireplace in his kitchen cast long shadows of the fiddler and his bow on the walls and ceiling, and as Breeda leaned in a little closer to the window she noticed a look of pure sadness on Finbarr's face.

Breeda had heard about Finbarr's wife. A few months ago he'd opened his heart to Margaret on one of his visits to her bedside. He'd sat with Margaret's thin hand in his own stocky fingers and spoke in a low and considered tone about his own experience with sickness and loss. Breeda knew that a man like Finbarr wouldn't uncork his aching heart very often, so she'd kept herself busy downstairs in the kitchen, curbing her own curiosity, and giving her neighbor and her mother the space they needed. Later, after he'd gone home, Margaret had filled Breeda in on some of the details. Her name had been Ellen. A young Canadian nurse who had been hitchhiking along the West coast of Ireland when one day fate had brought them together. Finbarr and Ellen had enjoyed seven years together, and it was only when they'd started trying for a child that cancer decided to lash its cruel claws into her. When at last it took Ellen from him, Finbarr could no longer face life on the farmhouse they'd together called home, and so he'd ended up moving next door to the Looneys.

Now, watching him through his window, Breeda wondered if his music, like her own mother's painting, was his way of managing his pain. As he continued to play he closed his eyes and Breeda suddenly felt improper. She shouldn't be trespassing on this private moment. She dropped her gaze and stepped back softly into the shadows where she turned her face towards the stars overhead. Finbarr's fiddle music wavered dizzily and took flight into the night sky above her and Breeda found herself wondering if there was anyone out there untouched by the burden of a heavy heart. She hugged herself for a moment, the air around her suddenly chilly, and turned slowly back towards the warmth of her own house.

Just out of earshot, Breeda's laptop chimed once on her kitchen counter. An email had arrived from her past, and a can of worms had well and truly been opened.

CHAPTER 15

Saturday morning was sunny and blustery, one of those perky days to blow away the cobwebs. Breeda's limbs felt fizzy as she walked the length of the pier, seagulls circling and swooping overhead. Her mind raced as she turned at the end of the pier, then retraced her steps back towards the village. Up ahead, potted nasturtiums twitched happily on either side of the red door to Grounds for Divorce. Breeda was in the mood for a coffee, and maybe a slice of cake. She allowed herself a small smile. The online ad she'd placed in *The Dunry Examiner* the previous evening had already got a response.

The email had come from Rita O'Hanlon – a name and a face Breeda hadn't thought of in many years. Dear old Mrs O'Hanlon. She'd taught Breeda for a while back in Dunry, in those days before Dervil Sneddon had made Breeda's school days hell.

Breeda picked up her pace. She would grab a skimmed latte and sit quietly in the back corner of the cafe and plan her reply to Mrs O'Hanlon. The woman had invited Breeda back to Dunry for lunch on Monday. Her email had been warm but pared back, and it was obvious she didn't want to put anything relating to Malachy Looney in writing. Breeda had been flustered with excitement since reading the email, her brain buzzing with a million questions. But now, as the thought of returning to Dunry settled in, she found her footsteps slowing a little. Dunry. The place she was born. The place they'd left hurriedly at the crack of dawn twenty-five years ago. A place full of pain and confusion and god-knows-what-else. Only three hours drive from Carrickross, it might as well have been a thousand years and a million miles away. She never thought she'd return to the place, and now the prospect of going back there made her a little queasy.

Breeda put a hand to her stomach and decided a pot of tea would be better than coffee. The cafe door opened as she approached. She heard his voice, that booming laugh of his. Another voice too. The American woman. Breeda grabbed her phone from her pocket, and stuck it to her ear, just as Brian and Alex-from-the-Boston-Office stepped out into the morning light. They stopped abruptly, all startled eyes and rictus grins. Breeda gave her best smile to them both, then talked into her mobile, as if mid-conversation.

'No problem, Mister Sheridan ...'

Brian and Alex-from-the-Boston-Office were still standing at the door, waiting. Breeda looked at Alex-from-the-Boston-Office's pristine white sneakers and willed them on.

'OK, Mister Sheridan. That's absolutely fine ...' Breeda was good at this. Maybe she should do an improv course. She looked at Brian and rolled her eyes. Would Mr Sheridan *ever* stop yakking.

Breeda stood to the side, hoping they'd take the hint and walk on. Brian had his hand in the small of Alex-from-the-Boston-Office's back, encouraging her to walk on, not wanting a scene. But the woman was resisting. Breeda could guess why. She was going to check that Breeda was okay after the humiliating episode in the pub the other night. Breeda couldn't face that – not sympathy from a relative stranger – well-intentioned as she might be. Breeda smiled again, and turned her back towards them, making nonspecific *mmms* and *ahhs* into her phone.

And then it rang. Her bloody phone rang. Brian and Alex-from-the-Boston-Office stood watching as Breeda's face turned crimson.

'Mister Sheridan, I'll have to call you back, I've another call coming through …'

Breeda turned, and pushed through the cafe door, the phone still ringing in her ear, her neck a network of prickles. She walked straight to the back corner and glared at the screen.

Nora.

Breeda jabbed at the reject button and stuffed the phone into her jacket packet. She sat heavily at the table and craned her neck towards the window. Brian and Alex-from-the-Boston-Office were walking slowly off down towards the beach. She could see him shaking his head, no doubt making a wisecrack about crackpot Breeda.

From her jacket pocket the phone rang.

Nora – again.

Whatever she wanted couldn't be that urgent. She could just bloody well wait. Breeda kept her finger pressed against the off button, then relaxed back into her seat, as she watched the phone screen pulse then die.

CHAPTER 16

After lunch Breeda glided around her bedroom. She hummed to herself, as she dropped random items into a tote bag, which gaped up at her from the top of the bed.

Phone charger - check

Smart outfit - check

Casual outfit - check

Comfy shoes, toiletry bag, sunglasses. Check. Check. Check.

She stood in her dressing gown, looking down into the bag, her hands on her hips and her damp hair wrapped in a turban towel. She gave a satisfied nod to no-one in particular.

When she'd gotten home from the cafe, she'd quickly composed a reply to Mrs O'Hanlon's email, and shot it off before she could change her mind. No going back now. Breeda would have to call in sick to Mr Sheridan on Monday morning. She'd do it on the three hour drive down the road. She felt her buzz die a little at the thought of lying to him. He'd been more than decent to her, always flexible with her shifts, up to and following her mother's death. She pictured herself being spotted by him – or worse – by Nora, or Myra Finch. She'd just have to set off a little earlier than required on Monday morning, and get back after dark.

As she pulled the bedroom door behind her, Breeda could hear Finbarr start up his hammering and banging next door. She smiled. For once she didn't mind. But as she came down the stairs, something felt not quite right. The hammering noise. It wasn't coming from Finbarr's roof, or even his side of the common wall. A blurry movement caught Breeda's eye through the opaque pane of the front door.

'What the …?'

Johnny Nesbitt, from O'Donoghue's Estate Agents, was in Breeda's front garden, dressed in a skinny navy suit, and smiling down at her from atop a three-step ladder. As he dropped his mallet onto the grass, he grabbed the post he'd been hammering with both hands and gave it a good shake.

'Now. That should hold. And a very good day to you, Breeda. I hope I didn't disturb your bath?'

Breeda stared up at him, open-mouthed.

'So, I'd expect quite a lot of interest. Good time of year. Exceptional views. Decent sized plot. Yadda yadda …' He jumped down, picked up the mallet, and turned sideways to her, practising his winning golf swing on an imaginary course. 'Nice!' He turned back to her. 'Floor plans are booked in for Monday afternoon. We'll do the photos then too - do try and clear away any clutter and tatt, OK? And we'll aim to get some viewings mid-week …' The young man pressed his card into her hand, picked up his ladder, and headed off. 'Cheers for now, Breeda. You have yourself an awesome day.'

Breeda looked up at the *For Sale* sign, then at the back of Johnny Nesbitt's retreating suit, then up at the

For Sale sign again. And then she heard herself laugh. She wished Oona was here to see this.

'Johnny - sorry - I think there's been a mix-up. You see I'm not selling …'

She walked after him now, his branded car parked cheekily across her driveway. The Estate Agent grabbed a file from his passenger seat and turned to Breeda as he riffled through the dossier of paper-clipped pages. Breeda found herself momentarily distracted by the slick hair and the brilliance of his teeth. The guy was a walking cliché. Well, his cocky smile was about to vanish.

'Yep. Here we are. Vendor's name: Nora Cullen. That would be your Aunt Nora? Look - she signed here – just this morning – all legit and above board.' He leaned in towards her. 'I have to say though, I've never seen someone so keen to get a place sold. Weird she didn't mention it to you though?' He flashed the smile again and tossed the folder back in the car. 'Anyhoo, I'll be in touch.' He climbed into the shiny black car and buzzed down the window. 'Remember Breeda - de-cluttering is our friend.' He winked and gave his horn a jaunty toot. 'Ciao ciao now.'

Breeda stood looking after the car as it sped off in the direction of town. With the sound of the engine fading, a surreal silence settled over the garden and even muted the birds. Breeda saw herself, as if from the perspective of a hovering drone, standing halfway along her driveway, the hem of her dressing gown being buffeted in the early afternoon breeze.

She turned to look up at the *For Sale* sign. So Nora must have heard about the ad in the paper. And now she was trying to thwart Breeda's attempts to find her father. But this? Who the hell was Nora Cullen to try and sell Breeda's family home from under her? These four walls had been Breeda and Margaret's home for the past twenty-five years. Nora had lost the plot – this wasn't her house to sell. Breeda pictured a version of her future - the one Nora fancied - mapping out in front of her. A future spent in Nora's poky spare room with its creaky single bed and the crucifix hanging above it. Breeda would rather die than live a claustrophobic life under her aunt's watchful eye. She looked down to her slippered feet and shook her head.

A low cloud had moved overheard and drained the light from the ground around Breeda. And now as her chest tightened, she felt her pulse quicken. A fiery ball of anger pounded at her rib cage. The years of put-downs and insults and judgements - Breeda had had enough. The woman needed to show her some respect.

Breeda pulled the phone from her dressing gown pocket, her anger level surging, and marched towards the sign. She hit the dial button.

'Pick up … Pick up!'

With the phone clamped to one ear she used her other hand to pull and push the signpost, but it wouldn't budge. A few more rings, and Nora's voice mail greeting kicked in. Breeda hung up and kicked the post as hard as she could in her slippered feet. She kicked it again. And again, harder this time. She flung the phone on the grass and took a run at the stubborn bastard of a sign, determined to get the thing out of the ground and off her property. She ran full pelt at it, hit it at the wrong angle, and landed heavily in the flower bed. A rock hidden

103

among the daffodils jabbed into her lower back. But she lay still, her panting the only noise. The cloud moved off, and she closed her eyes against the glare of the sky. And then she heard it, a throat being cleared. A shadow flitted above and she looked up. Finbarr was observing her from the roof, his face etched with confusion.

'Miss Looney? You're not selling …?'

Breeda sprang to her feet and glared at him, her face like thunder.

'Selling, Finbarr? Selling, my arse!'

Finbarr flinched, startled at her anger, and stepped backwards on the roof. But Breeda had no time to feel bad. She stormed into her front hall, her heart thumping, and grabbed her car keys from the hook by the door.

Nora Cullen had crossed the line.

CHAPTER 17

Nora squinted up at the sky above St Colmcille's church, and seemed satisfied that there was no rain on the way. She smoothed the starched white cloth on the trestle table in front of her and felt the warmth of the reflected sunlight catching her face from below. Standing in the neatly maintained church grounds she imagined she looked beatific. She surveyed the clipped bushes and tidy lawn in front of her book stall and allowed herself to relax a little. Everything was in order. It was all going to be fine.

She leaned over to straighten up Nelson Mandela in the memoir section, and then, with her heel, firmly slid a box of undisplayed books – tatty and questionable donations – further under the table. It was tempting to crawl under the table herself, to stretch out amid the cool shadows and close her eyes. It had taken ages to get to sleep the night before, worries about her wayward niece needling her thoughts and chasing comfort from the bed. But at two thirty in the morning, Nora had settled on a plan, making a note on the pad by the bed – *Call Estate Agent* – after which she'd plumped her pillow and fallen fast asleep. Breeda would just have to learn who was boss. The absolute audacity! Asking for information on Malachy Looney in *The Dunry Examiner*. Did she really think she could get anything past Nora Cullen?

Nora pulled at a button on her tweed jacket and looked up at the sky again. The day was warming up, and her mouth was now officially parched. She looked across the heads of the middle-aged parishioners who were starting to arrive.

Where was Myra with that cup of tea?

'Splendid as always, Nora.' A man's voice. A rich baritone.

Nora turned, a hand to her heart.

'Oh, Father McFadden. Isn't it only a glorious day …' She knew her cheeks were pink. The priest flashed her a smile and walked a couple of well-manicured fingers along the spines of a few books, humming a hymn to himself. There was something about Jim McFadden which slightly undid Nora. He was over six-foot-tall, and his thick dark hair was greying at the temples. Nora looked up from his hands to find him smiling at her.

'Nora, where would we be without you?'

'Father McFadden … what do you mean?' She raised a hand to her ear and knew her cheeks were blushing.

'You're an absolute trooper, Nora. The fundraising, the committee, the meals on wheels …'

She let the priest continue. Nora hadn't done meals-on-wheels in years. But he was on a roll. He was talking now about an interdenominational weekend next month. Nora watched his lips move and nodded. His foot seemed to connect with something under the table, and he bent down to move whatever it was out of the way. When he stood back up, he was holding some of the tatty paperbacks from one of the donated boxes. He proceeded to stack them on top of Nora's good gardening section. He continued to talk – fixing Nora with his dark eyes – about the importance of cross-border initiatives. His hands found one of the books, and he picked it up absentmindedly, and bounced it lightly on top of the stack as he spoke. The back of the book was facing Nora. She squinted and turned her head ever so slightly. The back cover had a naked woman with her hands in cuffs and a ball gag in her mouth. The blood drained from Nora's face. With every fibre in her body she willed the priest to not look down.

'So, what do you think?'

'What's that, Father?'

'The fundraising walk? Would you be able to donate a couple of hours?'

Father McFadden had raised the book, and was now tapping it lightly against his chin, his bottom lip curled over the top of it, his puppy-dog eyes daring Nora to turn him down. Nora's gaze darted between the naked woman and the priest's mouth, feeling like she'd stumbled into a kinky threesome. She nodded furiously to the priest, her heart pounding beneath the tight tweed jacket.

'Good, good. I knew I could count on you, Nora.'

Mission accomplished, the priest sat the book back down, patted the table and headed off with a winner's smile – next stop Mrs Kelly and her homemade chutneys. Keeping her eyes on the milling crowd, Nora nimbly grabbed the offending item and the other tatty books and flung them back into the cardboard box under the table. She wiped her hands on her jacket and stood up straight, willing herself back into a state of chaste composure. She rubbed her silver crucifix between thumb and forefinger, and at last there was Myra with her cup of tea.

'The queue, Nora! The queue!'

Myra handed her a cup (no saucer) and placed her own cup clumsily on the table, where it slopped over the rim and onto the white linen tablecloth.

'Oh, for goodness sake, Myra Finch, have you no sense …'

But Myra wasn't listening. A stirring amongst some of the meandering crowd had caught her attention, and she followed the gaze of a few well-coiffed heads, now turned in the direction of a commotion at the churchyard entrance.

CHAPTER 18

Breeda had arrived in a satisfying spray of gravel and as she crunched up the path towards the church she locked eyes on her target. Parishioners scattered, a Red Sea parting to make way for the crazy woman in her muddy dressing gown. Myra Finch was mouthing something to Nora – nothing new there – and now Nora was looking up too.

It was a thing of beauty to witness. Nora's mastery of her reactions was exceptional, better than any Vegas poker player. As Breeda marched towards the book stall it was as if Nora could conjure up some Wiccan hocus-pocus and stretch the very essence of time to compose herself. Within a second of seeing Breeda storming towards her, Nora had worked through shock, fear, and penny-dropping, and was now planning damage limitation and dignity retention. Before Breeda even got to open her mouth Nora had raised a guiding hand in the direction of the side of the church.

'This way, Breeda …' She was smiling at the curious onlookers and rolled her eyes in her best 'Oh dear, what has Breeda been up to now …?' expression. With her smile locked in place, her eyes gave extra crinkle to Father McFadden, as she turned from her book stall, and set off down the side path of the church yard.

'Nora, slow down! I want to talk to you …'

But Nora moved swiftly. Breeda could see her hands were balled into fists. She powered on, taking them deeper into the graveyard, towards a bank of Ash trees near the crumbling stone wall. Breeda knew about the old unmarked graves on the other side of that wall – the graves of paupers and babies born out of wedlock.

'Nora. Stop!'

She reached for her aunt's shoulder, and Nora spun. Breeda flinched and stopped in her tracks. Inches in front of her Nora glared with devil eyes and a pulsing temple from beneath her perfect blow-dry. Breeda, unnerved, cast a glance back the way they'd come, but the two women were alone among the headstones.

'Aunt Nora, I don't understand what's happening? You can't sell the house.' A brief pause as Breeda watched the rise and fall of her Aunt's shoulders in their tweed armor. She decided to push on, 'Anyway, it's not yours to sell.'

Nora's eyes widened at the challenge and when she spoke the words came clear and controlled.

'Oh, but you see Breeda - the house *is* mine to sell.'

The eyebrows raised now, inviting Breeda to contradict her.

'That house is indeed most definitely mine to sell. It's in my name. I bought it when we moved here and charged your mother a nominal rent. A pittance. She was my tenant, I was her landlord. I looked after her. That's what family do, did you know that Breeda? They look after each other.'

Breeda dropped her eyes from Nora's hawk like stare. She wracked her brain for some proof, something – anything – to disprove what Nora was now telling her.

There would be deeds, or bank statements, or some damn thing in the back of a drawer somewhere. There had to be. Breeda felt a cold sweat on the back of her neck. This couldn't be happening.

'But Aunt Nora, you can't do this.' The statement came out more as a question and Breeda hated the whiny desperation she could hear in her own voice. She lowered her gaze to her aunt's shoes, 'I'll have nowhere to go ...'

'Well, you probably should have thought of that before you disobeyed me.'

So she *had* seen the online ad. Breeda looked up now. Nora nodded at her, unblinkingly.

'Oh yes, Breeda. I know you think I'm a daft old biddy, but nothing gets past your Aunt Nora. I have my contacts.'

'But Nora, what will I do?'

Nora leaned in towards Breeda now.

'Here's what you'll do. You'll leave the past in the past – as I instructed you to do. You'll pack your bags tomorrow. And you'll unpack them in my spare room on Monday.

A show reel flickered to life in Breeda's mind now, her future plotted out so clearly. The stifling spare room, the front door bolted at ten each night, the snippy comments, the tuts and sighs - death by a thousand put-downs. She couldn't do it.

Nora was giving her a dry bath.

'Would you take a look at yourself!'

Breeda looked down at her faded purple dressing gown, patchy with mud from her earlier run-in with the *For Sale* sign. She couldn't think of anything to say.

'If you can't behave like an adult, then I have no choice but to keep you on a tight leash.'

'Nora, I'm not a dog!'

'I told you! I told you to drop this whole thing,' the eyes were blazing again. 'How could you do this to your poor mother? Raking up the past like that …'

Nora turned towards the grave at her side and blessed herself. Breeda followed her gaze, and a bitter taste of sick arose from her stomach. She had been so distracted, so rushed, that she'd not even registered that they were standing by her own mother's grave. Mere weeks ago she'd stood at this very spot, and laid a small bunch of native flowers on the coffin. And now, here she was, standing in her dressing gown, having a row with her only living relative. She lowered her eyes in shame. Nora had turned back to her now.

'Your poor mother. If she knew what you were up to she'd be turning in her grave.'

Nora closed her eyes and made the sign of the cross. The laugh left Breeda's mouth before she could stop it. Her whole life had flipped upside down, every aspect now so bloody surreal. Nora's fist was fast. The whack to Breeda's face was sharp. Her right ear stung and Breeda staggered backwards. Her hand grappled for something to steady herself, but she stumbled over a small lip of concrete and landed heavily on the grave.

'Pack your stuff. Vacate that house. Be at mine by 5pm Monday sharp.'

Breeda looked up from where she was sprawled on her mother's grave, but Nora had already turned and marched off, leaving her alone under the eerie stillness of the Ash trees.

At the end of the path – the last part in shadow – Nora stopped for a moment. Breeda watched as she smoothed down her jacket, patted her hair, and then walked around the corner to her awaiting parishioners.

CHAPTER 19

Westerly light bathed the front of Breeda's house in a surreal pink chalkiness. Oona twisted the screw cap off a bottle of pinot gris as Breeda walked towards her, unwrapping two wine glasses from newspaper cocoons.

'Rookie mistake, my friend. Always pack the wine glasses last.'

'I know. I know. Wine glasses, loo roll, teabags, kettle ...'

Oona poured them both wine, then shimmied her backside onto the hood of her car to sit beside Breeda. A few swifts wheeled and divebombed in the side garden and the two friends watched them in the twilight. In front of them, the *For Sale* sign stood by the front door, like a joykill bouncer.

Breeda had spent the last few hours in a frenzy of packing, trying not to think too much, as she emptied out kitchen cupboards, then pulled boxes of god-knows-what from the attic. But a heaviness had clung to her as she'd walked from room to room, slowing her down so that she'd moved like a wounded animal looking through resigned eyes for somewhere to lay down and die.

In the weeks following her mother's death, Breeda would experience a blissful few moments of ignorance each day — first thing, as she'd awaken — before the sad reality of her new life would thud heavily into her awareness. And each morning, she'd find herself staring vacantly at the crack in her bedroom ceiling, as the deafening quiet of the house would forcibly shoulder her heart into a clumsy realignment. She'd lie there, unmoving, and make herself pull up a fresh memory of her mother, a simple cognitive exercise to stop Margaret from running off and forever hiding in the shadowy corners of her mind. In those first few weeks a deluge of images had readily presented themselves — Margaret putting candles on cakes, or draping tinsel, or whispering *a chuisle mo chroí* as she'd tucked young Breeda in at night. But over the past few mornings Breeda had found her archive condensing, shrinking in on itself, so that she struggled to find anything other than recent memories with Margaret gaunt, bed-bound, half-gone. To make matters worse, Breeda could no longer remember her mother's voice — the subtle drawl of her Dunry accent or her off-key singing as she'd sat at her easel. She cursed herself for not having had the wherewithal to record her, to capture something, *anything*, on her phone. And it frightened Breeda, this fading — it frightened her, and it saddened her to her very core. But when she'd experience those struggles in conjuring the younger Margaret back, she'd simply stand at the kitchen counter, or open the cap on the shampoo bottle or plonk herself on the back step, and those distant memories, those ones from more carefree times, would come tumbling back to her.

This house, which has been Margaret's refuge from the world, and where they'd begun again after fleeing from Dunry, it was Breeda's key to those million memories which echoed in its bricks and mortar. And now Nora was cruelly prising it from her grip. Breeda took a long sip from her wine and looked down at a patch of grass.

'So, what are you going to do?'

Breeda turned to her friend and shook her head.

'I have no clue, Oona. Finish packing everything tomorrow. Look for somewhere else. I can't go to Dunry on Monday morning. I'll just have to knock that whole thing on the head. I don't know what I was thinking.' Breeda looked back up at the house and tried to ignore the lump in her throat. 'Nora wants me to move into hers on Monday. But I can't face that. Not after today.'

'Bree, you do know you can always crash at ours for a while? You have a spare key. I mean it.'

'Thanks Oona. I appreciate that, really. But I think it's time I stood on my own two feet.'

Oona sighed beside her.

'Christ, Bree, that's your home right there. You've lived within those four walls since you were twelve years old …'

As the two friends sat on the warm bonnet of the car and watched the setting sun reflect in the windows Breeda knew her heart was breaking. She'd made an absolute mess of things. Her shoulders began to shake.

'Ah, love. It's OK. Come here. You're not on your own …'

Breeda felt Oona's arm around her shoulders. She wiped her eyes with the back of her hand. Oona's sentiment was sweet, but she was wrong. Breeda *was* on her own. There was no knight in shining armor, no rich relative, no hero who was going to ride into town and save the day for Breeda Looney. She needed to fix this mess herself.

Oona tilted Breeda's face to get a better look at the red marks.

'I can't believe Nora did that to you …'

'Yep.'

'Friggin' nutcase.'

'Yep. I was lucky she didn't take the head off me.' Breeda took another sip of the chilled wine. 'I'm still in shock. I've never actually seen such vitriol in another person's face. It was like she was possessed.'

'And your Aunt Nora of all people … you just can't tell. A lot of these devout old ones are fierce into their threesomes and whips and stuff.'

Breeda started to choke on her drink. 'Would you stop! I do not need that image of Nora right now, thank you very much.'

The two friends nestled their wine glasses against their bosoms and regarded the ugly *For Sale* sign as the first of the evening stars appeared overhead. Breeda realised that this would be one of her last ever sunsets here. Part of her wished she'd never found that damn birthday card.

'Well, you know my theory, Bree …' Oona wiggled her bum on the car, preparing herself for lecture mode. 'In Western society anger is often the go-to emotion for people not able to deal with other negative, more painful, emotions. Anger's addictive. It can feel empowering. But it's usually a way of avoiding something difficult. You know – shame, hurt, anxiety, sadness …'

117

Breeda's mind often wandered when Oona quoted self-help books, or talked about her visits to ashrams, and unblocking her third eye. But something in her words was calling at Breeda's attention, like ginger cat hairs drawn to a black evening dress.

'Say that again, Oona.'

'Well, I just mean, what else might she be feeling if it wasn't anger? I mean, is it possible that you've done something that is making her feel threatened? Or scared?'

As Oona expounded on her theory Breeda raised the wine glass and tapped it gently off her bottom lip. Her pulse started a subtle quickening. Nora wasn't *angry*. She was bloody terrified. She was hiding something, and she was determined to stop Breeda from meddling. The birthday card from Mal Looney had been the trigger. At that moment a chill ran over Breeda's body.

'Bree?'

'Hmm?' Breeda looked up. Oona had hopped off the car and now stood waiting.

'I just said we could go in if you're getting cold?'

But Breeda sat for an extra moment, staring at the front of the house. She knew now what she had to do on Monday morning. She shimmied off the car, linked her arm through Oona's, and the two friends ambled towards the front door of number one Bayview Rise.

'You know what, Oona? I actually think I'm getting warmer.'

CHAPTER 20

On Monday morning, under a clear sky, Breeda's car clipped along the deserted roads in an Easterly direction. She had set off a little before eight, not long before the Nora Cullens and Myra Finches of the world would be flicking on their kettles and riffling through their post. She had filled the cat's bowl to overflowing ('Ginger, you don't need to eat it all now') and shoved a last-minute note under Finbarr's front door asking him if he'd mind her for a little while.

A little while.

How long was a little while? She'd love to know, herself. There was no reason she wouldn't be on her way back home from Dunry before teatime. Surely her lunch with Rita O'Hanlon would only take an hour – but who knows what she might find out, and where it might lead?

Breeda geared down into third as she overtook a refrigerated van. She looked at the stretch of country road ahead of her, the odometer on the dash ticking slowly but steadily. With every extra kilometer she put between herself and Carrickross, she was getting one kilometer closer to a place she never thought she'd return to. She had no clue what awaited her in Dunry. All she knew was that if Nora wasn't going to tell her the truth about her father she had no choice but to meet Mrs O'Hanlon.

Breeda's thoughts turned to Nora and she remembered how the woman had stood in the graveyard on Saturday, wound-up like a tight spring in her tweed two-piece. A woman who'd always had so much control and discipline, now reduced to a desperate bully. Breeda nudged the accelerator. She glanced at herself in the rear-view mirror. A graveyard-brawling, soon-to-be-homeless stranger blinked back at her. Was this the start of her slow descent into madness? Or was it something else? The finding of a missing piece – a piece that, deep down, Breeda had always sensed was missing?

She flicked on the radio, and turned up *Smooth FM*. *Chris deBurgh. The Lady In Red.*

Breeda settled back in the seat and allowed herself to hum along. At least she still had Oona. And her job. Speaking of which … Breeda needed to call Mister Sheridan to tell him she wouldn't be coming in today.

Up ahead she could see a quiet petrol station and Breeda pulled off the road. It was one of those places where a chap would still come out in overalls to *fill her up* and squeegee the windows. It was just before nine, and the forecourt was devoid of any other cars. Breeda parked, pulled out her phone, and scrolled through to Cork! It would be better to call the shop directly – Mr Sheridan wouldn't be in until ten-thirty or so – so she could just leave a message. Besides, she didn't want to speak to him. Breeda knew she was the world's worst liar.

He answered on the first ring.

Shit.

'Oh hi, Mr Sheridan!' *Double shit.* She'd forgotten to sound sick.

'Breeda? And a very good morning to the wonderful Miss Looney. And for the umpteenth time will you please call me George …'

She could hear him set his mug of tea back down.

'Now, I've made a start on those Nebbiolos. I'll wait until you get in before I get those Fianos shelved – you know me and ladders when I'm on my own …'

Breeda closed her eyes, pictured herself in a hospital gown, and dug deep for an Oscar-winning performance. She forced a slight croak into her voice.

'Ah, Mister Sheridan. I'm really sorry. I won't be in today. I'm coming down with something.'

Silence down the line. Breeda pressed on.

'Yeah, I think it's a viral thing. It's doing the rounds.' Should she attempt a cough? Probably best not. 'I reckon I picked it up at yoga …'

Breeda opened her eyes. She knew she was wincing at the pisspoor lie. She pictured the birthday card he had gone to the bother of sending her the other day. She slithered further down into the car seat and heard him sigh down the line.

'Well, Breeda. You better rest up. No point coming in here and spreading germs. Do you need me to bring you over anything?'

'No, no. I'm just going to sleep it off, hopefully. I'm really sorry, Mister Sheridan…' And she was. He was a decent man, and he deserved better. She'd make it up to him when the whole thing had blown over. Breeda pressed the phone closer to her ear. She could already hear the forgiveness in his tone.

'Just you focus on getting yourself shipshape, Breeda Looney, and we'll see you in a day or two.'

A sharp rap on the car window. Breeda jumped and let out a high-pitched whinny. The attendant in his oily overalls was motioning for her to wind down the window.

'Breeda - are you OK there?'

'I'm fine, Mr Sheridan. It's just the cat.'

'That front tyre's a bit flat. D'ya want me to put some air in it for ya?'

'Breeda?'

Breeda scrunched her eyes closed, trying to block out her reality. She shook her head violently, hoping the guy on the other side of her window would just shut the hell up.

'It's just the radio, Mr Sheridan. OK. Speak soon.'

She jabbed at the *Call End* button, then turned with a fixed smile to find the interrupting attendant staring brazenly at her tits.

By the time Breeda commenced her slow descent into Dunry the sky was dark and hanging low. She shifted in her seat and felt a pointy ache across her shoulder blades. A few drops of rain patterned her windscreen and as she rounded a bend in the road the township in the valley down below opened up before her like a grey patchwork quilt. Breeda's eyes flitted over the concrete jumble of slate roofs and old steeples – at once depressingly familiar, yet alien. The bread factory, the leisure complex, the shopping center and the schools, all seemingly unchanged from twenty-five years ago. There were no modern high rises, no flyovers, no churches re-imagined as destination Michelin-starred restaurants. It was as if the town had warded off the eye of any investors or developers. It was exactly as she remembered it. Maybe greyer. Maybe smaller. All Breeda knew was that she felt not one ounce of nostalgia, no heart-string pulled, no misty-eyed yearning in her bones for this place; just a sense of tightness at her throat, a pressing need to turn this car around, before descending any further into the valley.

Up ahead the traffic light turned red. Breeda watched as a young couple, both in their late teens, pushed a pram across the road. The orange-faced mother had several plastic shopping bags hooked over the handle of the pram. Breeda could make out the ready-meals, liters of coke, the sliced white, and the crisps. Not a single piece of fruit or veg in sight.

That poor baby, thought Breeda. *Already sentenced to a life of insulin, rotten gums, and leaving school at sixteen, to get a job in a supermarket two hundred meters from home, where it would end up stacking shelves with junk food for the next generation.*

Trailing a couple of feet behind the woman, the father held a cigarette in one hand and a super-sized can of energy drink in the other. As he knocked back the dregs from the can he spilt a little down his chin. He cursed as he wiped the front of his tracksuit top. The girlfriend turned to see what the fuss was about. As she turned back to the pram to shush the baby, she looked at Breeda. The woman smiled at her and rolled her eyes.

Men!

Breeda smiled back and felt an instant flush of shame. Who was she to judge these people? Weren't they just doing the best they knew how? The light turned green and Breeda moved off slowly, straining to catch a

123

final glimpse of the new family in her rear-view mirror, and silently wishing them the best of luck.

A few minutes later Breeda found the street with the pub where she was to have her lunchtime meeting. She pulled into a space in front of a betting shop. It was still a few minutes until midday. She took a look in the mirror, gave her hair a quick brush, and fingered on some lip balm. She knew she still had time; still had time to change her mind, to start the car and drive back to Carrickross. Still had time to not make this whole thing worse than it could be. She looked at the front of the pub further along the pavement. But no, whatever she might or might not find out, she owed it to her father. She owed it to herself.

She stepped out of the car. The hum of televised horse-racing droned out of the bookies onto the pavement, and Breeda stretched her hands overhead. An empty crisp bag cartwheeled past her ankle and she followed it towards the bridge. She trailed her hand along the rough pebble-dashed wall, and then stopped to look down on the slate grey river below, a murky graveyard of barely submerged shopping trolleys, abandoned bikes, and God-only-knows what else. Breeda closed her eyes, drew in her breath, and let the place wash over her – the wall under her fingertips, the chill breeze on her neck, the traffic noise in the distance, the smell of the algae from below – all of it. She wanted to be present, to remember this place and this moment, to lock it away in her sensory memory vault, in case she ever needed to return to the time before the Pandora's box was opened.

Over the rooftops the Cathedral bells commenced their midday clang. Breeda turned and walked quickly back down the street and pushed open the door of the pub before she could change her mind.

CHAPTER 21

Nora didn't mind the gays. In fairness, they were few and far between up here in Carrickross. And anyway, the few that did exist kept themselves to themselves. Apart from a few years ago. Then, there'd been an awful rake of them, strutting around the village in their 'YES' t-shirts, demanding votes, and wanting gay *this* and gay *that*. Nora checked her watch as she rounded the corner onto Main Street. She had no doubt that most of Breeda's generation considered her a dinosaur, a relic of another time. And they would have rolled their eyes behind her back and assumed she'd voted No in the referendum. Nora felt a smug little smile flit over her face. Well she hadn't voted No. Nora Cullen was a progressive woman. As she came to a stop outside the doorway of Cork! she watched George Sheridan lost in his cryptic crossword. He was standing at the counter, his tongue protruding in concentration, his poor belt straining to corral his generous paunch. What did Nora care if the likes of George Sheridan wanted to tie the knot with some fella? Not that he had a fella to walk him down the aisle anyway. Nora put her hand to the door. She hadn't voted Yes either. But that wasn't the point.

The bell trilled above Nora's head. George Sheridan looked up with a mild panic, and his hands moved to straighten the tie hanging over his belly. Nora suspected she scared the bejesus out of the man – and a part of her secretly delighted in the fact.

'Miss Cullen – and how are you on this fine day?'

Nora fixed him with a civil smile and moved towards the counter.

'Mr Sheridan. I was wondering if I might have a quick word with Breeda?' Nora sat her purse on the counter and started to remove her white gloves. She craned her neck to try and see beyond the man's bulk into the storeroom out back.

'Oh, it's young Breeda you're after? And I thought you might have finally rejected your teetotal ways.' He forced a guffaw but seemed to instantly regret it.

Nora looked him in the eye and felt her smile tighten. She hesitated for a moment and then sighed briefly – she could afford to throw the fool a scrap.

'Breeda is moving in with me later today. I want to check everything is in order …'

She folded her gloves neatly and laid them on the counter, then flipped open her purse and extracted a key. A small bronze figure of Saint Francis of Assisi dangled on the end of the key chain.

'And I need to give her the spare key. Is she on a break?' Nora tried to peer past the man again. 'Where is she?'

George Sheridan's face had taken on a most unpleasant moist pallor. His lips parted, but his fat tongue lolled over to the side of his mouth, and for a fleeting moment Nora wondered if the man was having a stroke. A noncommittal hum left him and hung in the air between them.

Nora flipped her purse shut, a fresh crease between her eyebrows.

'Mister Sheridan, I said where is Breeda?' She enunciated slowly and watched him closely. His beady eyes darted around the shop until he could avoid her gaze no longer.

'Breeda called in sick this morning. Bit of a viral thing.'

Nora stared at his chubby lips. 'So she's at home?'

'She's at home, yes. Tucked up and probably fast asleep. I dare say—'

But Nora was already at the door, the bell shrilling dramatically above her head. She stood still and silent, her body half-turned to the street. Her eyes studied the pavement at her feet for a second, then she turned and set off briskly in the direction of the Looney house. She bypassed pavement dawdlers glued to their phones. This just wouldn't do: the girl was scheduled to move in to Nora's this afternoon. The spare room was ready. Nora had left out two pork chops. She slowed her pace.

What if Breeda wasn't shivering under a mountain of blankets at this very moment …

What if …

A storminess passed across Nora's face. The toe of her shoe found a dip in a paving slab and she stumbled and lurched, then righted herself. At the side of the post office she stopped to catch her breath. Her shoulders heaved in her tight jacket and her hand troubled the crucifix at her chest. She looked up uneasily towards the house on Bayview Rise, then started up the hill.

CHAPTER 22

The chowder was a good recommendation – thick with fresh seafood, rich and comforting. Breeda wiped the last of her wheaten bread along the remaining cream and looked up from her bowl. Mrs O'Hanlon's eyes crinkled back at her over the rim of her teacup. She still had the same ruddy cheeks and wild hair, the same couldn't-care-less attitude, which had stood her apart from the other teachers back in the day. The woman sat her teacup down and burped softly into the back of her hand.

'And you've never been back since?'

'Not once.'

Under their table the old lady's golden retriever stretched and readjusted his heavy head against Breeda's ankle. She patted his haunch distractedly and gazed at the flames in the fireplace in the corner. A log cracked, a spark shot out, and the dog raised his head for a moment before giving himself back over to the call of slumber. Breeda glanced around the dark pub, its swirly carpet and smoke-stained ceiling a remnant of another time. At nearby tables locals sat murmuring to each other over soup and sandwiches.

'Well. It's good to see you back now, Breeda. And I'm sorry to hear about your poor mother. She always carried herself like a real lady.'

This brought a wistful smile to Breeda's face. Margaret Looney was a lady.

'But I have to admit to being a bit intrigued when I saw your ad in the paper. I do know–'

Mrs O'Hanlon sat back from the table as a lithe teenage girl with long red hair approached to clear their plates. The waitress eyed Breeda, in a not-unfriendly manner, obviously trying to place her.

Mrs O'Hanlon leaned in towards Breeda, once the waitress had left them again.

'And I'll be honest, Breeda. It was always thought strange. A family disappearing like that, and so soon after your father's–'

Breeda sat forward herself now. My father's what? *Drowning? Disappearance?* His what?

But Mrs O'Hanlon had gone silent again. The waitress was back with bloody dessert menus.

'Thanks,' Mrs O'Hanlon stood to button her jacket and untie the dog's lead, 'But I think we'll take Coco for a walk.'

Breeda stood too, suddenly feeling too hot and confined in the small low-ceilinged parlor. She'd be glad of the fresh air. And the chance to talk uninterrupted.

Behind the pub, the street climbed, then narrowed, and led them to a walkway into the overgrown grounds of a long-abandoned convent. Nettles and dandelions stood on either side of the well-worn steep track, and, looking up, Breeda could see what looked like an old mausoleum, now covered in tags and graffiti. Mrs O'Hanlon launched a chewed tennis ball from her stick, and Coco bounded after it, towards some long grass up ahead. Breeda unbuttoned her jacket and watched the old lady push on up the hill, the steepness of the track no bother to her.

'Nearly there, Breeda. There's a bench at the top with our names on it,' she said over her shoulder.

Breeda's breath was heavy and ragged. She stopped and rested her hands on her waist. 'Be there in a sec. Save me a spot.'

She turned to take in the view down below. Her eye was drawn beyond the briars and brambles, to the old convent building itself, down below her. Its walls were veined in dark ivy and the few unbroken windowpanes stared sullenly back at her, devoid of human life.

As Breeda stared down at the stark facade of the building, a memory came to her.

Hadn't Nora spent some time in there?

Above the weeds a Red Admiral flitted and tugged at her attention. Breeda watched its aerial dance, haphazard and angular, then looked back at the somber building below her.

She had! Nora had spent a few months in there.

Breeda's eyes slowly scanned the upper floor of the building, and she wondered if Nora had slept behind one of those windows, wondered if Nora had found whatever it was she'd sought within those high stone walls?

A wry smile played over Breeda's face. It was funny the things that got lost along the way. But being back here was bringing stuff up, and now it felt like old memories were queueing for oxygen. Her senses were being stimulated, and the archives were opening. Maybe it was hearing the dialect, with its languid nasal drone, the smallest trace with which Breeda still spoke. Maybe it was the permanent cloud hanging over the valley, and the end-of-days quality it afforded the daylight. Or maybe it was just *being* here.

Breeda turned to take in the wider tapestry of town down below her, the roof of the pub where they'd just had lunch, the bridge and the river, all now surprisingly distant. She followed the rooftops, from the spire of the cathedral, up a distant drumlin of squat, boxy houses. Her eyes fixed on a familiar roof. To an unfamiliar eye, just a random terraced house, but to Breeda, one with a million memories and twisted emotions. From up here she could see her old bedroom window. That very same window she had hidden behind, when a disgraced Father Peter Green had come over to try to make amends. Even now, she felt her throat rise and fall. She turned and carried on slowly up the track.

Mrs O'Hanlon was sitting on the bench, her legs stretched out, her ruddy cheeks threatening to explode.

'Isn't it a fabulous view, Breeda?'

Breeda shirked off her hot denim jacket and collapsed onto the bench.

'Sure is. Lovely.'

'So. What do you want to know?'

Breeda sat up straight. She could work with direct.

'Well, you know I'm looking for information on my dad. Mal Looney …'

'Mm-hmm …'

'Well …this is going to sound weird, so bear with me …' Breeda fidgeted on the hard bench and tongued at the dryness along her bottom lip. 'You see, I feel a bit of a fool saying this …' She rubbed her palms along the top of her jeans, 'But I'm not convinced my Dad died when I was a kid.'

Rita O'Hanlon extracted a packet of mint lozenges from her jacket pocket and slowly unfurled a wrap of foil, letting it dangle like pared apple skin. She popped a lozenge in her gob, then held the packet out to Breeda.

'No thanks.' Breeda cleared her throat, a sudden need to keep things moving. 'I found a card. A birthday card.' The words slid out as her eyes fixed on her old roof in the distance. 'My Dad sent it to me. I'm pretty sure he did. Anyway, my Aunt Nora—'

'Is that oul one still alive?'

'Yes. Aunt Nora tore—'

'I can't say I was ever a fan of Nora Cullen. She had tickets on herself, that one. Always a bit up herself, if you ask me. Wrecked my head any time I talked to her.'

Breeda sat back and waited. The mint lozenge cracked under Rita O'Hanlon's premolars.

'Well, what about your Aunt Nora?'

Breeda shuffled herself up straight again.

'Nora burnt the card. My card.'

At this, Rita O'Hanlon turned, aghast.

'Why would she–'

Breeda pressed on.

'I can't help but feel the card was legit, and if it is – was – then my dad might still be alive out there somewhere, not knowing I was kept in the dark. And he would most likely think I couldn't be bothered getting in touch …' Breeda paused and turned to look at the old teacher from her childhood. 'Nora won't help me. I'm kinda hoping you will …?'

Coco chose that moment to exit the long grass and sit in front of them. He splayed his back legs and dragged his arse across the ground. Mrs O'Hanlon laughed, but Breeda looked on vacantly. She needed answers, not laughs. Mrs O'Hanlon flung the tennis ball down the hill, and the dog disappeared after it, leaving the two women sitting in silence once more.

The old lady leaned forward, and twisted her wedding ring, modest and tarnished and fifty years old.

'Breeda, it was always considered a wee bit queer how youse all upped and left – you and your Mam and Nora. Vanishing at the crack of dawn like that, in the middle of winter, only days after your father's death.'

Breeda sat motionless, trying to ignore that last word, wanting Rita to continue.

'I'll be honest, I haven't seen hide nor hair of Malachy Looney since you all moved away.'

Breeda stared at the woman's wedding ring, tight against the fleshy finger.

'But if I was you, I'd trust my gut. I responded to your ad for a reason. Now, it might mean nothing …'

At this Breeda turned to face the woman. She stared at her moving lips, not trusting her ears alone to deal with what words might come next.

'There were rumors,' she nudged Breeda with her elbow, 'as there always are in wee backwaters like this. Anyway, apparently your Dad wasn't backwards at coming forwards, if you catch my drift.' A quick sideways glance at Breeda, 'He had a bit of a reputation as a *ladies' man* …'

Breeda shook her head. 'You mean …he–'

'Yes. Your old man was a complete slut. He'd probably be diagnosed with some trendy condition today, and be off to sexaholics anonymous, or whatever it's called. Am I being a bit insensitive?'

The color had drained from Breeda's face and she was grateful for the seat beneath her.

'No, you're OK …I'm just …well, it's all news to me. You know?'

A sympathetic hand landed on Breeda's knee, and gave it a reassuring pat. At the same moment her phone buzzed in her jacket.

Nora.

Breeda hit the *Reject Call* button and stuffed the phone back in her pocket. Mrs O'Hanlon had taken her hand off her knee and now Breeda noticed an insistent twitch in her own foot.

'Anyway,' the old lady continued, 'And do not quote me on this, Breeda, or I will deny it… One of Malachy's floozies was a bit tipsy a couple of years ago, when we were having Christmas drinks – at that very table in that very bar where we had lunch today …' Mrs O'Hanlon made a funny grunt and took a moment to ingest the cosmic significance of this coincidence. 'Anyway. She told me that she'd been back and forth over to London over the years, to see one Mal Looney.'

Breeda's legs now felt jumpy. She stood up quickly and paced.

'You mean, since he …?'

'Yes, love. Since he …' The old lady did the air quotes, 'died…'

Breeda sat again, just as quickly.

'So he didn't …he's still—' Breeda closed her eyes against the view below her. Her hand tightened on the arm of the bench.

'I believe he's still alive, yes, love.'

'And this woman, from the pub …?'

135

'Mmmm …'

Breeda cracked open her eyes and turned. 'What do you mean – *mmmm*?'

'What I mean is that you might be lucky to get any sense out of her these days. Poor thing has dementia,' Mrs O'Hanlon blessed herself, and whispered *please be to God* to the sky. 'But it would do you no harm to pay her a visit.'

'You mean she's still here, in Dunry?'

'Right over there.' Mrs O'Hanlon had stood and was pointing to the main road down into town, the one Breeda had driven down only two hours earlier. Breeda stood now too.

'And who is she?'

'Oh …' Rita O'Hanlon chuckled to herself as Coco dropped the slobbery tennis ball at their feet. 'I think her daughter was in your class. It's Mrs Sneddon. Mrs Mona Sneddon.'

CHAPTER 23

Breeda cut the engine and slid off her seatbelt. She had never been this close to the Sneddon house before. As a kid, any time they'd driven past, she'd never failed to look up at it. She'd imagined a grand staircase, maybe a music room, most likely family breakfasts around a swimming pool out back, where a maid would bring freshly squeezed orange juice which no one would ever touch. It had been Southfork Ranch in her impressionable mind. But now, looking at it from the driveway as a weary adult, it was shrunken and tired and past its heyday. Like everything else in this godforsaken place.

Her hand hovered on the latch of the car door, but the thought of moving her body suddenly seemed like too much effort. She was aware of a dull thrum which had started up in her temple, a pulsing swoosh and suck. Everything was moving too fast. She took a deep breath, and stared at the front of the house again, a streak of rust below the overflow pipe, the bruises of moss under the sills.

Had her dad ever been here? Had he and old Mona Sneddon—

But she stopped herself, batting the thought from her mind before it became a visual she couldn't unsee.

Breeda slipped her phone from her pocket.

She swiped away the missed calls from Nora and opened her photo gallery. It was in her favorites folder, a copy of a photograph she'd once found in an old yellowing album. A total gem of a picture; not just for the rarity of having a photo of her Mam and Dad together, but because they looked so happy, so vibrant. Her Mam's thirtieth birthday, the pair of them standing side by side at a tall table, an iced cake in front of them, a knife poised in her mother's hand. Their eyes clear, their faces glowing, their whole lives ahead of them …or so they thought.

Breeda fingered in closer to their faces. Her dad's green eyes, just like her own; his ever-so-gappy smile, just like her own. And her heart lifted when she looked at her mother, the slash of red on her lips, the dark eyes with the movie star confidence. Breeda zoomed in closer.

Where had all that confidence gone?
Where did this version of her mother fade to?
Did she know about him and—

The image vanished as the phone shook in Breeda's hand. Nora's name flashed up. Breeda rejected the call and yanked the door open. It was no wonder Nora had wanted to scupper Breeda's – how had she put it – *raking up the past*? This was exactly what Nora wanted to keep from her. That her parents' marriage had been less than perfect, and that Mal Looney was a philandering bastard who should be cut out of their lives like a cancerous growth. Breeda walked to the front door and stood with her finger frozen at Mona Sneddon's doorbell. She was getting accustomed to hesitating at Sneddon doorsteps recently. She sucked in some air and held it in her lungs. She had no clue as to what she was going to say.

Hi Mrs Sneddon. Is it true you and my Dad used to knock knees?

Up above her a magpie skittered along the guttering, its head a robotic twitch, the black eyes examining the stranger below. Breeda stared back, part of her hoping for advice.

Christ, things are bad when you need a bird to tell you what to do.

The magpie turned, the inky plumage on its wing shimmering cobalt for a fraction of a second. As it hopped further along the gutter, an old rhyme from her childhood played through Breeda's mind.

One for sorrow, two for mirth,
Three for death, and four for birth
Five for silver, six for gold
And seven for a secret never to be—

The front door swung open. Breeda jumped back and raised her hand to her heart. Standing in the doorway, an old woman in a tatty cardigan stared back at her – the dark brown eyes unmistakably Sneddon. Behind her a young woman hurried up the hallway, all the while looking at Breeda warily.

'Who is it, Mrs Sneddon?' The young woman had finished drying her hands on a tea-towel, and now had a protective arm around Mona Sneddon's shoulder. Was that an accent Breeda could hear? Polish? Czech?

'Oh, hello!' Breeda looked from one woman to the other. 'My name's Breeda–'. She held back the surname, not yet ready to surrender it. 'I was hoping to have a quick word with Mrs Sneddon?'

Tea-towel woman squinted out at the car and its Donegal number plate, and then frowned back at the stranger before her.

'Mrs Sneddon is about to have nap. She – we not expect anyone …'

'Oh, it'll only take a minute. I'm a friend of her daughter's…' Breeda felt a squirt of hot bile threaten to rise at the lie.

The woman leaned into the silence, her eyes narrowed, a password needed.

'Dervil. I went to school with Dervil.'

At this the woman's face softened somewhat.

Mona Sneddon lurched forward, grabbed onto Breeda's forearm, and started guiding her into the hallway.

'Dervil's my daughter. She lives in Australia.'

'Is that right, Mrs Sneddon?' Breeda smiled at the home help, who had stood back to let her pass.

'Five minutes. Then she need rest.'

Breeda nodded a silent thank you in reply.

Mrs Sneddon continued, as she led Breeda into the living room, 'I'm going to live with Dervil. In Australia.'

The home help shook her head, winked at Breeda, then walked down the hallway to the kitchen out back, mumbling something in her mother tongue. Mona Sneddon coaxed herself and Breeda onto a large pink settee, too many throw cushions, not enough arse space. Breeda nudged a cushion out of the way with her elbow. In the corner a TV showed an advert for incontinence pads. Breeda pointed the remote and muted it and then glanced around the room. The walls wore a silver-patterned wallpaper – all reflective fleur-de-lis and over-busy border – and had redundant nails protruding on either side of the chimney breast. The taken-down pictures stood stacked at an angle against the far wall. One of the pictures was jutting out from the stack and was facing back into the room. It was a framed family photograph. Mr and Mrs Sneddon standing proudly in their Sunday best, a teenage version of Dervil, chesty and older than Breeda had known her, her gangly legs disappearing out of view into the collection of picture frames to her right. And – Breeda cocked her head – a slice of someone else. She squinted and leaned forward for a closer look.

'I'm going to have my own room.'

Breeda turned back to the old lady, whose hand, mottled with sun damage, was tenderly stroking her arm.

'And I'll have all my pictures, and my good chair to sit in, and my knitting.'

'That sounds lovely, Mrs Sneddon.'

The clatter of a dropped pan lid came through from the kitchen. The old lady's eyes flicked over to the TV.

'Listen, Mrs Sneddon. My name is Breeda. Breeda Looney …'

The side of Mona Sneddon's face didn't twitch. Nothing.

'I think you maybe knew – know – my father?'

The papery hand continued to stroke Breeda's sleeve.

'Mal. Mal Looney.'

The fingers jumped, almost imperceptibly, but Breeda felt it, a speed bump on her denim sleeve. The woman's brown eyes didn't leave the television screen.

'Did you know him, Mona? Mal Looney? I really need to get in touch with him?'

The old woman had closed her eyes now and turned her face slightly towards the window and the mid-afternoon sunlight. A song was humming gently on her lips, and her body swayed, lost in thought. Breeda looked down at her jacket sleeve, the frail fingers stroking once more. She patted Mona's hand into submission and the humming stopped. She tried again.

'Do you know Mal Looney, Mona?' The words came out louder than Breeda had intended. Mrs Sneddon turned and pulled back her hand. She stared at Breeda with wide eyes.

'Lemonade! Would you like a glass of lemonade?!' Mona had shimmied herself off the settee, and now stood beaming proudly at Breeda from the door.

'Dervil loves lemonade. But we always brush our teeth afterwards!' She winked at Breeda, then smacked her lips, both coquettish and disturbing for someone in her seventies, before disappearing off to the kitchen.

Breeda allowed her body to sag back into the fussy cushions for a moment, tipped her weary head back, and let her eyes rove the painted ceiling whorls overhead. In the momentary silence she found herself wondering if Dervil's childhood bedroom was on the other side of that ceiling; if up there was where Dervil had diligently written party invitations to everyone in their class – everyone apart from Breeda. She wondered if young Dervil had lain up there at night, planning Breeda's demise. And for the first time she pondered if Dervil's abject loathing of her had been due to a long-ago affair between one Mona Sneddon and one Malachy Looney.

A muffled argument came through from the kitchen. The home help was attempting to soothe Mona, but Mona seemed to have switched into truculent toddler mode and wouldn't be appeased. Drawers were being tugged and slammed. Cupboard doors were banging. Footsteps hurried down the hallway and Breeda pushed herself up off the cushions. The living room door opened, and the home help stood looking harried.

'Sorry, you have to go. Too excited. Too excited.'

Breeda hopped to her feet just as something glass smashed out the back.

'Of course. I'm so sorry. I hope—'

The woman shook her head, the front door already opened for the unplanned guest. 'Not your fault. Just too much excited.'

'OK, I'm sorry.' Breeda stood outside on the doorstep as the woman rushed back down the hallway towards Mona and her mayhem. In the dull light, at the back of the house, Breeda could just make out Mona, shaking a book by its spine, a cat throttling a sparrow. Breeda took a final glance at the old woman, then pulled the front door quietly, and turned with a sigh.

She stood with her hand on the car door and turned to survey the houses and streets of Dunry town down below her, one last time. Across the valley she could see the convent grounds where Rita O'Hanlon had sat with her only an hour ago and given her a surge of hope. Breeda sighed. A dismal realization was distilling in the atmosphere above her. She closed her eyes, and gave into it, letting it slowly condense and enfold her. There was nothing more to be done. It was time to go home and get on with whatever semblance of life she had left.

Climbing into the car, her bones suddenly heavy, Breeda felt drugged by the stifling air inside, stale and fuggy from the afternoon sun. She started the engine and lowered her window, her tyres crackling on the gravel driveway as she pulled away. If the roads were clear she should be home by six-thirty, in plenty of time for a glass of wine and a cuddle with Ginger on the back step. But then – like a punch to her gut – Breeda remembered she had no home. No more sundowners on the back step, no more eye rolls at Finbarr's clattering on the roof, no more view of the bay and the pier and majestic Muckish mountain in the distance. Nora's box room awaited.

Something in the rear-view mirror caught her eye. Breeda braked and stuck her head out the window. Mona Sneddon was chasing the car, her stick-thin legs driving her forward with wild abandon. Trailing behind Mona, the frazzled home help was calling her back, and struggling to keep up. Breeda unbuckled her seatbelt and turned to open the car door, but in the side mirror she saw Mona's approaching face, agitated, flushed and crazy-eyed. The woman had her arm aloft and was shouting something after the car. Had Breeda upset her? Breeda leaned away from the open window, too late to close it, and prepared herself for an incoming slap.

'M.L.!'

Breeda cracked open an eye. Mona stood there panting, a strand of grey hair wet on her forehead. She was thrusting something through the open window at Breeda, nodding excitedly for her to take it.

'M.L.!', she repeated, a wheeze from her lungs.

Breeda took a postcard from Mona's scrawny hand. She squinted at the writing on the back.

144

In the top corner was an address - Hartland Road, Camden, London – and a phone number. As the home help reached them, out of breath too, Breeda read on.

Dear M.
New place is decent. Hope to be here for a while.
Come visit me soon?
M.L. xx

Breeda flipped the postcard. A landscape of buildings she knew by sight, but not by name. A view she'd probably seen on telly once. She turned the card again.

A view over London from Primrose Hill.

Breeda made a frantic rummage in her handbag for the folded envelope from the birthday card. She held it and the postcard side-by-side, her hands trembling. The handwriting was a perfect match. Breeda's vision blurred and when she pulled her eyes away she found Mona Sneddon looking back at her, as pleased as punch.

'M L?'

A fat tear escaped Breeda's eye, as she grabbed the old lady's hand and rubbed its papery mottles in gratitude.

'M L, Mona,' she nodded. 'M L.'

CHAPTER 24

The tide had ebbed far out, and the rippled sand it left behind shone warm and golden under Breeda's bare feet. She hadn't meant to come here. She hadn't even thought of the place. But after leaving Mona Sneddon's, Breeda had found herself heading south, instead of northwest back to Carrickross. And she had kept driving, until she saw signs with a place name she'd not seen in decades.

Breeda raised a hand to her brow and looked out beyond the shoreline. A thin grey cloud hung on the distant horizon and she played with the notion it was the coastline of England. She lifted Mona Sneddon's postcard to her face and inhaled the slightly musky scent. Mal Looney was across there somewhere and his only child was going to find him and make things right.

She closed her eyes for a second, a smile playing over her face, as she pictured her younger self, sitting proudly atop her Dad's shoulders.

'Who's the apple of my eye?' he'd shout up to her, as they'd strolled this very beach.

'I am!' she'd squeal, knowing what was coming.

'Who?'

'Me! Breeda Looney!'

She'd pummel his chest playfully with the back of her bare sandy feet until he'd bite a chunk out of an imaginary apple, and then toss it up to her to take a bite too. Young Breeda had felt invincible up there on Mal Looney's shoulders, queen of the world, safe and loved.

She turned and strolled slowly back in the direction of her car. The beach was hers this afternoon, utterly deserted but for a few hunkering seagulls which grumbled out of her way as she cut through them. Scanning the grassy dunes off to her right she wondered if the caravan park still existed back there on the other side. She thought of the little yellow caravan they'd owned back in the day, the thick brown stripe around the middle, so very seventies. It had been simple and basic, a perfect little getaway for school holidays and long summers. There was never a need to go abroad – not that you'd ever get Mal Looney on a plane — flying was an accident waiting to happen, he'd always said. Breeda took in a deep lungful of air and let the memories wash over her. Near the caravan had been the toilet block where a seven-year-old Breeda had got stuck in the cubicle with the stiff bolt. Too timid to bang on the door she'd instead waited quietly until her dad had come searching for her hours later. And further along there'd been the old amusements with the breakneck waltzer and the penny arcade. And the red-roofed sweetie shop where Breeda and the wee girl from the caravan two doors up (*Maura? Moira?*) would blow their winnings from the one-armed bandits on white chocolate mice and sherbet dips.

Those few summers Breeda and her parents had come here had allowed her to run free, to be a bog-standard kid. Their modest little caravan and this sweeping beach were only an hour south of Dunry now, but back then – before the motorway was built – it had seemed to take most of a day to get here. She remembered the feeling of excitement building in the car as they got closer until Breeda would squeal and clap at the sight of the little red roof of the sweetie shop. But then, all of a sudden, those visits to the beach had come to an abrupt end.

Breeda reached her car and turned to regard the strand one last time. This place, just like Dunry, had long ago been swept under a rug by her mother and Nora. After Mal had died, when they'd started afresh on the other side of the country in Carrickross, both places – Dunry and the strand – had been shoehorned clumsily into Breeda's past and labelled *taboo*. But now, looking at the golden sand stretching out in front of her, Breeda felt a futile sense of yearning. She was hungry for an alternate past, the one from which she hadn't been unfairly wrenched, the one where she hadn't been lied to, the one where she hadn't been denied her father.

Her mother never spoke of the incident, and back then young Breeda had known better than to ask her. She'd pieced it together, nonetheless. In the cold, sleety, post-Christmas days, following Mal's death, Breeda had overheard the odd snippet from neighbors. The rumors that he'd had a few drinks, that he'd been spotted wading into the bitterly cold waters at last light, that the car had been left unlocked at the top of this very strand, his licence discarded on the driver's seat.

She could feel a hardness setting into her face now, a belligerent little fist pounding in her ribcage. An anger was inside her, dormant no longer, and she was going to coax its flames and let its roar guide her forward. She thought of Nora's dramatic seething, back at the graveyard. Pathetic, in hindsight. Nora's anger was fake, built on a crumbling bedrock of concerns for reputation and worries about tittle-tattle from behind twitching net curtains. This anger that Breeda was feeling, here and now, was different – it was justified. A man had been forced into exile for a dalliance with a local woman, and a young girl had been denied her father. Someone was going to have to pay for this.

And her mother? What of Margaret Looney in all this? Had she known? Or had she just been a gormless fool, allowing Nora to pull her strings and make her dance blindly through her depressive haze? But Margaret wasn't around to ask any more. And Nora might as well be dead. There was only one person left in the world who could shine a light on this whole tragic state of affairs and give Breeda the answers she craved.

Breeda sat into the car and looked at the postcard once more. The phone number was a land line number. She took her phone from her pocket and slowly tapped in the digits. With her breath held, she hovered a finger over the *Call* button. She touched the button, clasped the phone tight to her ear, and stared off towards the chop and spray of the white horses in the distance.

In North London a phone began to ring. Breeda imagined her father walking into a hallway, getting closer to it, maybe setting down a mug of tea. She rubbed her palm along her jeans. The ring tone pulsed in her ear and she realised she was still holding her breath. Breeda flung open the car door – the air stifling again – and exhaled slowly.

'Hello?'

149

A woman's voice. Unexpected. The dialect jarring. Breeda sat up.

'Oh. Hello. I'm looking for Malachy Looney?'

'Mal's not here at the mo.' In the background a dog barked. 'Trixie – be quiet!' A pause. 'Who's this then?'

Breeda stood out of the car, an itch of sweat prickling her scalp. She hit the rewind button in her brain and replayed the woman's words.

Mal's not here at the mo.

Breeda put out a hand to steady herself, all doubt gone. He was alive. Her father was alive. Her legs wobbled, a newborn foal at its first tentative steps.

'I said who's this?'

'That's OK. I'll call back later.' She turned and gripped the side of the car with one hand.

'Here, just—'

Breeda killed the call and flung her phone onto the passenger seat. Her gut spasmed, and for the second time that afternoon, she found herself looking at creamy chunks of seafood chowder.

CHAPTER 25

Nora stood across the road from The Treasure Chest in her least-favourite two-piece suit. Through the large shop window she could see Myra stepping back from her display of Donegal tweed blankets and lambswool throws, an index finger tapping at her lips. She observed as Myra swapped out a pink throw for a mustard one, before walking back behind the counter to answer the phone. Nora wiped a clammy hand along the side of her skirt. She felt frightened of what she was about to do. But needs must.

And now Dougie Mahon, the lanky shrink's browbeaten husband, was pulling up outside the shop. He locked his car, then walked his toolbox inside, probably there to fix the flickering strip of lights under the shelves. Nora watched the silent interchange between them both: Dougie laying his tools out on the floor; Myra casting a sly glance at his bum crack as she twiddled the phone cord.

The quiet fury that Nora had experienced earlier — as she'd stood catching her breath in the doorway of Breeda's empty bedroom — had shapeshifted into a steely pragmatism over the past few hours. Nora realised she couldn't really blame the girl for pretending to be sick so she could slink off to Dunry. She was just being true to her nature, after all. Crafty and obstreperous, that was Breeda's way. Nora patted a hand to her hair. She wasn't the type of woman to make mistakes. But in this instance, well, Nora was going to have to shoulder the blame for this mess. She thought once more of the promise she'd made to Margaret on her deathbed: she was to look after Breeda. Keep her safe. Mind her. Nora cleared her throat, now dry and tight, and looked back towards the shop. There was still time. She could still make things right.

From Nora's right came the slick glide of tyres – a small peloton of men on expensive bikes going way too fast through the village. They seemed to be bloody everywhere these days, fleeing their midlife crises along the bends and inclines of the *Wild Atlantic Way*. What had Myra called them once? *MAMILS* - that was it. Middle-aged men in Lycra. Nora stood her ground at the edge of the pavement as the collective prostate of Mamils whizzed past her, a blaze of sweat and bulging calves.

She looked back to the shop window. It was actually good that Dougie Mahon was there. The sooner Oona Mahon heard about it, the better. Any second now they'd look out and spot her. She had to be ready, she had to go through with it. Behind her a young boy was shooing away a couple of pestering seagulls from his bag of chips. Nora tried to ignore the scrawk and flap of the birds, the smell of fat and vinegar wafting past. She closed her eyes and whispered a *Hail Mary* to herself.

And then from around the corner came the huff and chug of McGuigan's coach.

For the love of God!

She hadn't factored that in. The blasted coach would park in front of The Treasure Chest and block their view of her. Nora glanced to her right again. No more cyclists, but a campervan was coming towards her, a couple of young foreigners sitting up front. She looked straight ahead now with a singular focus, ignoring the bulk of the tour coach arriving from her left, blocking out the campervan approaching from her right. Myra and Dougie were chatting at the counter. Nora rubbed at her crucifix and willed them to look out, to see her. And just then, Myra did. She turned and looked, their eyes met. The moment stretched, the seagulls paused, and the sky above Nora Cullen held its breath as she clutched her chest and fell into the path of the campervan.

CHAPTER 26

Breeda pegged the last of Nora's knickers to the clothesline and tried to ignore their mocking dance in the mid-morning breeze. She kicked her foot against the plastic laundry basket on the ground, and watched it scoot across the backyard where it hit the step with a satisfying smack.

She stood for a moment, thinking back to the awful blur of Monday evening: Oona and Dougie's panicked phone call and the ensuing cross-country mercy dash to the hospital, a ton of guilt in the passenger seat keeping Breeda company during her frantic drive home. The subsequent five nights in Nora's box room had brought a dull crunch to the discs of her lower back, and now Breeda quietly cursed the torturous wrack of a spare bed upstairs. She reached her hands overhead, forced an arch into her stiff spine, and looked up at the cloudless sky overhead. A thin white contrail smudged the blue in an Easterly direction. Breeda stared at it and found herself wondering if it was bound for London, a place where she should be right now. She swallowed hard. There was an impatient excitement yearning to come up, but right now it had to be pushed down deep inside for a while longer. Just until Nora had recovered from the heart attack.

A bell tinkled from deep inside the belly of the house. Breeda snatched up the laundry basket.

Lady Muck wants a fresh pot of tea.

She paused at the back step, put her hand to the wall, and forced herself to remember that it wasn't Nora's fault. The poor woman had been under huge strain – no thanks to Breeda – and now she lay upstairs, holding on for dear life. Breeda was all she had left, and this was when family overlooked their differences, buried their squabbles, and pulled together.

Breeda climbed the back steps slowly, sat the basket inside the laundry door, then stuck the kettle under the cold tap. Her phone lay sleeping on the kitchen windowsill. There was still no word from Doctor Chakraborty: Breeda had left the woman three voice mails since collecting Nora at the hospital on Monday. She remembered how she'd burst into the hospital's reception area, fearing the worst, her shoes squeaking on the polished lino and her wild eyes searching for someone to direct her to Nora's deathbed. But she had simply found poor Nora deserted in the waiting room, a blanket draped over her knees and not a doctor or nurse in sight — an absolute disgrace. Now Breeda picked up the phone and willed it to ring. She needed to discuss Nora's care, to understand the longer-term prognosis of her heart condition. From upstairs the bell rang again. Breeda sat the phone back on the windowsill, planted the kettle on the hob, and clicked on the gas.

'One minute, Aunt Nora!'

Looking out at the garden she slowly chewed at her bottom lip. The initial excitement at knowing Mal was alive had quickly brought on a restlessness that had permeated every cell of her body. And now she desperately wanted to get the hell out of here, to go to

London and throw her arms around her father. To get on with her new life. Her true life.

But since fetching Nora from the hospital five days ago, Breeda had felt a stone-like heaviness in the pit of her stomach, anchoring her to this house. It wasn't just the rigid springs of the spare bed keeping her awake into the dead hours of the night. It was the bitter acknowledgement that she, alone, had caused this; had brought her aunt to the brink of death; might, in fact, still push her over the edge. She was beyond ashamed.

Breeda imagined the little butterfly heart beating erratically in the old lady's chest cavity upstairs. She filled her lungs, and then exhaled a long breath of acceptance. She would simply have to be on her best behavior. Any upset or stress could kill Nora. Breeda would simply play the good girl from now on.

She unfolded the postcard from the pocket of her apron and looked at the view from Primrose Hill once more. Her dad was still there, she just had to be patient. She flipped the card and traced her finger along the phone number and considered ringing it again. But that woman, whoever she was, might answer again, and Breeda was a bad liar at the best of times. What she really wanted was to turn up and surprise him, and not have anyone else in the world tarnish or taint or put a spin on their reunion in any way. She folded the postcard and slipped it back in her pocket. Just another few days.

As Breeda poured the water into the teapot her phone rang.

'Oona!'

'How are ya, chica?'

'Oh … you know …'

'Is Nora doing your head in?'

'Understatement of the year, love.'

'Well, I might have something to cheer you up. Are you doing anything this afternoon?'

Breeda listened to Oona's proposal, doing her best to block out Nora's bell, louder and more insistent now.

'Well, what do you say?'

'I would love to, Oona,' Breeda turned in the direction of the bell. 'But I'll have to run it past her ladyship first…'

'Barbecue?'

Nora looked from the bedroom doorway where Breeda stood, to the edge of the bed where Myra Finch was neatly perched. After a moment she looked back to her wayward niece.

'Barbecue?'

The word took on a sourness as it left Nora's mouth, and now it hung incredulous in the air between the three women. Myra Finch was studying a freckled hand in her lap, her pinched face the epitome of a seasoned lemon-sucker. Breeda looked down at her own chipped nail polish, feeling like a teenage girl asking the Pope for a cherry-flavored condom.

'It would only be for an hour or two, Aunt Nora …'

Breeda heard the grating grovel in her own words and cringed. How in hell had she managed to stuff up her life so spectacularly that she now had to seek permission to go out for a sausage and a salad? She looked up and caught Myra Finch shaking her head not-so-subtly and felt a sudden urge to stride across the room and deck the bitch.

'And who, may I ask, is hosting this "barbecue"?' Nora was looking at Myra now, their coiffed heads both shaking to the same harmonic at the girl's impudence.

'Oona. And Dougie. They're just having a few people over. It's such a lovely afternoon.'

Breeda gestured like a hammy actor with an open hand towards the window. Nora ignored the blue sky outside, instead fixing Breeda with a hard stare.

'I want you back by six at the latest. Six. Do you hear me?'

The woman was obviously playing up for Myra; a martyr milking her role as invalid on a moral crusade to keep her niece in check. As Breeda looked at her aunt propped up against a wall of pillows, unsaid words bubbled up from within her. She wanted to tell her aunt to take a run and jump. To tell her to treat Breeda like the grown woman she was, and to take some responsibility for her own heart condition. And part of Breeda wanted to fling other words at her aunt too and watch them sting and shock her pious face. She could tell her that Mal Looney was alive and well in London, and that she'd be getting the hell out of this house as soon as Nora was back on her feet. But Breeda bit her tongue, remembering her aunt's delicate condition, and forced a smile.

'No problem, Aunt Nora. Six it is.'

Nora shuffled herself more upright in the bed.

'Now, take this tray downstairs. And you might as well bring myself and Myra up some soup. Good girl.'

'Alright, Aunt Nora.' Breeda cast a glance around the gloom of the bedroom, then looked once more out the window. A shock of pink cherry blossoms jostled in the warm afternoon breeze, and carried in a sweet scent, like a childhood friend asking Breeda out to play.

'And a plate of cheese and ham toasties.'

Nora mumbled something to Myra, and Myra mumbled something back.

'And the packet of Jaffa Cakes.'

As Breeda turned to leave she spotted something familiar lying flat on Nora's dresser. Her foot caught on the carpet, and the cups on the tray clattered as she put a hand out to steady herself.

'Aunt Nora—'

The rest of the words caught in Breeda's throat, as she stared at the painting of the swimmer – her mother's wedding present – out of place in Nora's bedroom. Breeda shook her head, waiting for it to make sense. Nora must have let herself into the house when Breeda was in Dunry. Breeda swallowed hard. That painting was hers.

'Oh that. Well, it's too valuable to be hanging there in your mother's bedroom, with God-knows-who traipsing in to view the house over the coming weeks. I'll store it somewhere safe. Out of harm's way.'

Breeda turned around. Nora was staring back at her with a look of pure defiance. They locked eyes as the blood pounded in Breeda's head. She dropped her gaze to the trembling cups on the tray in her hands. Nora's cup had a smear of lipstick on the rim and it seemed to sneer back at her. Breeda took in a deep lungful of air and forced herself to remember that her aunt's health was precarious at best. Now wasn't the time. Breeda needed to get out of here for a few hours. She needed to clear her head. She needed a drink. Her mind was already picturing Oona's ice bucket of wine and beers in the back garden.

'I'll just fetch those soups.'

Breeda threw a dead-eyed smile towards the women on the bed and turned to leave. And as she descended the stairs, she felt a hairline fracture run through her. A ticking time bomb had begun its countdown.

CHAPTER 27

Breeda parked outside Oona and Dougie's semidetached terraced house and stepped out of the car to the strains of music and laughter drifting up the side path from the back garden. She smoothed her dress down over her tummy. It would do the job: floral and flattering, and with just the right amount of exposed arm. She brushed some bronzer across her cheeks and as she tottered off down the driveway on a pair of wedge shoes Breeda decided to give herself permission to let her hair down, if only for a few hours: the Noras and the Myras, the Brians and the Dervils of the world could all go to hell. Breeda's head was well and truly wrecked, and what she needed right now was a relaxing afternoon. A few drinks, and a good old natter with Oona on her swing chair would be like sunlight to a seedling. And at that moment, as if by magic, Oona's telltale hoot bounced up the side path to Breeda, and a long overdue smile bloomed on her face.

As Breeda rounded the corner, she came face to face with Dougie. He stopped in his tracks, a plate of lamb kebabs in one hand, a champagne flute in the other.

'Sorry, love. The supermodel convention is two doors up. But you can stay for a sausage if you like?'

'It's a bit early for a sausage innuendo, Doug. I haven't even had a drink.'

'Here, take this. I was bringing it over to my good wife.' He turned to nod in the direction of the far back corner of the garden, 'She's probably had enough, but she's demanding another.'

Breeda craned her neck and glimpsed Oona on the far side of the garden. Between Breeda and Oona the lawn was jammed. Oona hooted again and Breeda slowly navigated her way through the crowd.

'Breeda!'

Oona's face was flushed, her eyes already a little glassy. She wobbled herself off the swing seat, and raised her arms in the air, sloshing the remains of her glass onto the ground.

'You look only gorgeous! Marie, take a look at Bree.'

While Oona yanked Breeda into an embrace, Marie Boyle, the woman from two doors down, tapped Breeda's glass with her own.

'Cheers, Breeda. You are looking well.'

Oona released Breeda, then looked past her shoulder, as someone else approached.

'And I believe you two know each other?'

As Breeda turned around her smile morphed into a lunatic grimace, and she felt an urgent need to evacuate her bowels. She opened her mouth but had no words. A faked smile was being bitched down at her, eyebrows raised in a porcelain brow.

Marie Boyle piped up from beside Breeda.

'Yeah, Dervil was telling us you went to school together. Was she a dark horse? Was she, Dervil?'

Marie nudged Breeda in the waist, then looked playfully towards their new friend.

Dervil bit her bottom lip, then looked conspiratorially from Marie to Oona. She leaned in a couple of inches, lowered her voice, then nodded to Breeda's legs.

'Let's just say young Breeda didn't get those knees from saying her prayers.'

Breeda stood dumbfounded, a mute player in her own life, as they caught the joke lobbed their way. Oona squealed, and Marie doubled over in a laughing fit which drew a curious look from Dougie across the garden.

'Sweet Jesus. I'm going to wet my knickers.' Oona jiggled on the spot with a hand to the crotch of her jeans. Neither Marie or Oona noticed the red blotches on their friend's face. Breeda was the butt of the joke, the loner schoolgirl once more.

'Who was that young priest you were chummy with, Breeda? Remember the guy who left the school all of a sudden?'

Dervil took a slow sip from her glass, and tilted her head, a faultless serve across the net. The chitchat and music in the garden ebbed into the background now, and a stench of awkwardness hung around Breeda. She suddenly realised she had nothing left, that she'd been running on fumes these past few days.

'And what's going on over here? You sound like a coven of witches.'

The women turned. Dougie had arrived with a bottle of prosecco and a jug of water and was leaning in to top up their glasses. He filled Oona's empty flute from the water jug.

'Drink that or no more of this.'

He waggled the prosecco bottle in front of her. She started to protest, but instead skulled the water, then held her glass out triumphantly for a proper refill.

As the women busied themselves with top-ups, Breeda saw her opportunity to scarper before Dervil could make any more wisecracks.

'Back in a sec. Just popping to the loo.'

She kept her head down as she pushed through the crowd. Someone called her name, but Breeda ploughed on, pretending not to hear. There was color in her cheeks, but it wasn't from embarrassment alone now. Anger surged through her. She was livid. She grabbed a fresh glass of bubbles from a tray on the kitchen counter and headed straight for the downstairs loo. She turned the lock, slammed the seat on the toilet and downed the glass in one go.

The absolute bitch.

So this was how it was going to be. The gloves were off and Dervil was going to try and destroy her all over again. Breeda banged the side of her hand against the tiled wall, vexed with herself for not saying something. But she knew that only would have created a scene, and she couldn't do that to Oona. Breeda forced herself to sit back against the cistern, her jaw tense. Her eyes found a little crocheted doll she'd bought Oona as a joke one Christmas, now squatting over a loo roll, on the shelf above the basin. As she sat listening to the slow drip of the tap she tried to slow her breathing. Her future was mapping itself out and solidifying with each passing minute: a future with Dervil chipping away at her by stealth and poisoning her name amongst the inhabitants of Carrickross. Breeda closed her eyes and tilted her head back. The champagne swilled and bubbled in her stomach.

Yes, her dad and Dervil's mother had had an affair twenty-five odd years ago.

Yes, it was wrong.

But it was in the past. They'd been grown adults.

And the sins of the father didn't belong at Breeda's feet. Besides, hadn't Mona Sneddon been just as complicit?

Someone tried the door handle and her body jumped.

For God's sake. Couldn't she just have one minute!

Breeda got to her feet and quickly smoothed her hair. She forced an empty smile at herself in the mirror, then opened the door.

'Oh, hello.'

It was that guy. The flower buyer. The yoga guy with the arse. He was standing inches in front of her, his familiarity still confounding her. He smiled and Breeda noticed a space between his two front teeth. She opened her mouth to say hello but the bubbles she'd just knocked back chose that particular moment to make their presence felt in the form of a thunderous belch.

The stranger stood back, startled. Breeda rushed a hand to her mouth, her eyes wide, only managing to shake her stunned head at her vulgarity. They stood regarding each other for a split second, the silence after the burp more absolute. Then he laughed. He threw his head back and laughed.

'Well, there's something you don't see every day.'

'I'm so, so–'

'I'm Aidan,' He stuck out his hand. 'Pleased to meet you So-So.'

Breeda bit her bottom lip, and felt the heat evaporate off her cheeks.

'I'm Breeda. And I'm really sorry about that. What must you think?'

He nodded to the empty glass in her hand.

'I think you're probably allowed just one more of those. Any more and we might need to issue a storm warning.

He stood aside to let her out, then shuffled past her into the loo. Breeda turned to hurry off down the hallway, but he called after her, through the half-closed door.

'Breeda - will I join you outside for that last glass?'

He was looking at her with his dark eyebrows raised.

What the hell, Breeda thought. *It's not like the afternoon could get any worse ...*

CHAPTER 28

On an old bench near a laurel hedge in a quieter part of Oona's back garden, Breeda and Aidan sat and observed the crowd on the lawn. Aidan had begun to tell Breeda a little about himself. He was a cop, on stress leave after an incident down in Dublin a few months prior. As Breeda listened to this she noticed a shadow cross his face. He leaned forward and slowly turned the beer bottle in his hand, momentarily lost in thought. Breeda shifted slightly on the bench. He looked up and shot an apologetic smile her way.

'Sorry. Didn't mean to be a party pooper. Here – feel this …'

He took her hand and slowly ran her index finger along the hairline of his forearm as far as his wrist. Her fingers traced the grooves and hollows under his flesh. She kept her eyes on his wrist, could sense his eyes on her.

'What is that?'

'Just some plates and pins. A souvenir from my job.'

'Are you, like, some kind of bionic man.'

He took his arm back and slugged from his beer. 'I like to think of myself as The Terminator, actually'.

'Ah, OK, well I guess I can call you Arnie.'

Across the garden, a group of tipsy women — with Oona as their ringleader — were gathered around a makeshift dance floor, hellbent on getting Finbarr Feeley to throw a few shapes for them. The poor guy's face was flushed with embarrassment, and Breeda felt an urge to run over and rescue him. But she remained on the bench, a dull wariness holding her back. Earlier that afternoon, after leaving Nora's, Breeda had swung by Bayview Rise to pick out her summer frock from storage. On parking the car she'd noticed the grass on their front lawn was uncharacteristically long, longer than Finbarr had ever let it grow. If Nora saw the state of the garden she'd fuss and fret about it putting off prospective buyers, and as Breeda had stuck her key in the front door she'd wondered if Finbarr's nose might be out of joint. He had every right to be off with her, after she'd been so short to him the day the *For Sale* sign went up. The man deserved better, and an apology was overdue. But now, back at the barbecue, as if reading her mind, Finbarr looked over from the dance floor. Breeda smiled at him, he nodded a smile back, and she instantly felt her shoulders soften.

Beside her on the bench, Aidan took another swig from his beer bottle.

'Who's that fella?'

'Who, Finbarr? He's just my neighbor.'

'Have you noticed he keeps looking over here. He's been staring daggers at me since we started talking.'

She turned to look at Aidan, then back over at the farmer.

'Finbarr? God no, he doesn't have a bad bone in his body. He's probably just wondering who you are …'

At that moment Finbarr gave into the surrounding pack and started to unleash a few dance moves to their whoops and cheers. He caught Breeda's eye again and they both started to laugh. Breeda watched for a moment, weirdly proud of him, glad to see him enjoying himself. Even from this distance she could see the plucked cuffs on his old jacket from years of snagging his sleeves on barbed wire fences up the back fields. And as she sat watching him she wondered if the gentle giant in his torn tweed jacket might find himself someone special someday.

'How's the lemonade going down?'

Breeda glanced at Aidan. 'Much better than the bubbles, thanks.'

'Well, hopefully it stays down too this time.'

She went to swat his shoulder but shifted on the bench and brushed her fingers through her hair instead. She barely knew this guy. Yet something …

'So Aidan …'

He gave her a look.

'Sorry. So *Arnie* … what's a nice cop from Dublin doing in a place like this?'

'Ah, you see, it's such a lovely afternoon and Dougie—'

Now she did push his shoulder.

'No, you dope. I mean what brings you to Carrickcross village – the official center of the known universe – are you on holiday?'

'Oh …' He laughed, and settled back against the bench, 'No, not on holiday exactly. I guess you could call it a confluence of events. The incident down in Dublin,' a brief pause, 'then a death in the family …'

Breeda put a hand to his arm.

'I'm sorry … I didn't mean to pry …'

'No, no, you're grand. I'm just—'

They looked up. Oona had come over, breathless from laughing so much, and collapsed onto the spare space on the other side of Aidan.

'Do you mind if I sit for a minute? That Finbarr one cracks me up.' She fanned her glowing face, and then turned to them. 'So it looks like you two have met then?'

Aidan answered for them. 'Yeah, but we actually crossed paths earlier in the week.'

Breeda shifted in her seat again.

So he'd remembered her from that day when he was buying the flowers.

Then she realised with horror that there was an alternative, and a flush of heat reddened her face …

He'd noticed her checking out his arse at yoga.

He was watching Breeda now, his eyes narrowed, a cheeky smile threatening to erupt.

'You don't remember?'

Breeda opened her mouth, then closed it again.

'The other day, on the road. You threw me the filthiest look as I passed you,' he turned back to Oona, 'Granted I was probably going a bit too fast for that road…'

'On the motorbike. That was *you*!'

He turned back to Breeda and laughed, a laugh she was already beginning to like hearing. Just then an annoying chime interrupted them. Breeda took out her phone, killed the alarm, then groaned as she closed her eyes and slumped down the bench. Her pumpkin carriage awaited on the street.

'Guys, I'd love to stay but I have to make a move.'

'Ah, Bree! Nora?'

'Nora.'

'And how is the patient?'

Breeda grimaced at Oona. She thought of Lady Muck propped up in her bed, the servant's bell never far from her twitchy fingers.

'Oh. You know …'

'Can't you stay for one more? Aidan here will think you're very rude for running off …'

'Sorry, but I best not. I don't want to end up in the naughty corner.'

Breeda forced herself to stand and smoothed down her dress. Aidan stood too, leaving Oona glued to the bench.

'Well, it was lovely chatting, So-so.'

He gave her hand a single firm shake.

'You too, Arnie. I might see you again if you're in town for a bit.'

Oona piped up from the bench, not one to be ignored.

'So, how's the new place going, Aidan? Dougie says the electrics are all finished now? Bree, you know that big house up on Riley's Hill …?'

Breeda turned to Oona, then looked back at Aidan.

'Riley's Hill?'

Oona again, 'Yeah, himself and Dervil took over that big empty house. They got it for a steal. But once—'

Oona kept talking but Breeda could no longer hear her friend.

Aidan was watching Breeda with a look of confusion to match the one on her own face. His hand was still wrapped around hers. A sharp voice made Breeda jump, and her bowels clenched again.

'Aidan, fetch the car please. I'll see you out front in a second.' Dervil's eyes were fixed on Breeda, and Breeda, in turn, dropped her own eyes to the lawn.

Aidan let go of Breeda's hand, then touched Dervil gently on the shoulder.

'Are you alright, Derv?'

She gave a barely perceptible nod. 'Migraine.'

Aidan walked off, then turned at the corner to give them a farewell salute. 'Catch youse soon,' he shouted, 'And thanks for a great barbecue, Oona.' And with that he was gone.

Breeda shriveled at Dervil's continued glare, and when Oona stood up Breeda's hand found her arm and held on, grateful for her presence.

'Oona, be a sweetie? I'd love a glass of water so I can pop a couple of painkillers … Would you mind?'

'Of course, Dervil. Not a bother. Wait here.'

Breeda looked after Oona's retreating back and felt a fresh panic rising. She wanted to cast a hook, to yank her friend back, and stick onto her like a barnacle about to weather Armageddon. Her eyes darted around the people nearby, but they were all totally oblivious to her predicament. The awkward silence stretched in front of her, and Breeda turned her eyes back to Dervil.

'I didn't know he was your husband!' she blurted, louder than she'd meant to.

The eyebrows raised a fraction, but Dervil held her tongue – an invitation for whatever was the next nugget of wisdom about to leave Breeda's mouth.

'What I mean to say is, we were only talking. I have absolutely no interest in Aidan, Dervil. I'm not that sort of girl.'

She went to speak again but Dervil silenced her with an upheld hand. Over Dervil's shoulder, Breeda could see Oona rushing back towards them, a pint glass of water slopping in front of her. Marie Boyle was merrily traipsing after her with a tray of vol-au-vents fresh from the oven. Breeda suddenly didn't want them near her – she didn't want witnesses for what now might be about to unfold. Oona presented the water glass, but Dervil ignored it, her eyes still locked on her prey.

'Breeda, I want you to stay away from me.'

Breeda made a single silent nod, keenly aware of Oona and Marie sensing tension in the air.

'I want you to stay away from Aidan too.'

'No problem, I didn't—'

The raised hand again.

'And I most definitely want you to stay away from my elderly mother.'

Three pairs of eyes now regarded Breeda, and the blood rose to her cheeks once more.

'You see, Breeda, in my lexicon, the Looney name is synonymous with scum. Filth. Crud. Excrement. You know, like a steaming dog turd in a piss-stenched back alley, best to be avoided.'

Breeda didn't know, but she found herself nodding, desperate for this to be over.

'We're both adults. We both know about your *father*.' Oona and Marie looked from Breeda to Dervil, then back again, spectators just lacking some strawberries and cream.

'And the thing is, Breeda, every time I have to look at your face I think of that pig and the havoc he wreaked on my family.'

Breeda's tongue flailed inside her mouth, a salmon out of water. She wanted to interrupt, to explain that she'd only recently found out about the affair herself, to say it wasn't her fault. But she stood silent and shamefaced.

A frustrated sigh came from Dervil, and Breeda watched with relief as her kitten heels turned and walked away. Breeda looked up just as Dervil stopped to consider something, and then turned back to face them.

'Incidentally, Breeda – Aidan isn't my husband. He is in fact my brother.'

The three women watched on intently, and now other people standing nearby had picked up on the drama and were looking on too.

'But I strongly suggest you give up any notions of romantic dabbling on that front...' then with a parting shot over her shoulder, 'Unless you're into incest.'

The words hit Breeda's brain, but their meaning lagged behind, and she felt something shift under her feet as Dervil strode off. She steadied herself with a hand to Oona's forearm. Her eyes found the patch of lawn where Dervil had been standing just a moment before, and she heard the words echo in her head. And then it rammed into her with full force – why she'd always felt a curious pull towards Aidan. From the moment she'd spotted him outside the florists there'd been something about him; the shock of black hair, the familiar side profile, the gappy smile, their ease with each other. Breeda felt her body start to go and she latched her other hand onto Marie's forearm. She thought of Aidan's eyes. The same as hers. The same as her fathers.

'Sweet Jesus,' said Oona.

The tray in Marie Boyle's hand tipped, and the three women watched as a suicide of vol-au-vents raced down to the grass.

CHAPTER 29

The drive back to Nora's must have logged somewhere in the depths of Breeda's dazed brain, but the people and buildings which drifted outside the car window were beyond her vision, part of another world. It was Aidan's face alone she could see now, and her mind's eye pictured his features, as she remembered him sitting on Oona's garden bench only twenty minutes before. She tried to deconstruct his face, to calculate the ratio of Sneddon to Looney hidden in his DNA. From her mouth she forced a slow deep breath. A jittery little disquiet had started to vibrate deep inside her and it was now swelling and breaking in the shallows of her limbs. Her fingers twitched on the steering wheel, and she gripped it more tightly, trying to anchor herself to a shifting reality.

I have a brother.

She mulled this fact over, let the word play out on her tongue, a hovering sommelier awaiting her verdict.

Christ. I have a brother.

Her head shook at the utter craziness of the last week, at the new normal which had marched unannounced into her life. A father found and a brother discovered, all in the space of a few days.

What was she going to discover next – a meth lab in Nora's attic?

Breeda parked the car outside her aunt's house, killed the engine, and listened to the ticking of the cooling motor. The clock on the dash read *17:55*. She needed a moment to sit and let it all wash over her, to let the news soak into her bones and become a part of her.

Had Nora known about Aidan? Was that the reason all along for the tantrums and threats, the fight at her mother's grave, the heart attack – had she been so revulsed at the shameful prospect of Breeda uncovering a bastard child in the stale depths of the family closet? The clock on the dash blinked over to *17:56* and Breeda looked towards the house. On either side of Nora's front door the two olive trees stood sentry, resisting the early evening breeze. She just wouldn't mention it. How could she? It would simply have to be another topic on the list of things to be avoided at all costs. After all, she'd never forgive herself if she caused Nora another coronary.

As Breeda climbed out of the car her phone began to ring. She rummaged it out of the bottom of her bag and squinted at the screen.

'Hello?'

'Breeda. It's Doctor Chakraborty. I believe you've been trying to get hold of me.'

In the background Breeda could hear papers being shuffled, the doctor already contemplating her next call. 'Apologies for the delay in getting back to you – just a lot going on. What were you after?'

Breeda leaned against the car, wishing she had a pen and paper so she could take notes. Instead she closed her eyes against the evening light and tried to focus.

'Well, Doctor, obviously my Aunt Nora's situation is quite serious, and I'm keen to understand how I should be caring for her.' Breeda lowered her voice, ashamed at even having the next thought. 'And I guess, to understand how long she has left?'

A pause on the other end of the line.

'I'm sure you're doing a fine job of looking after her, Breeda. Just the same meds as she's always been on …'

'OK …'

'At the end of the day her condition is stable. It hasn't gotten worse over the years, and – as I told her at the hospital – she just needs to keep doing what's she's doing. Meds and light exercise.'

Breeda opened her eyes now.

'Doctor, I'm a bit confused. Surely a heart attack is pretty serious. Doesn't she—'

'A heart attack?'

Breeda turned to look at the house now.

'I'm not sure where you got that idea. But it's just a bit of heart arrhythmia and high blood pressure – stuff she's lived with for years. Nothing new and I don't expect any change if she stays on her meds. Apart from that she's as fit as a fiddle.' The doctor was chortling now, 'She's a tough old bird, is Nora Cullen. Nothing to worry about, Breeda. Nothing whatsoever.'

Breeda rubbed a hand roughly on her prickling scalp.

'So, Doctor… are you telling me she didn't have a heart—'

'I'm sorry, Breeda, I do have to go. I have a patient to attend to.' More shuffling of papers.

'Of course … I … Thank you—'

The line went dead, but Breeda kept the phone pressed to her ear, expecting more words to materialize and make sense of it all. Yet as she looked at the house she felt it rise up, the truth of the matter rushing to the surface, barging its way past her naivety and gullibility. Breeda looked to her phone, now trembling in her hand. And she finally realised what an unheeded part of her had suspected all along: the old bitch had been playing Breeda for a fool.

Breeda stormed up Nora's pathway. This was war.

CHAPTER 30

Breeda had already climbed the stairs by the time the front door bounced in its hinges and slammed itself shut. Nora's bedroom stood empty. Breeda pulled back the quilt and felt the sheet with the back of her hand. It was cold.

She turned, her eyes blazing.

'Nora!'

She bounded down the stairs and flung open the kitchen door. Nora stood spooning loose-leaf tea into the pot, the radio playing in the background. She didn't turn to look.

'For goodness sake, Breeda. I thought a heifer had escaped from McGinley's farm. You're making an awful din on the stairs.'

A half-eaten Jaffa Cake sat waiting on a side plate, and Nora popped it in her mouth.

'Feeling better, Nora?'

Something in Breeda's tone brought a quick glance from Nora now, the eyes narrowed, shrewd and calculating. The toaster popped, and Nora turned back, now focused on buttering her toast. She wore her poker face, but Breeda was convinced she could see a subtle rearranging of her features.

'Well, while you were off gallivanting, I was parched upstairs.' Nora arranged the tea and toast on the tray. 'The tongue was hanging out of me. But I'm not one to complain ...' She reached into the fridge for the milk jug and a look of tight anguish played over her face. Breeda watched from the hallway as the pathetic charade unfolded for the audience of one. Nora set the jug down on the counter, and now raised a hand to her chest. She winced at some imaginary pain and steadied herself with a hand to the counter. It occurred to Breeda, at that moment, that this was just the end of a long line of guilt trips that Nora had taken her on over the years. The woman was pure shameless.

Nora turned from the tray and walked slowly towards the hall. She avoided Breeda's eyes and just shuffled slowly past her.

'Now bring that tray up, there's a good girl. I really shouldn't be moving around in my condition.'

Breeda remained in the doorway, facing the empty kitchen, the stage now clear. She let her aunt's words hang in the air for a moment, while Nora continued her slow retreat down the hallway behind her. Breeda turned and watched the back of her head. She wanted to savour this.

'Your condition, Nora? I was just talking to Doctor Chakraborty about *your condition.*'

The tiniest falter in Nora's gait, and then she had her hand to the banister. She kept her face toward the front door.

'Doctor Chakraborty? Yes, nice woman. A very nice woman.' Nora put her foot on the bottom stair. 'Now, bring up my tray before the tea goes cold. Good girl, Breeda.'

'For Christ's sake, Nora!'

Nora stopped. She took her foot off the stair and turned, contempt flashing in her eyes.

'You do *not* blaspheme in my house, child!'

'To hell with your house, Nora. You're a bloody liar!'

The heat had returned to Breeda's veins, and now a rage curled her fingers into fists. Nora stood tight-lipped and simmered at the foot of the stairs. She was working out her next move. But it was Breeda who spoke.

'Well? Have you nothing to say for yourself? The other day I rushed back here to your supposed deathbed. But according to our good friend Doctor Chakraborty you've got a manageable heart condition. No heart attack. Just a conniving old bitch who likes to play her gullible niece for a fool!'

'Now, just you wait a minute!' Nora's spittle caught the evening sunlight as it launched, then fizzled, on the hallway tiles.

'No, Nora. *You* wait a minute!'

Breeda felt her shoulders rise and fall, and briefly worried that the blackness was waiting in the wings, about to descend on her with its full suffocating force. But this wasn't a closing-in. This was a rising up – something primal and powerful forcing itself up and coaxing Breeda to sweetly submit to it. In front of her was the cause of so much pain. Nora's deceit simply knew no bounds. For a borrowed instant Breeda could see beyond the pursed mouth, birdlike eyes and thunderous scowl and could sift away all the crud to find the faintest memory of the younger Nora. The Nora from the photograph, all linked arms and laughter on Old Compton Street with Breeda's own mother. A happy carefree version from a distant time. Not this bitter old bitch standing in front of her. How hard she must have worked to sink this low.

Breeda opened her mouth to let her have it, but this was beyond words. There was simply no point in talking to Nora anymore. Instead she just shook her head, stunned at the havoc that could be wreaked by one person. Nora mistook the silence as the regret of a hothead.

'Look at you, throwing a tantrum, after all I've done for you?'

Breeda couldn't help but laugh. 'You know what, Nora? I just don't care anymore. To hell with you. Sell the house. Enjoy the money. With any luck you choke on it.'

She pushed past Nora and climbed the stairs. She would just pack her bag and get the hell out of here. 'I'm getting on with my own life. And that includes making amends with my own father.'

Nora was following her briskly up the stairs, no evidence of a heart attack now. 'What do you mean by that?'

'*What do I mean*? Well, I'm not exactly being cryptic, am I, Nora?' Breeda turned quickly on the landing and Nora stopped abruptly at her heels. 'I'm going to London to find my dad.'

Nora's face tightened at this and she put a hand to her chest. Breeda laughed in her face.

'Oh drop the act, Nora. And don't worry – I know all about the bastard son too. He's actually a really nice guy. You see, it's all out in the open now. Feels good, hmm?'

Breeda turned and grabbed her canvas tote bag from under the spare bed and started pulling her clothes roughly off the hangers in the heavy old armoire. She sensed Nora hover in the background, and then move quietly around her. She was fiddling at the framed sepia picture of Saint Brigid. But Breeda focused on the job at hand, balling and ramming her clothes into the bag, needing to get away from this house and its poison. She checked under the bed and then remembered her toiletry bag in the bathroom. She turned, but Nora had already moved quietly back behind her, and was now blocking the bedroom doorway. Breeda looked up. Something had changed in the old woman's face, and she was clutching a handful of papers.

'Now, Breeda. I wouldn't act in haste, if I were you.' There was a quiet triumph in Nora's tone, and Breeda felt it pluck at her curiosity. She watched on silently from the foot of the bed as a smug smile broke over her aunt's face. Nora tipped her index finger to her tongue, and then slowly leafed through the bunch of pages in her hand, enjoying the sense of regained control. Breeda noticed a faded logo on the top of each page, something familiar yet long forgotten.

'Did you never wonder where the money came from?'

'What are you talking about *now*, Nora?'

Breeda's patience was up. She wasn't going to be sucked in. She pushed past Nora, rounded into the bathroom, and swept her toiletries into her bathroom bag. In the mirror she could see Nora had a hand on the bathroom door frame, the other hand wafting the papers aloft, as she looked up at the walls and ceilings.

'This house. Your house too. How do you think they were paid for?' Nora's voice had grown thick with condescension and she was slowing her words for the backward child in front of her.

Breeda pushed past her again and shoved her toiletry bag into her tote on the bed. Angled on the floor the framed picture of Saint Brigid regarded her coolly and Breeda looked up to where the picture usually hung. A concealed safe was gaping open in the wall. Inside were what looked like neatly stacked rolls of cash – Nora never did trust the banks after the near collapse – and lying flat on top of the cash rolls was a familiar ornate gold picture frame. It was the painting of the swimming man from her mother's bedroom. *Breeda's picture.* Breeda shook her head and looked back at her bag. She was officially beyond caring. She zipped her bag closed, surveyed the spare room for the last time, and turned to leave.

'Nora, I really have no clue what you're talking about. This is goodbye.'

Breeda went to push past her, but this time Nora held her ground.

'Nora – move.'

'Life insurance.'

Breeda's eyes dropped to the clutch of papers in Nora's bony hand. A crease etched her brow.

'What are you talking about?'

'Life insurance, Breeda. A policy he took out a couple of years before he died. On my advice, might I add. The most sensible thing that man ever did.'

Breeda snatched the papers from Nora's hand, and turned her back on her aunt. She riffled through the pages, noticed the logo again, a company long gone or re-branded or absorbed by another. Her eyes strained to scan the small, faded print. But then she saw it on the last page – his name, the date, his signature.

'But Nora. He didn't die.'

The words came out as a near-whisper. She looked once more at Mal's signature, imagined the day he would have scrawled it, Nora no doubt hovering at his elbow, circling like a vulture and planning his demise. The logo drew her eyes once more. Hadn't that been the insurance company Nora had worked for in London? Hadn't there been a branch beside the opticians in Dunry too? The paper suddenly felt filthy against Breeda's fingertips, and she forced the pages back into Nora's arms. Breeda turned and stood silently for a moment. She just wanted to weep, to collapse in a heap on the hardwood floors beneath her, and to bow out for good.

'Maybe he didn't die,' said Nora from behind her, 'But he may as well have. He was dead to your mother after he got that Sneddon whore up the pole. He had to go. There was no way I was having him sniffing around after that. Besides, he wasn't good for her … for her moods. The Sneddon incident was just the straw that broke the camel's back.'

Breeda forced herself to turn and face her aunt.

'But Nora, this is wrong.'

Now it was Nora's turn to laugh.

'Are you worried about the insurance companies? Don't be! They're a pack of shysters. I should know – I saw how they operated from the inside. No harm done if they make the odd mistake in a customer's favour.' The breeziness in Nora's voice made Breeda want to retch.

She continued with a sigh. 'Look, it's not my proudest moment, Breeda. But we needed that money. It was our only chance for a fresh start.'

'But there was no body. How could—'

Nora folded her arms against her dressing gown, unable to hide the tiny glint of pride from her eyes.

'Things were a wee bit different back then, Breeda. I knew people. The local Guards, the priest – Father Mitchell.' Nora stood her ground but gazed out the window. 'They liked me and your Mam. They never took to Malachy Looney and his gambling, his boozing, his *womanizing*. As far as they knew he actually did drown at the strand that day. He had vanished, and his car had been found there.'

Breeda raised her eyebrows and Nora nodded back her confirmation.

'Yes, I may have helped. I drove his car down, then got the bus back. So with Malachy out of the picture it just took a little convincing to get a couple of reliable members of the community to act as witnesses – Mal had been seen drinking at the shore, later was seen wading into big water – that sort of thing. After that it was pretty easy. A bit of paperwork, the policy paid out, your mother had given me her power of attorney, end of story.'

Breeda walked to the window and looked out over the back garden. A butterfly had settled on the sweet-pea plant at the side wall. She stared at it, envying its innocence, its clutterless brain. She heard the exhaustion in her own voice.

'Was he in on it?'

'Who?'

'My dad. Was Mal in on the whole scam?'

'Oh, not at all! He was clueless. Why do you ask?'

Breeda turned. A hot little ember still glowed in her, and now she felt it spark into life.

'Well, why would he have abandoned me? He wouldn't have just left me!'

Nora shifted slightly and looked around the room.

'Nora. Why did he leave?'

Nora looked back, her voice lowered. 'I told you already. He got Mona Sneddon pregnant.'

'That doesn't explain why he left.' A steadiness had returned to Breeda's voice now.

Nora relented. 'When we found out about the Sneddon woman, I told him he had to leave. He laughed at me – told me to mind my own business. But it *was* my business, Breeda. I've always put this family first.' She challenged Breeda with an unblinking stare. 'He left me no choice. I had a word … with a few of the local lads…'

'What do you mean – *local lads*?'

Nora rolled her eyes. 'You really are a bit slow sometimes. You know, *the lads* …' Nora quietened her voice, 'The IRA. Anyway, I may have told them a few things about him.' Nora scattered her words more quickly now, 'Might have said he belted your mother … did a bit of stuff to you … Anyway.' She composed herself again. 'He got a visit that same evening and was put on the ferry to Holyhead. If he'd stayed in Dunry, he'd have never walked again.'

Nora glanced over at Breeda, but quickly dropped her gaze.

'Sweet Jesus, Nora. Is there no end–'

Nora slapped her hand off the wall. 'Do not blaspheme in this house! I did it for you! I did it for your mother!'

Breeda felt hot tears trip down her cheeks. She wiped them roughly away with the back of her hand and gripped the handles of her bag.

'And where are you going, you daft girl. Haven't you heard a damn word I've said?'

Nora had squared off in the doorway again, zero intent of letting Breeda escape.

'Get out of my way!'

Nora held out a hand.

'If that bastard gets word of this he'll want his share. That's the sort of person he is. We'll both be homeless. He'll probably tell the insurance company, the cops!'

'Nora, I don't care. Now move!'

Breeda shouldered her way past Nora and heard a satisfying whack as her aunt's elbow hit the door frame.

'If I go down I'll take you with me, girl!'

Breeda swung around. Nora was stood rubbing her arm, her face flushed with rage. But Breeda could see what looked like fear creeping into her eyes too. She moved towards Breeda now and gripped the bag straps over her shoulder.

'Please. They might send me to prison, Breeda. Is that really what you want? For giving your mother and you a roof over your heads?'

Nora's beady blue-grey eyes darted over Breeda's face, scanning for some sign of comprehension. She pulled tighter on the bag strap and brought herself closer to Breeda's face. A crumb of buttered toast was lodged in a little crevice on the side of her mouth, and her hot little breaths broke over Breeda's face. Breeda needed away from this diseased house and this toxic woman. She yanked the bag, and Nora lost her grip, stumbling backwards a few paces along the landing.

Down below her, beyond the black and white tiled floor, Breeda could see the front door. She thought of the fresh air and freedom waiting outside. She turned from the top of the staircase to take one last look at this terrible woman, someone who now might as well be a stranger.

'You wanna know something, Nora? For years I felt intimidated by you, like I was never good enough, like I was a constant disappointment. But looking at you now … I actually feel nothing but pity. You're just a spiteful old woman who wouldn't know decency if it slapped you in the face.' Breeda adjusted the bag on her shoulder and turned her back on her aunt. 'You won't see me again.'

Breeda's feet found the stairs, but Nora hadn't finished with her. A hand pulled tightly on the collar of Breeda's jacket.

'Think of your poor mother. Her name will be all over the papers!'

Nora's hand now pulled hard on Breeda's hair, and Breeda cursed and tripped backwards up the top stairs. She grabbed for the banister rail, and flailed her other hand back, managing to break Nora's grip on her hair. She felt the old woman's hand grasp and latch onto the bag strap again.

'For Christ's sake, Nora. Let go!'

Breeda pulled on the banisters, swift and hard. Her body swung, and she stumbled forward, her ribs connecting hard with the handrail. She clung with one hand as she willed her body not to launch. Her foot left the stair, and her knee whacked the rail, but she knew she'd managed to avoid toppling over. The seconds slowed and off to her left a shape blurred in her periphery. Something was lurching and scrambling through the air, a gangly bird failing to fly. Its limbs wheeled wild, as it grappled past her, and Breeda felt her bag strap leave her shoulder, as the bag too took flight. Nora traced a slow arc into Breeda's line of vision, a look of wonderment hanging on her face. Below her, the pendulum of the grandfather clock swung in slo-mo, the black and white floor tiles waited patiently. Breeda shut her eyes, and time resumed. The thud pierced the silence, and Breeda's stomach seized at the thought of what lay down on the tiles. She cracked open an eye and looked over her shoulder. Nora's legs were trailed along the lower stairs, but her upper body had landed on its side on the hard-tiled floor. Even from Breeda's vantage point she could see the arm and shoulder on the floor looked mangled. The old lady blinked her eyes open and Breeda heard herself exhale. Nora was facing the skirting board and a low animal groan was coming from her. The paperwork she'd been clutching only moments before had fluttered down and was now settling around her like oversized confetti.

Breeda skittered down the stairs, careful not to disturb any limbs. She squatted and gently stroked her aunt's hair, then leaned forward, dreading the sight of an expanding pool of claret on the tiles under Nora's head. But no blood was evident, her upper arm having buffered the impact to her skull. Nora continued to groan, and was moving her upper arm around, trying to pull herself off the stairs. Her legs shifted and brought weight onto her crushed arm. She winced at the pain and sucked air in through her teeth.

'I think it's broken. Don't move, Nora. Just don't move, OK?'

Breeda stood and paced over the scattered pages. An ambulance would take at least half an hour. She would just have to take her to the hospital herself.

Down near her feet Nora's face was set rigid and her jaw jutted out. Breeda realised the woman was shaking her head.

'What would your poor mother say? The mess you've made – of everything.' A small defiant laugh left Nora's tight mouth. 'I'll tell you what, girl – you can drop any plans of going to London – cos I'll be needing you here, now more than ever.'

Breeda looked down and felt a shift in her core. In Nora's face a sense of victory had already crept in, relegating the pain to second place.

Breeda's eyes drifted over the random pattern of black and white at her feet. The little faded insurance logo taunted her from the pages. She bent and slowly gathered them up and placed the pile on the phone table near the front door. Above the table, on the wall, hung a small round mirror, and now she found herself staring at it. In the background, Nora's voice prattled on, but Breeda was listening no longer. All she could do was stare at her reflection and seek advice from the person looking back at her. To her left lay Nora, to her right the front door. Breeda lifted the phone from the hall table and dialed.

'Please state your emergency.'

'I need an Ambulance please. Suspected broken limbs. An elderly lady has fallen down the stairs. Her name is Nora Cullen.'

'What's the address please?'

Breeda squatted down beside Nora and gently smoothed her hair.

'It's number three, Muckish View, Carrickross.'

'And your name please.'

Breeda looked at Nora and the stubborn set of her face. Her belted dressing gown had ridden up her legs and Breeda gently smoothed it back with her hand. Only last month Breeda had sat by her mother's side, stroking Margaret's thinned hair and papery skin, as she lay wasting away in her own dressing gown. Now Breeda watched Nora's face, and could suddenly see so much of her own mother in this person by her knees. A sorrow echoed in the depths of her heart, and she felt her chin weaken as she bent forward and kissed her aunt on the temple.

'Your name please?'

Breeda looked back at the phone in her hand.

'Oh, I'm just a neighbor. The front door is open. Please hurry.'

Breeda hung up the phone as Nora shifted beside her on the floor.

'What do you mean – you're just a neighbor?' She attempted to turn to look at Breeda, but even the smallest movement brought her body further down the stairs onto her smashed shoulder and arm.

Breeda placed the phone within Nora's reach, then stood and walked to the hall table. She took one more look in the mirror then folded the insurance papers from the side table and slid them into the top of her bag.

She opened the front door and looked down as the diluted gold of the evening light stretched weakly along the hallway floor.

'Goodbye, Nora.'

Breeda's chest tightened and she forced herself onward, blocking out Nora's angry words as they chased her down the steps and along the front path. She drew in a deep lungful of cool air and looked up, ignoring the tears spilling down the side of her face. The flashing white wingtip lights of a plane were heading into the darkest patch of sky, heading East.

I'm coming for you, Dad.

In the background, Nora's anger had dissolved into gulping sobs.

'Breeda!'

Breeda clicked the gate neatly behind herself, then set off into the darkening streets.

CHAPTER 31

Breeda leaned her backside on the high cushion at the end of the carriage and looked along the two rows of seats stretched out in front of her. There were no suits among the other passengers – it was a Sunday after all – just Londoners going about their business and tourists on their way to Camden market. She was too flustered to take a proper seat, her left leg twitchy, a fidget in her fingers. She slid her hands under her arse, closed her eyes against the artificial light, and listened to the rhythmic clack underfoot.

She was on her way to him. She was actually on her way to him.

Breeda tried to picture his expression when she'd turn up on his doorstep. But her father's face eluded her now, and in its place an image of Aidan presented itself. It was hard to believe she hadn't picked up on the resemblance before. But then again, she hadn't any reason to suspect she had a half-brother, let alone one wandering around Carrickross village. She smiled at the craziness of the situation.

The train came to a halt at Camden Town station. Hers was the next stop. As people left and entered the carriage, Breeda took out the postcard from her jacket pocket. She traced Mal's handwriting with her fingertip, then turned it over, and looked at the view over the city from Primrose Hill. A man in a tailored jacket and skinny jeans had perched beside her, and she sensed him look at the postcard, then glance at her, before losing interest and turning back to his phone screen.

Her eyes flitted over the faces of the fresh batch of strangers who had just boarded. She thought about the millions of lives, the millions of stories, in this one city - each person the center of their own universe. Hotels and houses, parks and apartments, were passing by overhead, every life intertwined and rippling from the impact of others. As the train sped on, she saw herself being swept along. Leaving Nora's house last night had been like leaping off a bridge, and now here she was being buffeted down a river, an insistent rapid pulling her forward, nothing to cling to, the bank too far away. But she had chosen to jump in, and this was her river, after all, one she'd never even been able to dip her toes into before now.

As the doors opened at Chalk Farm station, she picked up her tote bag and allowed herself to be carried out of the carriage on the tide of passengers heading for the exit. A southbound train had stopped at the same time and when the doors of the lift opened the waiting crowd surged forward and pressed around her. She clutched her bag tight against her chest and willed the lift not to break down. Carrickross village felt a million miles away and she tried to ignore the drumming of her heart against her hand. From behind Breeda, tinny noise spilled out of a cheap pair of headphones. In front of her a middle-aged Indian man held his young daughter firmly in his arms. Breeda focused on the flakes of dandruff on his shoulder and tried to slow her breathing as his pretty daughter stared intently at her. At last the lift shunted to a stop, the doors opened, and a moment later Breeda found herself blinking in the mid-afternoon sunlight.

Turning onto Hartland Road a few minutes later Breeda's pace slowed. She'd eaten nothing since the day before, but now felt like something needed to come up, her gut clenching, her hands sweaty. She glanced up the street. Some of the houses had planter boxes outside their first-floor windows, one or two had scaffolding out the front, but the street was eerily devoid of people. Breeda checked the address on the postcard once more, then carefully counted the houses up ahead on her left. She could see it. The canary yellow door stood out like a sore thumb amongst the neighboring houses with their muted palettes. It was all now so real, and she seemed to feel the gravity of the situation – the risk and recklessness – for the very first time.

Would he even recognize her after all these years? Was she turning up years too late for any bridges to be built? Would she be a nuisance to be shooed off his doorstep? Breeda reached the yellow door but kept walking. A short distance ahead was a railway bridge. She crossed the road and stood under it, desperate for a moment to gather herself, to let her heart and head synchronize. It was just over a week since she'd found the birthday card from her supposedly dead Dad, and now here she was, stood on his street, wondering which window he slept behind.

As she turned to look back towards the house with the yellow door her phone buzzed into life. The number wasn't familiar, but it was someone from home.

'Hello?'

'Hi Breeda?' A brief pause. 'It's Aidan.'

She shrugged her bag off her shoulder and leaned her back against the rough brown wall of the railway tunnel. The bricks vibrated her body in time to the slow rumble of an approaching train.

'Oh, hi …'

Across the road a ghost figure moved behind one of the net curtains, observed her for a moment, then vanished. Aidan cleared his throat and Breeda closed her eyes, pressing the phone tighter to her ear.

'So … the craziest thing … I've got a sister I didn't know I had …'

His voice was tentative, tired, warm.

'You didn't know?'

'No clue. Dervil told me yesterday after the barbecue. She has a way with words, that one.'

Breeda felt a tug of sympathy. 'I can only imagine.'

'Yeah. Look, Breeda, I'm sorry I didn't call you yesterday. I'm a bit shell-shocked to be honest. It's not every day you discover your Dad's not your biological father.'

A jogger idled past Breeda, and she turned her body sideways to the brick wall. She'd been so caught up in her own drama with Nora and her need to get to London that she hadn't stopped to consider reaching out to Aidan. Down the line she could hear ice cubes clink in a glass. She couldn't blame him.

'I should have called you, Aidan. I'm sorry.'

'Not at all. You'd only just found out about me yourself. It was Dervil who's been sitting on this for years. She only filled me in yesterday.'

She could hear him refilling his glass and the bottle being set back down.

'Your Mam? Your Dad? Never told—'

'No. My poor Dad knew – God rest his soul – as soon as he took one look at me. But he made Dervil promise never to say a word. He never wanted me feeling unloved in any way.'

She heard him take another swig.

'He was a decent soul, was Frank Sneddon. Dervil thinks he died of a broken heart. And as far as I'm concerned, well, he'll always—' A waver had started up in Aidan's voice and now a lump rose in Breeda's throat too. She wished she could put an arm around his shoulder.

'And Dervil knew all this time?'

Aidan laughed wryly down the line. 'She was twelve years old when my mother got pregnant with me.' He groaned, then paused, unsure whether to continue. 'Dervil walked in on your dad and my mam.'

'What?'

'Yeah. One afternoon when she ran home from school for her lunch box. Caught them at it. So you could say she knew about me since day one.'

Breeda leaned her back against the brick wall and exhaled slowly through her cheeks. Now it made sense. She'd always thought Dervil's hatred of her had arrived from nowhere. But now she understood where it had seeded from. She could imagine twelve-year-old Dervil at her mother's bedroom door, lip trembling, eyes brimming, as she watched Mal Looney's pasty arse thrusting away between Mona's legs. And now Breeda tried to imagine how it must have been for Dervil in school after that – to have to look at Breeda's face each day and be reminded of the man who'd broken her father and destroyed her family.

'I'm speechless. I just don't—'

'Breeda – are you free to meet up?' The idea had perked Aidan up. 'A coffee? Scrap that – a proper drink?'

She looked at the yellow door across the street.

'Aidan, I'm actually in London.'

'London? What are you doing there?'

Breeda took a deep breath.

'It's where he lives …'

Aidan paused. Breeda could hear him put his glass back down, then shuffle forward on his seat.

'You mean …'

'Yeah …'

'So you're there to …'

'Yeah …'

'Wow …'

'Yeah…' She sucked in through her teeth. What she wouldn't do for a tumbler of whiskey right now. 'I'm standing here like a fool, looking across the street at his front door.'

'What are you waiting for?'

'I don't know.' She heard her own mumbled words. 'I'm kinda terrified.'

An ice-cube cracked in his glass.

'When was the last time you saw him?'

'Twenty-five years ago.'

'Well, is it any wonder you're a bit freaked out. If you want my advice, seize the day. If you overthink it you'll chicken out.'

She stood up straight and locked eyes on the front door. He was right. And besides, she hadn't destroyed her relationship with Nora and lost the roof over her head just so she could lurk under a railway bridge in North London. Overhead the train had arrived, and she had to shout to be heard.

'Thanks, Aidan. I'll call you back in a bit. You take care, OK?' She swung the bag over her shoulder. 'Wish me luck.'

She strode out onto the road, the yellow door in her sights. The screech of tyres hit her before she even saw the white van. She raised an arm to protect her face. Her phone fell and bounced off the ground. Inches away the driver blasted his horn. His shaved head stuck out the window.

'You stupid cow! What the—'

Breeda grappled for her phone, near the driver's front wheel, and staggered backwards, gasping an apology to the man. She stumbled her way between two parked cars, and stood on the pavement, her legs jelly. He was glaring at her, his face puce.

'I'm so sorry—'

Breeda looked up and down the street, suddenly fearful he might jump out and punch her. But the engine revved three times and he was gone, another screech of tyres in his wake.

Behind her a dog gave a single bark.

'Trixie!'

The canary yellow door had opened and a woman with spikes of grey hair and red-framed glasses stood watching her.

'Alright?'

Breeda nodded, her face misted with a cold sweat. She approached the low front wall, behind which two wheelie bins barely hid. The woman stayed in her hallway, protected by the half-closed front door. To one side of her feet sat the dog, a small white Terrier. Both woman and dog regarded Breeda silently.

'Well, that could have been worse.' The train had rumbled off and now Breeda's words came out overloud, her accent alien in the quiet street.

A flicker of something crossed the woman's face, but still she held her tongue. Her eyes looked Breeda up and down, and Breeda self-consciously raked a hand through her hair.

'I'm sorry to disturb you – I'm looking for Malachy Looney. Is this … is this the right house?'

The door opened a fraction wider and the dog tilted its head to the other side.

'Oh, it's the right house, alright.' Something close to a smile materialized on the woman's face, and Breeda felt her legs drain of stability once more. Her hand found the low front wall.

'Is he in?' All moisture had gone from Breeda's mouth, each word a struggle.

''Fraid you've missed him, love.' The door opened a few inches wider, one foot still planted firmly behind it. The woman nodded slowly, nothing else forthcoming. Breeda started to sense she was relishing the intrigue.

'Any idea when he'll be back?'

A slow lick of the bottom lip.

'Thing is, love – old Mal's upped and left. All a bit sudden, if you ask me. I've already rented out his room to someone else.'

She seemed to note the confusion on Breeda's face.

'I'm a landlady – not a charity. So, anyway, off he goes. Mentioned jetting off to Florida for a change of scene. Sick of London, so he says.' A nod to the darkening sky overhead. 'Can't say I blame him!'

'Florida.' It wasn't a question so much as a sound that Breeda felt compelled to make at that moment.

'Yeah,' the woman continued, after a quick look up the street, and the slightest lean forward. 'Between you and me, I think he got spooked. Someone called up last week – some woman – wouldn't leave a message.' Her eyes held Breeda's a fraction of a second too long. 'But anyway. I'm not one to gossip. As long as my lodgers pay on time then Mrs Bennett's as happy as a pig in the proverbial.'

The dog, Trixie, had lost interest, and had tacked off down the hallway floorboards. This seemed to be the cue for Mrs Bennett too.

'Anyway. Must get on. If you do track down old Mal, tell him Mrs B says hello.'

The door started to close before something else seemed to occur to the landlady.

'By the way, who should I say was asking? Just in case he gets in touch?' Her eyes had narrowed, and she stood motionless.

Breeda's words came out as a long, deflated sigh.

'Breeda. Just tell him Breeda was asking after him.'

The woman gave a single nod.

'Alright, Breeda. Well, you watch yourself crossing the road. Tara, now.'

The brass knocker bounced once on the closed door and the street once again settled into its Sunday afternoon stillness. Breeda picked up the bag from her feet and turned back to survey the street. She had no clue what to do next. She hadn't even a hotel room in which to sit and cry. Her empty stomach felt leaden and she needed to sit somewhere and think. And she needed a drink. A bloody big drink.

CHAPTER 32

Nora stood in her late sister's upstairs bathroom and tossed another two painkillers into her mouth. She struggled on the cold tap with her left hand and forced the pills down, trying to slow-breathe away her frustration. Oona Mahon – well-intentioned but annoying as hell – was bellowing something up at her from the living room. Only half an hour before she'd turned up unannounced with a fruit basket at Nora's front door and when she'd caught Nora struggling her one good arm into her coat she'd insisted she would drive her over to the Looney house herself. So now Nora stood at the bathroom sink, willing herself to calm down, but feeling disgruntled at the interfering do-gooder hovering around downstairs. She glanced at herself in the mirror and shrunk back from her reflection, her eyes sunken and bloodshot.

Another shout came up from downstairs.

'Are you sure I can't get you whatever it was you needed, Nora?'

'Thank you, Oona, but no. I won't be a minute.'

She winced at the effort of shouting back down the stairs. It was a pain to raise her voice above a whisper. They could set her arm in plaster, but no neat little white cast existed for her three broken ribs. Bed rest and patience, they'd told her last night at the hospital. They hadn't wanted to let her out today, of course, but when Myra had visited her at lunchtime, Nora had threatened to create a scene if they tried to keep her in. She couldn't face another sleepless night in that public ward, with its phlegmy coughers, the stench of bleach, and the superbugs lurking on every surface. Nora looked down at her broken arm in its virginal sling. She'd been lucky, they'd told her. It could have been so much worse, they'd told her.

If only they knew ...

She crossed quietly to Margaret's old bedroom and scanned it from the doorway. Breeda had packed everything as instructed, only leaving Margaret's paintings on the wall and the photos on the dresser. The bed was stripped, the wardrobe was emptied. All else was boxed-up and ready to go. Nora sat slowly onto the bed and let her sore body sink onto the feathery softness of the mattress. From this level the view was one of only mountain and sky. No wonder Margaret had loved daubing at her watercolors here, keeping her troubled mind on an even keel.

Nora ran her left hand slowly along the stripes of the mattress and stared vacantly at the bare floorboards. She didn't really know why she'd come here today – but she'd had to come – something had compelled her to. And she'd needed to get out of her own house. Too many memories had been raked up now and had been chasing her from room to room. Her body had been in shock from the altercation with Breeda yesterday as well, and her mind had steadily caught up with the violence, so that it too now felt battered and bruised. Telling Breeda about the insurance policy had been beyond stupid, and she felt alarmed at her own lack of discretion. She fingered the little crucifix at her neck, queer in her left hand. Who could she trust if not herself? Now she stroked the cast on her broken arm, but no sensation penetrated the plaster, the soothing useless.

A shock of color from behind the bedroom door drew Nora's eye. She recognized it immediately – Margaret's yellow coat from Portobello Market. She unhooked the hanger from the door and bunched the material in her left arm, burying her face in the bright yellow wool, and seeking even the slightest scent of her younger sister. It was like running into an old friend from happier days, and now Nora was conscious of a lump in her throat. The bottom of the coat was muddy, along the hem, and she walked over to the window, and picked distractedly at the little clumped tufts with her one good hand.

It had been while Nora was working at the insurance company, over the summer of 1975, that her younger sister had come to London for a week. Margaret had adored London, of course, her first time in the Big Smoke. She'd been raring to get out and explore the city bright and early each morning, even after a cramped night on the lumpy two-seater settee in Nora's tawdry bedsit. One morning, as Nora was making ready to head to the office, Margaret had stated rather matter-of-factly over a piece of toast that she was sick of looking like a dowdy culchie, and that she was going hunting for a new dress. She promptly scrounged a few quid off her big sister – with a promise to pay her back – then caught the Tube to Westbourne Park, and from there walked down

207

to Portobello market. But it wasn't a dress that caught her eye that morning, but a beautiful coat of sunflower yellow, the likes of which she'd never seen. It demanded to be bought, so she'd later tell Nora, and she'd dreaded to ask the man behind the counter just how much it cost. She'd haggled, of course – the shopkeeper a total curmudgeon who was having none of it – but she'd wangled a smile out of him, then a laugh, and five minutes later had walked out with change in her pocket. Her Ma and Da would have been proud.

That same afternoon, while Nora had been filing away policies in a stuffy Haymarket office, Margaret had popped into a pub in Soho to use the ladies. The barman had insisted that she buy a drink if she was to use the facilities, so she'd paid for a Britvic and was sipping her glass when she felt a pair of eyes on her from across the bar. The man had held her gaze as he folded up his copy of the racing fixtures, and walked over confidently, hand extended, his eyes never leaving hers. He'd introduced himself – a London boy from Irish stock – but he was more interested in learning about Margaret. He wanted to know what she was doing in London, if she was a model, and how had she not been snapped up yet. Margaret Cullen wasn't green, and had someone tried such a routine back in Dunry she'd have laughed in his face. But this fella, this Malachy Looney, there was something about his persistence, his self-belief, his fascination in her, that swept her up as a willing participant in the game.

And so, ten minutes later, when she'd finished her orange juice, she'd permitted him to buy her a Babycham – just the one – and the banter had continued.

As they'd talked, she became aware of herself observing the little vignette playing out in the timeless bar. What would they say back at home? She imagined how the tongues would wag, but to hell with all that. She felt womanly. She felt wanted. And she relished the sense of impropriety of having a drink with a strange man in a strange city on a Thursday afternoon.

Three drinks later, and feeling tipsy from lack of lunch, Margaret realised with a shock how late it was. She had already agreed to meet Nora at the Eros statue after work. As she'd pulled on her coat Malachy Looney had looked so crestfallen that she'd agreed to meet him again the next evening, same place. He'd stood with her on the street, outside the pub, and as they shook on it his hand had not wanted to release hers. She allowed herself to be drawn into him for the quickest of embraces. Her new coat flashed golden in the evening sun, and in that moment, in the warmth of his arms, she felt like everything and anything was possible. As she'd walked off towards Shaftesbury Avenue Margaret had felt his eyes on her back, and she couldn't hold back the grin which broke over her face.

Just after five pm the next day the two sisters had strolled down Old Compton Street, Margaret bubbling over with a nervous energy and turning heads in her new coat. Beside her, Nora was failing to fight the infection of her sister's giddiness. She was happy to be dragged along to check out Margaret's new beau and felt inwardly relieved to be getting out of her poky bedsit. But she was also aware of an uncomfortable little pang of jealousy in the pit of her stomach. Not one jot of interest had been shown her way in the three weeks she'd been in London, and here was her younger sister fresh off the boat, men already sniffing around her like flies around shite. Margaret had always been the stunner, of course, and the sting of envy lurking in Nora's mind was nothing new. She pushed the feeling down, suddenly embarrassed at her pettiness, and linked her arm tighter through her sister's. And so they found themselves traipsing through Soho, bent double every few meters to snort with laughter at something no one else in the world would get. Nora had brought her little Hanimex camera along, and they'd coaxed a cheery chap from the door of a book shop to take their picture, his clumsy fingers struggling on the button, which set the pair of them off into hysterics once again.

They'd fallen into the crowded bar, and weaved through the swell of Friday evening drinkers, finding a relatively quiet spot towards the back. Margaret stood on her tiptoes and glanced over the heads around the bar.

'I don't see him.'

'Well, he's hardly likely to stand you up, Maggie. Relax. We're a bit early anyway.'

The inside of the bar was clammy, and Margaret shrugged off her new coat.

'Take this, would you? I'm dying for a pee. Must be the nerves.'

As Margaret headed off to the loo Nora turned to look for two free stools, but instead caught her reflection in the tiniest gilt-edged wall mirror, buried in amongst prints of old Soho. She thought of her sister, who definitely looked nothing like a dowdy culchie, despite what she'd said yesterday. Margaret was all big brown eyes, long pale neck, and the fullest of lips. Nora leaned closer into the mirror. Her own eyes were more grey than blue today. Her mouth was just a tight little slash. And her hair – similar in color and length to Margaret's – was hatefully wiry and dry and a divil to tame. Nora glanced over to the ladies, then unfolded Margaret's yellow coat and slid her arms into it in one smooth movement. She buttoned it up quickly and stuck her hands in the pockets. Her fingers found something – Margaret's good lipstick – and she took it out and quickly filled in her lips before rouging her cheeks a little. She might be chaperoning her sister, but it didn't mean she had to look like an old maid while she did it. She turned discreetly to one side, then the other, then pressed her lips together once more in the mirror.

She froze. Two strong arms were around her, locking her in a tight embrace. Nora stood rigid, her hands still in the coat pockets, her arms clamped to her sides. She tried to turn but a man's face nuzzled her neck now, and a heady blend of cigarettes and shaving soap forced its way inside her nostrils. His grip tightened, arms like marble, and she knew she was powerless to escape. The bar was full of people, yet no one looked her way. She was drowning, only meters from the crowded shore. She squirmed her face away and cast a panicked glance at the gilt-edged mirror. And now she saw him, his eyes closed, his stubbled cheek pressed against her flushed face.

He whispered, his breath hot in her ear.

'You're a sight for sore eyes, Maggie.'

And as if sensing her eyes on him he looked up. Their eyes met in the mirror and the din of the pub dropped away. Nora saw something shift in the man's face as he realised his mistake. The moment stretched so that they both stood frozen in time. They stared at each other, Nora's breath shallow, his heart pounding against her, two strangers entwined in an accidental intimacy.

He released her, slowly, then took a step back, the spell broken. Nora pushed herself away, stumbling forward, and looked down at her feet as she tried to regain her composure. She shook the suffocating coat off her shoulders and when she looked up again she found him staring at her in the mirror, a bold smile on his face, his palms up in surrender.

'Sorry about that. A case of mistaken identity ...'

Nora turned to face him, her body shaking. She folded the coat over her arms to try and disguise a tremor, holding it in front of her like a barrier. It *was* just an innocent mistake, wasn't it? She could still feel the ghost of his stubble against her cheek and she forced herself not to raise her fingers to her face.

'You must be Mr Looney?' Her voice was dry. She needed water.

'And you must be the big sister, Nora. Call me Mal.'

From the side of her eye Nora could see Margaret approaching and now she took a step backwards. When Margaret reached them she appeared slightly miffed at having missed her chance to introduce them.

'Well, it looks like you two have met then? Hello.'

She leaned into Mal Looney's space and he planted a kiss on her turned cheek.

'Well, ladies, who's having what, then?' The Looney man had taken his wallet out of his jacket, but Nora pushed the coat into her sister's arms.

'Here you go. My turn.'

Nora fought her way through the crowd to the bathroom, her legs still unsteady, and once there, wiped all traces of lipstick from her face. She turned to go back into the noisy bar, but stopped, and instead held her wrists under the cold tap. She stood waiting for the water to cool the fire from her veins. But a minute later, with her wrists still under the tap, she looked at herself in the mirror and found herself wondering if it was cooling or cleansing she needed from the water.

The interfering blonde was now shouting something up the stairs and Nora stood up stiffly from the bed. She turned to the dresser and found the old black and white photo from that day in Soho. She picked it up and tilted it towards the window. The two sisters, arm in arm, about to have their destinies set in stone. Margaret's shining beauty smiled back at her from Old Compton Street all those decades ago, and now Nora realised why she'd had to come here today. This was the place where her sister's spirit lingered the most. She traced a finger over Margaret's features.

'I'm sorry, Maggie.'

Outside the sky had taken on a slate grey color and the window had started to rattle in its frame. Nora placed the photo on the sill and watched the foam forming on the bay down below. She lowered herself awkwardly onto her knees, made the sign of the cross, and said a silent prayer for what she feared was surely about to come.

CHAPTER 33

Breeda's feet drew her back towards the familiarity of Chalk Farm tube station. Once there, her gaze latched onto a young couple up ahead – disgustingly gorgeous twenty-somethings – the guy's arm hanging comfortably around the girl's pale shoulder, his other hand guiding a bicycle. Breeda followed at a distance, hungry for a distraction. She crossed the road after them and a moment later found herself on a smart wide street, boutiques and cafes drawing her eyes but registering nowhere in her brain. She could hear the thoughts clambering up, clamoring for attention. A part of her – she imagined a little internalized version of Nora – wanted to scream 'I told you so!' and shake her by her own stupid shoulders. But if she let it up now it would take over and she'd be done for. A dark room – a dark room and a bottle of something numbing – that's what she needed now.

A fat drop of rain found its way down her jacket collar and some blotches patterned the pavement around her. Up ahead on the far corner, beyond the well-heeled pedestrians who were picking up their paces, she spotted a pub. She pushed in through the side door, worked her way along the length of the busy bar, and found a stool at the far end. She hung her bag from a brass hook under the bar and tried not to think of the mess she'd created.

A young woman was leaning towards her from the other side of the bar, her nose pierced, her wavy hair rinsed a light blue. She looked up from the pint glass she was drying with a tea-towel and gave Breeda a smile.

'What can I get you?'

'A red wine. Please.'

The smile broadened, in a knowing *one-of-those-days* ways.

'Well, we've got Pinot, Shiraz, Malbec, Chian–'

'Shiraz. Please.'

The girl nodded, then turned away, before shouting over her shoulder.

'Large one?'

'Please.'

Breeda shrugged off her jacket and felt the heat from the fireplace behind her on the back of her arms. Every few moments the bar doors swung open to admit another person or two from the wet streets. Feet were stamped, umbrellas were tapped, and collars were turned back into place. Breeda glanced discreetly at the faces around her, hungry for the anonymity.

'There you go. Would you like to start a tab?'

That knowing smile again. No doubt the girl had seen enough middle-aged fools like Breeda prop up the bar one too many times. Breeda rooted around in her purse and handed over her only credit card. The girl gave it the once over.

'Thanks …' She tilted it to the light, 'Breeda? You just holler out when you want another of those, alright?'

Breeda shook a pill from the bottle in her bag and lifted it to her mouth. The glass of wine in front of her was huge – it had been poured up to the 250ml mark.

But wasn't that what she'd wanted? She slid it towards herself and swilled.

A quarter of an hour later the wine glass sat empty in front of Breeda. She realised she needed to eat. She caught the bargirl's eye and ordered a lasagna and a second glass of red, then looked down at her phone. The screen was a black mirror, smeared and newly cracked, and it reflected a pair of tired Looney eyes back up at her. How close she had come, missing him by a matter of days. If she'd only stood up to Nora sooner, if she'd maybe tried calling him again, or just left a proper message so he'd known it was his daughter looking for him. Mrs Bennett's words came back to haunt her now – he got spooked – by Breeda's stupid phone call from the strand. And now with thoughts of the strand bubbling up from her past Breeda shifted on the barstool and felt her eyes moisten. What she wouldn't give to be able to wind back the years and find herself at the little yellow caravan with the brown stripe around the middle, her dad hoisting young Breeda up on his strong shoulders, as they went off for fish and chips and a ride on the waltzer. But she'd stuffed it up – she'd let him slip through her fingers. Breeda flipped the phone over – sick of the sight of herself – and lifted her wineglass to her lips.

By the time she pushed her empty plate away twenty minutes later the bar was deafening. Bodies bumped her as she sat slouched on her stool. People shouted and laughed, a cheery Friday buzz to which Breeda was impermeable. And it occurred to her as she sat there that wherever she went in life she would always be the awkward loner, out of step with the rest of the world, a bad smell for people to smile through and ignore. A different bar tender, an older lady with a web of smoker's lines around her mouth, lifted the plate and empty glass away.

'Did you want a look at the dessert menu?'

The woman wiped the bar, the smell of her stale cigarette smoke drifting towards Breeda with every movement. Breeda thought she saw the woman's eyes rove over her bumps and tummy. She sat up straight.

'Cheesecake.'

'Good choice. Another wine?'

'Please.'

The *yeses* and *pleases* were tripping easily off Breeda's tongue that evening. She checked her phone again. It had just gone seven and she still hadn't sorted out a hotel. The combination of the food, the fire, and the wine was numbing her brain. She leaned forward on the bar as the third glass of wine was set in front of her. She should have ordered a coffee, but instead she took a gulp of the wine. It felt heavy and sickly on her tongue. She took another swig.

People eager for drinks had now nudged in either side of her. A guy on her right was waving a fifty-pound note. He seemed to know the chap on her left and was bellowing something across Breeda's head. The bar had become stifling and suffocating and Breeda had had enough. The older bar woman, Smoker, was coming out of the kitchen at the far end of the bar. She was carrying an over-sized white ceramic plate and Breeda could see faces along the bar turn to admire it, curious as to the identity of the lucky recipient. Breeda felt a sudden sense of dread, allergic to any attention. She willed the woman to stop, for the plate to be for someone else. But *Smoker* advanced and Breeda lowered her gaze, a low panic taking hold. The plate landed in front of her and she found herself looking at a slice of cheesecake drowning under a syrupy slash of raspberry coulis. Around her the chatting had subsided. She could sense them looking at the desert, then looking at her, their thoughts as loud as if they'd shouted in her face.

No wonder you're a porker, putting it away like that.

If only someone – anyone – would give her a friendly nudge, encourage her to enjoy it, tell her that you only live once. She needed some kindness, some niceness, someone to tell her she was OK. But the silence stretched around her, heavy with a million micro-judgements. She forced herself to sit up straight, doing her utmost to ignore the heat in her face. Two small forkfuls and she could pay the bill and get out of there. She picked up the fork while the bodies continued to press against her, the waved banknotes hovering inches from her face.

Her eye was drawn to something on the plate - a flourish on the wide rim. She craned her neck but had to slowly turn the plate to read it. Someone in the kitchen had piped something in a chocolate swirl.

Smile!

One word – *Smile!* She should have known that it wouldn't take much. She continued to sit without blinking and stared at the dark letters on the edge of the plate. It was welling up now, and she was too spent to fight it. The first tears arrived silently, without any fanfare, no warning to the people around her. Maybe on a better day she'd be able to read *Smile!* on a plate and interpret it as intended - a nice flourish that the pastry-chef did for everybody. But not today. They were all back there in the kitchen, she knew it, snatching glimpses of the fat, miserable old cow and pissing themselves laughing at her. And why shouldn't they? She was beyond pathetic. She was a screw-up, a reject, a wrecker of lives. Her shoulders started to heave in awkward spasms. Around her elbows were nudging, conversations were pausing, heads were nodding in the direction of the crazy woman at the end of the bar. The hush spread, people further away unsure of the source, but looking on nevertheless.

She needed out. Breeda tugged at the bag, struggling to release it from the hook, and stood abruptly. Already people had taken a step back, a need to distance themselves from the instability in their midst. The stool toppled and clattered on the tiled floor behind her. Now people at the far end of the bar had smelled blood and turned to gawp at the unfolding drama. She pushed through the sea of curious faces, her bag blundering after her. She managed to blurt out a couple of mangled apologies – her flushed face slick with tears and snot – and pushed through the door onto the wet street. The sense of embarrassment propelled her further, past a red mailbox and across a road, until at last she could stand on the corner of the pavement and gulp in the evening air. A black cab had just come down the hill and as it turned tight onto Regent's Park Road its tyres found a pothole and sent a spray of murky water over Breeda. She watched the retreating taxi and then looked down at her soaked legs. The denim clung in patches to her thighs and calves.

She remembered her credit card – her only means of a hotel room – was still back there on the shelf behind the bar. She looked off in the direction of the pub and imagined the punters theorizing about the lunatic who'd just had a meltdown in their midst. There was no way she could show her face in there again tonight.

On the corner was the entrance to a park. She walked in and slowly climbed the lamplit pathway and near the top of the hill she found a bench a short distance from the path. She surrendered her body to it and looked out over the view rolling away below her.

A view over London from Primrose Hill.

Overhead the rain clouds had moved off, leaving only wispy patches in the night sky. The air was still and mild, and apart from the blinking taillight of a bike down below the park was pretty much deserted. Breeda stretched out her tired legs in front of her and let the lights of the cityscape in the distance distract her tired eyes. She squinted and the lights from the cranes, buildings and monuments stretched and danced over her retinas. She held her gaze like that, then closed her eyes, just for a minute, a need to suspend the reality of where she was and the trouble she'd caused. If only she could open her eyes and see the lights on the pier from her own kitchen window, with the trawlers bobbing out for their nightly haul. If only she could climb into her own bed, with Ginger balled happily at her feet, and pull the sheets over her face. She imagined Finbarr, banging and clattering on his roof next door, and a sad smile came to her face. Maybe if she kept her eyes closed now this could all just be a bad dream, and there'd be no harm done when she awoke in the morning.

She sighed slowly and her weary body sank further into the bench. She'd come to London looking for the missing piece of the puzzle, hoping to feel whole for the first time in her life. But now she felt further from herself than she'd ever felt before, totally alone and beyond exhausted. She toed off one shoe, then the other, and blindly scootched them over beside her bag on the ground. The background hum of the city played in her ears and she folded her feet up beside herself on the bench. Her limbs were like lead and her head had started to loll.

One minute. She would just close her eyes for one minute.

CHAPTER 34

Trixie's little yelps chased Breeda through the narrow corridors of her dreams. The dog nipped at her heels and skittered in ever-decreasing circles, until at last it latched its fangs onto the hem of her jeans and tugged her back to a state of consciousness. Breeda woke up with a pounding skull, the barking now close to her head, and swept her hand to scare whatever it was away. She pushed herself up awkwardly on the bench, the daylight blinding, and squinted at the source of the noise.

'Benji! Come here!'

A tall skinny man wearing tracksuit pants and a stripy jumper was calling to his miniature Schnauzer from over on the main path. He glared at Benji while he raked a hand through his hair, studiously avoiding eye contact with the homeless woman on the bench.

Benji lost interest and snuffled off back to his owner as Breeda swung her legs stiffly onto the ground. She could already feel a tightness in her lower back from her night of sleeping rough. There was a crunchiness to her left shoulder too and her mouth was parched. She checked her watch – it was nearly eight already. How the hell had she slept so long? She thought back to the Diazepam pill she'd popped along with the three large wines the previous evening - the equivalent of a bottle –

and shook her head at her stupidity. Down the hill the last of a thin layer of mist was lifting from the lower part of the park. Breeda blinked in the view of London, familiar now in the light of day.

'Oh, no, no, no!'

Her bag was gone. And her shoes – correction – *one* of her shoes was gone. She stood quickly and scoured the area around the bench. Nothing. Benji was disappearing down the path after his grumpy master and Breeda wondered if the little shit had swiped her shoe and buried it in a shallow grave somewhere. She sat again and rubbed her hands roughly through her tangle of hair, the memory of the mess she was in lying heavily across her shoulders.

Through the slats of the bench she could see her one remaining shoe looking up at her accusingly. One minute awake and already it was going to be one of those days. She patted her jacket pocket – at least she still had her phone. And then she remembered her credit card too, still back at the bar.

Looking down at the city again she imagined all the millions of people out there, wolfing down cornflakes and dashing for trains. She didn't belong here. She'd been stupid to come. It was time to go back to Carrickross and face the music. She would lie down naked on a slab in the middle of Main Street and let them all have a go at flaying the flesh from her bones. Whatever they wanted her to do to atone she would do it. She rubbed a hand to her puffy face, doubting there'd be anything left to salvage with Nora. At the thought of her aunt an image of the old woman came back to haunt her now, Nora lying broken at the bottom of the stairs.

Breeda let out an audible grown. What an utter shambles she'd made of it all. She stabbed her right foot into the shoe, then stood and clomped back down the path.

There were no obvious signs of life in the pub. Breeda banged on the door anyway and pushed her face up against the glass pane. She could make out the shelf behind the bar where her credit card would be. That card was her ticket home. And right now it would also buy her a pair of shoes and something to eat. A couple of workmen were drilling up the road a few yards away, their noise assaulting her brain. Breeda hammered louder on the door. From behind her, through the din, came another familiar noise. She turned around to find her old mate Benji barking up at her. On the other end of his leash the grumpy owner held a sourdough loaf and a carton of almond milk in his arm. This time the man did meet Breeda's eye. He scowled at her with a withering look of disdain.

'For goodness sake, woman! Get some professional help.'

He marched on and tugged yappy little Benji in his wake. Breeda stood open-mouthed, the sting of injustice burning her face. She felt a desperate need to shout after him, to tell him he'd got the wrong idea, but instead she turned away from the prick and tried to convince herself she didn't care what he thought. She squinted in through the glass at the shelf once more, then decided she had no choice but to return later for her credit card.

She set off as evenly as she could, her eyes on the furthest point of the street. She was tired and sore and desperate to see a friendly face. As she walked, she remembered she was officially now homeless too.

Breeda hobbled weakly onwards, any attempted bravado long gone. A few meters ahead a mother with a severe black bob yanked her daughter out of Breeda's path. The mother glowered, and the daughter gawped, and Breeda looked down at her bare foot, grimy from the park and pavement. Her jeans still had flecks of mud from the encounter with the taxi. And no matter how hard she tried to pat down her hair it still stuck up at every possible angle. She caught her full reflection in the glass door of a boutique and had to turn her face away, ashamed at how she must appear to the Monday morning commuters of this respectable neighborhood. A small inner voice toyed with the idea of how deliciously freeing it would be to begin a long, slow descent into the depths of lunacy.

Familiarity guided Breeda's feet once more and she soon found herself on his street again. His *former* street. She trailed her fingertips over the railings of the front gardens and tilted her head back slightly, exhaling a slow, deep breath. She was saying goodbye, acknowledging that she had come to the end of her quest. Overhead a crisscross of contrails etched the sky and Breeda stopped and stared up at the white lines for a few moments. Her dad was gone, just like all those passengers, off to new horizons and a fresh start. In the background an approaching train rumbled. She looked back at the pavement and walked slowly on, a little tightening in her chest the only telltale sign that she'd just passed a yellow front door.

She walked slowly under the railway bridge, closed her eyes and let her fingertips play over the bumps and grooves of the brickwork. Breeda imagined the stories these bricks could tell, wondered how often Mal Looney had walked under this very arch. The rumbling train was louder, but the bricks at her fingers divulged nothing of its approach. Beyond the arch sat a boarded-up old boozer. She spotted some glass smashed near the edge of the pavement – a pint glass, or a car window – and she skirted it. But a small shard managed to find her bare foot and outside a school she rested her hand on a railing and inspected her heel. A small piece of glass glinted at her through the dried mud on her foot. Behind her the noise of the train was louder still. But then, with a halting chill, she realised what it really was. Her knuckle whitened against the railing.

Not here. Not now.

Without turning around Breeda already knew that there was no train. She tightened her hand harder still on the railing and with her other hand groped wildly in her jacket pockets. The pills weren't there – they were in her stolen bag. Her chest tightened, and she pleaded silently – maybe she could ward it off if she could just cling on to the physical realm. But deep down she knew it was useless. She'd been a fool, ignoring the background hum as it had stalked her up the street. It would no longer be ignored. The rumble was its calling card, the briefest of courtesies to let her know old blackness was on his way.

Breeda put her foot down, wincing as glass jabbed further into the broken skin. School windows stared down at her, a hundred pupils waiting in the wings, ready to gawk and point at the weirdo in the street.

She forced herself on, each step a struggle. But buried in the deafening static something else was fighting to be heard. She stopped and grabbed the railing again. Nearly drowned by the white noise battering her skull came something vague, something remembered. She closed her eyes and leaned into the railings, felt it wash away, then drift quickly past again.

'Mentioned jetting off to Florida for a change of scene ...'

Mrs Bennett's words played through Breeda's mind just once and Breeda clung to them and the deception they revealed. The faintest flicker of hope whispered in the distance: *He might still be here. He might still be here.* She turned and looked back down the street and now felt a shot of urgency in her veins. She wouldn't make it back in time. But she had to. Through the railway arch she could still see the front of the houses. She put one foot in front of the other, the landlady's lie fueling her back in that direction. Breeda's eyes watered and her temple throbbed as she grabbed at the railings and pulled herself forward, her body moving in surges. Blindly, she stumbled, clinging to the weakest of hopes that she wasn't too late. She forced her bare foot into the splinters outside the abandoned pub, anything to help her focus, anything to keep her from going under, just yet.

Snapshots scattered, and a million memories danced before her eyes. Her mind zoomed in, and there they were, at the strand once more. Their rainy family holidays at their little yellow caravan, and her father's annual insistence that it was better than going abroad. And Breeda remembered clearly the whispered truth behind it all. Mal Looney had been absolutely terrified of flying.

Breeda bumped her shoulder along the bricks of the arch. The glass dug its way into new parts of her foot,

227

but she stumbled on. The rumble was a roar now, closing in quickly. Meters away, the yellow door was still out of reach. But she lunged for it, fell against it, banged it three times with the side of her fist. But she was too late, had no fight left in her for the landlady. Her cheek was wet against the paintwork, and as the door opened she felt herself falling, saw the wooden floor coming up to meet her. A pair of hands cupped her head. But her vision was gone. The blackness was here now, and it washed over her and pulled her down. Only one word went with her; a man's voice:

Breeda. Breeda ...

CHAPTER 35

The mug of sweetened tea in Breeda's hand had started to shake. She watched as he leaned forward from the side of the bed to gently take it from her clammy grip. Breeda couldn't help but stare, afraid to move, terrified that this brittle moment might disintegrate, and she'd wake up back on the park bench on Primrose Hill.

'Dad.'

The word escaped her softly: a simple statement, no hint of question. The clouds from the blackness had been slowly clearing from her brain, and now Breeda felt the room around her solidify, become more real.

He was smiling at her, that old familiar crinkle in the corner of his eye, deeper now. Breeda continued to stare, drinking in every detail of his face. His brow was more deeply etched than she remembered, the eyebrows wild, his hair thinned of its blackness. But the eyes watching her were those from her childhood. And suddenly Breeda was a little girl again, propped up in bed and listening to him read Pinocchio. She'd found him. Mal Looney. Her father. Dad.

Mal leaned forward and took his daughter's hands in his own. Breeda skirted her thumb over the big knuckles of his manual worker's hands. These were the same hands that had hoisted her up onto his shoulders for childhood walks on the strand; the same hands that had tossed his special girl imaginary apples; the same hands that had cupped her embattled head just two hours ago.

They sat in silence for a moment, the clatter of a nearby train merging into the other city sounds outside the bedroom window. He continued to watch her, but she suddenly had to look away. If she looked up now she would lose control. He leaned towards her.

'Who's the apple of my eye?'

Breeda's heart caught. Her words arrived in a childlike whisper.

'I am.'

'Who?'

'Me. Bree—'

But she could no longer hold it together. Her face crumpled and her body crumbled into her father's embrace. She blubbered in his arms as a convulsion ran through her entire body. Mal shushed her and gently stroked her hair.

'It's OK, my darlin'. Your old Dad's here.'

Breeda collapsed deeper into him, allowing herself to drown in his woody scent. A sweet release surged through every cell of her tired body and her tears coursed freely now. Dark blotches spread down her father's light blue shirt. He cupped the back of her head once more and rocked her gently.

'Is the t-shirt really that bad?'

Breeda laughed into his shoulder, then pushed him gently away, grateful for the change of tack. He sat back from her and they both looked down at the faded *Madness* t-shirt which he'd dug out from one of his drawers. She reached for his hand and shook her head.

'Dad, I have so much to tell you. And there's so much I want to know.'

A noise interrupted them, and Mal cocked an ear. Breeda heard it too – the sound of Mrs Bennett's feet on the staircase. Mal rubbed the back of his neck and Breeda noticed a slight clench in his jaw. She patted the back of his hand, sat back against the pillows, and blew her nose into a tissue.

'Well, ain't this a lovely vision of happy families.'

The landlady walked across the room and sat Breeda's laundered clothes on the end of the bed.

'All washed and dried. I've left you a pair of shoes down in the hall too. Nothing fancy, but it's the best I could do. At short notice.'

Breeda sat up straight against the bed head.

'Thank you so much, Mrs Bennett. I really do appreciate it. I hadn't planned—'

Mrs Bennett shoved the window up roughly and the net curtain billowed in.

'It beats me why you didn't just say who you were. Could have saved yourself a lot of trouble.' She smoothed the curtain down, then turned back to Breeda. 'You nearly gave your poor Dad here a heart attack. Thought you was from Her Majesty's revenue and customs. Didn't we, Mal?'

'I'm sorry, Mrs Bennett. I guess I should—'

The woman had tuned out. She stood flicking the light switch by the door.

'Mal – that bulb wants replacing. And when you're ready Trixie needs a walk.'

Mal nodded, a sly wink towards Breeda, daring her to smile. 'No problem, Mrs B. I'll get right onto it.'

Turning from the door Mrs Bennett shot Breeda a crafty look.

'No handbag with you?'

'Well, I *had* a bag. But it was stolen when I was in the park.'

Mrs Bennett seemed to take this in and looked from Breeda to Mal and then back again.

'So you've no money, then?'

Mal dropped his eyes and sighed. Breeda dropped hers too, embarrassed on behalf of the woman and her clumsy insinuations.

'Dad, I left my credit card at a pub. Will you come with me to get it?'

In the background Mrs Bennett withdrew, her victory postponed, and stomped back down the stairs. Mal looked up at Breeda, the crinkle back in the corner of his eyes.

'Course I will, love. I can even buy my grown-up daughter a grown-up drink to celebrate. You get dressed and I'll wait for you downstairs.'

Mrs Bennett's voice carried up from the hallway, 'Malachy, Trixie. Walkies.'

Breeda and her father looked at each other wide-eyed and collapsed in silent shakes of laughter.

Twenty minutes later Breeda found herself strolling down the street, her arm linked proudly through her Dad's, and Trixie straining ahead of them on her lead. On Regent's Park Road Breeda caught their reflection in the window of a Real Estate Agents. She leaned her head into his shoulder and let her feet fall in step with his. None of what had come before this mattered in the slightest now. This moment, right here and now, had made it all worthwhile. Even the silliness with Nora could be forgotten. Breeda had her prize, a new chapter was beginning, and each step they took now was putting fresh words on the page. She filled her lungs and felt nothing but love for the world.

Outside a shop Trixie had stopped to say hello to another dog. The owner walked out to untie him and Breeda couldn't help herself.

'Hello, Benji!'

The dog cocked its head at her, as did the owner, and Breeda beamed back her best smile.

Inside the pub a few locals were dotted around. It was a different place in the midday light, the one constant being the girl with blue hair. Spotting Breeda she smiled and fetched the credit card from the shelf.

'Forget something?'

'Thanks a million. I'd forget my head if it wasn't screwed on.'

Mal had taken Trixie down to the low table in front of the fire. The bar woman's gaze followed him for a moment, before she leaned forward, and touched Breeda gently on the forearm.

'You were a bit upset last night. Everything alright?'

Breeda leaned forward too and patted her hand.

'Let's just say it's better than alright now.'

The bar woman gave Breeda a warm smile, which faltered slightly as Mal approached. She cleared her throat and picked some empty glasses off the bar.

'Well, what can I get you good folk?'

'I'd like to buy my girl her first drink.'

'Dad, it's hardly my first drink.'

'Shush. You know what I mean. What's your poison?'

'I'll have a white wine please. Pinot Grigio.' Breeda could see the bar woman's mouth open but cut her off. 'Better make it a small one, thanks.'

'And a JD and coke. Double please.'

As the girl turned to fetch the drinks Mal patted the pockets in his leather jacket.

'Oh, I'm a pillock.'

'What's wrong?'

'I left my bloody wallet at home. Listen, I'll just pop home and get it.'

'Dad, go and sit down. It's not a problem.'

That smile again. He did have something of a lovable rogue about him.

'I'll pay you back later. And here I was wanting to buy my lovely daughter a drink.'

As he sauntered off towards the fireplace Breeda's smile trailed after him. She could see how he would have been a heartbreaker in his day. How he would have swept her mother off her feet in this very city, before following her over to Dunry. Out of nowhere an image of old Mona Sneddon came to mind. Breeda glanced towards Mal – sitting at the table and scratching Trixie behind the ear – and when he looked up he smiled back at her. She would store the Mona conversation away for another day. One thing at a time. She took a sip of her wine and handed the credit card back over.

Sitting by the glowing coals of the fire Breeda relaxed as the words flowed easily between herself and her father. She ordered another round of drinks, ignoring her empty stomach, and marveled at how easy it already was between them. She learned of his arthritis – his hands destroyed after years of bricklaying – and his plans to finally sell his building business. She told him how she'd packed in her corporate job so she could spend precious time with Margaret. He hadn't known of Margaret's passing, and he'd sat distracted by the fire for a moment, before they raised their glasses to her memory. Feeling the mood becoming too serious, Breeda changed the topic to the waste-of-skin also known as Brian O'Dowd. As she spoke his name his image was invoked, and now Breeda could picture him strutting into Heeley's Bar back home, with Alex-from-the-Boston-Office following on his heels. She turned to glance at her father and choked back a laugh – the similarity was uncanny - even down to the leather jacket and the glass of JD and coke. She couldn't wait to tell Oona about her not-so-subtle daddy issues.

They fell into silence for a moment. A log crackled and drew Breeda's attention back to the fire.

'Dad, I never knew …'

The words arrived unprompted, in the quiet of the pub, and he looked at her, waiting.

'They told me you'd drowned. They said you were dead.' Breeda shook her head at her own words, but the absurdity clung on. 'For years they lied to me. I found out, just last week, that you didn't die back then, all because of an eighteenth birthday card.' She turned and saw the ageing in his face now, the cost of Nora's lies carved in his skin. How much could a man forgive, she wondered. She sat back from the fire, aware that a different type of heat was beginning to burn her face now. 'I never received it, Dad. Nora never passed it on.'

A mask settled over his features. He was withdrawing, from right in front of her, and she felt as if she was going to lose him all over again. Reaching over she pulled his hand towards her.

'Dad, it's OK. We found each other, in the end, yeah?'

'I figured you hated me, just thought you wanted nothing to do with your old man.' He snorted, and now it was his turn to shake his head. 'Christ. Good old Nora.'

'I know, Dad. I know.' Breeda rubbed the back of his hand again, annoyed with herself for stumbling them both into this place already. But it was out now, and she'd started, so she was going to finish.

'Dad, I know why you were forced to leave Dunry.'

He raised an eyebrow but held his tongue.

'The other woman.' Breeda felt embarrassed by her turn of phrase and looked down at the burning coals.

Mal sat back in his chair and rubbed the back of his neck. She turned to look at him again, a sudden need to witness his expression.

'I went to visit her last week. I saw Mona Sneddon.'

A softening came over his features at the mention of the name. Breeda imagined his relief, having his adult daughter accept his shortcomings so ungrudgingly. His little indiscretion – his and Mona's peccadillo – was no longer a dirty secret to be hidden from his daughter.

'How is Mona?'

'Not great, to be honest. You knew about the dementia?' Breeda drained her glass.

'Yeah. She was due to pay me a visit. Unlikely now though.'

Breeda sat up straight.

'Dad, why don't you come home with me?'

'You what?' He drained his whiskey and pushed the glass away.

'Come home with me, for a visit. You can see Mona, I'll show you Carrickross. You can meet my friends.'

The idea took hold of Breeda, the cogs of her brain running at full speed. He'd come back for a quick visit, and she'd make him love it, and he'd end up staying. She'd use the last of her savings to rent the little two-bedroom apartment above the wine shop. Mister Sheridan might give her a few extra shifts, and in the meantime, she'd apply for that project management role in Letterkenny. She found herself nodding at him, her eyebrows raised expectantly.

The blue-haired girl had come to clear their glasses. She nodded to the empties and Breeda nodded back, before adding, 'Make them large ones please.'

'Right you are.' The barmaid flicked her tea towel over her shoulder and went to fetch the drinks.

'Go on, Dad. I want to show you off to everyone! And we've so much catching up to do. And anyway ...'

He was shaking his head, but he stopped at Breeda's hesitation, and his smile faded. 'And anyway what?'

Breeda examined her chipped nail polish. 'Well, I just don't think your Mrs Bennett is thrilled to have me here. I get the impression I'm in the way.'

'Oh, to hell with Mrs B. She's a little possessive, that's all. But in fairness, my life is here. Going back there ... there's just too many unhappy memories.' He leaned towards her, and quickly grabbed her hands in his. 'There's great memories, too, of course.'

She found a smile and hoped the tears would stay away. How naive she'd been to think that the act of tracking him down would be a swift solution for their years of forced separation. Breeda kept her eyes on the table as the two fresh drinks arrived. The girl went back to finish pouring a Guinness, and Trixie resettled her drowsy head on her front legs.

'I hate her so much.' Breeda could taste something metallic and blood-like on her tongue.

'Nora?'

She nodded and wiped her cheek with the back of her hand. There weren't supposed to be tears now. He turned his glass slowly on the table.

'Old Nora has a lot to answer for, alright. All those wasted years ...'

Breeda could picture Nora's beady little eyes now and remembered the easy lies she had spread to get her boys to threaten Mal onto the ferry that night, painting him as a wife-beater and a kiddie-fiddler. She pictured the uptight, pious hypocrite, and remembered her as she lay broken on her hallway floor. Remembered her as she lay surrounded by the scattered pages of the life insurance policy.

Breeda took a liberal swig of wine and stared into the flames. Something hot inside her was growing engorged. It needed a good lancing.

'Dad, I think there's something you should know about Nora Cullen.'

CHAPTER 36

Ginger stretched along the back doorstep and submitted the furry arc of her belly to the morning sun. Sitting beside her, Breeda leaned against the whitewashed wall and tilted her face to the cloudless blue above. She cradled the phone to her ear.

'And he's upstairs?'

'He is.'

'Wow, Bree. You don't do things by half.'

Oona's laugh came down the line and conjured up an easy smile to Breeda's face. She looked down to the bay and watched a kite surfer scud effortlessly across the water.

'So how does six o'clock sound? We'll have some champers, then eat at seven?'

'Sounds great. Anyone else coming?'

'Just you and Dougie, me, my *dad*...' Breeda emphasized the last word and heard Oona laugh again. 'And I'm thinking of asking Aidan as well...'

There was a slight pause on the line.

'So Mal knows he has a son?'

'He does now.' Breeda had let it slip to Mal – two days before – at their lunchtime drinking session in London. At the time, with the glow of wine in her empty belly, Breeda had felt her tongue slip out of neutral and had taken on the role of champion of the truth, raking up everyone else's dirt for them. By that night, after a day of boozing, her father had agreed to come back with her to Ireland for a quick visit. Malachy Looney had a daughter *and* a son.

'Well, I feel like I should film the whole thing, just in case it goes tits up.'

'Ah, thanks Oona. I've missed your supportive chats. Ever think of becoming a therapist?'

'That's a great idea! Listen, I have to go and drop the kids to school.'

'Okay, Love. Bring nothing but yourselves. See you at six.'

Breeda brought the phone back inside and glanced around the bare kitchen. She'd been awake since just after six, a buzz of excitement in her brain coaxing her to get up and get cracking. Before talking to Oona she had spent a few hours updating her resume for the project management role in Letterkenny. Her finger had hesitated over the *Submit* button on the website, and she had found herself getting up from the chair again and again, looking out towards the mountain, and fussing over the cat, trying not to think of her disappearing guest house dream. But after one final lingering look out the window she had forced herself back to the laptop, hit the *Submit* button, then slammed the laptop shut.

She flicked on the kettle, walked along the hallway, and listened. There was still no sign of life upstairs. Mal would be wrecked after yesterday's mammoth drive. Cracking open the front door she looked out to the driveway. His white van was still parked as they'd left it the night before.

Looney & Sons - Builders

When she's seen it for the first time, parked on his street in London, she'd laughed, and had wondered aloud who these sons were.

Better for business, he'd told her. *People like a family man*, he'd said.

The previous morning Breeda had sat in the passenger seat of the van, trying her best to ignore the filthy looks of Mrs Bennett. The landlady had been standing at her yellow front door, with her arms folded and a simmering grimace. Mal had gone in for a peck on the cheek, but Mrs B was having none of it, and had slammed the door in his face. Breeda had felt a twinge of guilt at the time, but a steadily increasing wave of excitement had replaced it. And even with the length of the journey - five hours to Holyhead, the ferry crossing to Dublin, then four hours drive up to Donegal – she'd felt herself becoming more and more animated with each kilometer they ticked off. By the time they'd reached the main road into Carrickross that night she couldn't help herself from leaning over and blasting the horn.

The Looneys were in town!

Now back in the kitchen Breeda poured a mug of tea and tiptoed up the stairs. She tapped softly on the door of her mother's old room.

'Are you awake, Dad?'

She nudged the door open to find him on the bed, pulling on his socks, his face still puffy from sleep.

'I am, Breeda, I am. Come in.'

'Still milk with two, right?'

He smiled and patted a space on the blanket beside him. Through the open wardrobe door she could see his backpack. But as she glanced around at the sparseness of the room she felt a sudden embarrassment. The place was too stark. She wanted him to feel comfortable. Her eyes settled on the framed photos and watercolors on the wall. Mal followed her gaze.

'She had a talent, did your old mum.'

'She did, Dad. She loved the light here.' Breeda walked over to the paintings and leaned in towards her favorites. She studiously avoided looking at the bare patch of wall with the lonely nail where the swimmer used to hang.

Damn Nora.

'Yeah, we'd talked about turning this place into a B&B ... thought it might be a good base for artists, or cyclists, or anyone wanting to escape.' As Breeda sat back down on the bed beside her father, she thought of the *For Sale* sign stuck into the front lawn. 'But, anyway, it's not meant to be.'

'Nora?'

'Nora.'

She turned to look at him now. The lines from the pillow still creased his cheek, and his hands holding the mug looked worn and sore. She had a sudden urge to wrap her arms around him and promise to look after him forever. All those years when she'd been denied the chance to care for him were now coming to the surface.

'Dad, what would you think if I had a couple of friends over this evening? I'll make us something nice.'

He fidgeted slightly beside her on the bed.

'Don't worry, just my best friend Oona and her husband Dougie. You'll like them a lot.'

She thought of Aidan too, but would say nothing until they'd spoken.

'Alright, love. But don't go to any bother on my account.'

'It's no bother, Dad, really. It would be my pleasure.'

She caught him looking at his watch, and she gently nudged him.

'Is there somewhere else you have to be?'

'I just need to get to the bank at some stage. I don't have any Euros.'

'Well, I'm heading into town shortly to pick up a few bits for tonight, so I can always get you some cash, and you can sort me out later? Unless you want to come with me now?'

She noticed him frown and put a hand to his arm.

'Are you worried about running into Nora? Don't be. She changes the flowers at Saint Colmcille's, every Wednesday morning, regular as clockwork.' Breeda could just imagine Nora standing on the altar with her blocks of oasis and fresh stems, the ultimate martyr with her broken arm. 'She won't be anywhere near the shops, Dad, I promise.'

Mal stood and walked to the window, taking in the view of the bay down below.

'No, I wasn't thinking about Nora. It's just a bit weird being back, that's all. Listen, you go ahead. I might have another cuppa, then I'll head into town on foot. I could do with stretching my legs after the drive. I might even have a flutter on the old gee-gees.'

'OK. Well, if you're sure …'

'I'm sure.'

He turned and Breeda leaned in to kiss the grey stubble on his cheek. When she was a kid he'd joked

243

that the odd bet on the horses was his only vice. Breeda cast a sly glance at him now, knowing that that wasn't strictly true.

Nearly hidden behind the bedroom door, Breeda spotted her mother's woolen coat. She unhooked it and headed downstairs. At the front door she paused for the briefest moment, wondering if she'd forgotten something, her fingers uncertain on the handle. She shook her doubt away, then glanced back up the stairs.

'I'll be back in an hour or two, Dad. Don't do anything I wouldn't do!'

Breeda pulled the front door neatly behind herself, leaving her laugh to echo in the silence of the hallway.

CHAPTER 37

The hanging baskets outside Flynn's were bursting with color that morning and Breeda stood on tiptoes to take in an exquisite faceful of perfume. She smiled as a father came out through the automatic doors, his young daughter trailing after him in a bright pink princess outfit. Breeda's gaze followed her, and then took in the jolly shop fronts behind her on sunny Main Street. It was as if someone had suddenly cranked up the saturation all around her, everything now more vibrant, life in *Technicolor*. This was probably how it had been all along. But now her blinkers were off, and here she was, Dorothy opening her door to the colorful land of Oz.

She picked up a basket from inside the sliding doors and grabbed a bottle of Veuve Cliquot from the chiller cabinet. At the butchery counter she ordered five grass-fed sirloins. To hell with the expense, she thought. This was the first meal she'd ever cook for her father.

As Breeda placed the steaks in her basket she fantasized how it would be to bump into Nora right now. Or Myra Finch. Or even Fuckwit Brian and Alex-from-the-Boston-Office. She was ready for them all. Nothing and no one could bring Breeda Looney down today, and as she walked past the boxes of breakfast cereals she felt invincible.

Breeda spotted the blonde ponytail a split second before Dervil turned and saw her. The two women froze, Dervil in mid-appraisal of an avocado, Breeda in mid-Pavlovian bowel clench. She could still turn to the display of porridge oats on her left, set her basket on the floor and scarper outside. She could, but she wouldn't. Instead, Breeda stood her ground, an inner resolve arising from somewhere, and bringing an unexpected steadiness to her body. Breeda adjusted the basket on her arm and stepped forward. She had no clue what she was going to say. But she was going to say something. Dervil seemed to sense the shift, a disruption to their established dynamic, and coolly cast the avocado back onto the display. She turned to leave.

'Dervil, wait. Please.'

The ponytail halted, and Breeda watched the shoulders rise and tense.

'I just wanted to talk to you …'

Dervil didn't turn around. Instead Breeda looked at the back of her black leather jacket and guessed at the curl of contempt on her lip. Over the intercom Mick Jagger was singing about seeing someone today at a reception, and in the background the self-scanner beeped with an irregular heartbeat. Breeda sucked in a deep lungful of air. This wasn't going to be easy.

'I know you hate me. Or at least, I know you think you hate me.'

Breeda saw the fists clench but decided to press on.

'But the thing is, Dervil, I don't really think your hate belongs at my feet.'

Dervil held her rigid stance and Breeda took a step forward.

'Your Mam. My Dad. What they did all those years ago …' Breeda watched the shoulders rise again, 'What they did had consequences for you, for me, for Aidan …'

The woman in front of her had the look of a coiled spring, and Breeda sensed that at any moment she could spin and slap her face. She lowered her voice into a soothing tone and carried on.

'And what they did hurt my mother. And your father too.'

At the mention of her father, Dervil's shoulders seemed to drop slightly and a softening came to her fists. For a moment a loaded silence hung between the two women, and Breeda pondered just how exhausting it must be to carry around all those years' worth of hate and anger. Breeda lifted a hand and let it hover a couple of inches from Dervil's back, afraid of being scalded.

'But you and I have a brother in common now …'

She took another breath, and gently placed her hand on Dervil's shoulder, steeling herself for a whack from a flying fist.

'I think it would be better if we could try and bury the hatchet? For Aidan's sake?'

Under Breeda's fingertips, through the black lambskin jacket, she was sure she could feel the smallest tremor in the woman's shoulders. Suddenly Dervil pulled down her sunglasses and marched through the sliding doors. Aidan was watching on from the bakery aisle and now he looked from Dervil's retreating back over to Breeda. He abandoned his trolley and rushed over.

'What was that about?'

247

Breeda exhaled and turned to him.

'I'm really not sure. Hopefully it's the start of a thawing process. Time will tell.'

Aidan had a tiredness in his eyes that hadn't been there at Oona's barbecue. Breeda could only guess how challenging the last few days must have been for him.

'You OK?'

He looked down at his feet and shook his head.

'I'm getting there, but it's been a tricky few days. We've had a couple of chats, Derv and me, and to be honest I think it's been eating away at her for years, the guilt of knowing about my dad, but not telling me. I don't blame her though.'

He looked Breeda in the eye now, needing her to hear him.

'Do me a favour – go easy on her? I know you two aren't exactly best buds, but she's had it tough recently. Her husband died in January.'

'What?'

'Knocked off his bike. Not far from their house in Sydney. That's why she's back here, a fresh start …'

Breeda dropped her gaze. She thought back to Oona's barbecue and the brief mention of a death in the family which Aidan had made. And now the Australian twang in Dervil's accent made sense too. She looked back up at him.

'I'm really sorry to hear that, Aidan. I had no clue.'

'Yeah, well, she's quite a private person is our Dervil. Just tread carefully around her, OK?'

Breeda nodded, then looked silently towards the avocado recently abandoned by Dervil.

'What?'

'Nothing.'

'Breeda, what is it?'

She looked up at him, at the same eyes as her father's.

'He's here.'

Aidan frowned, then his eyes widened.

'You mean—'

'Yep. We came over together yesterday on the ferry.' She put a hand to his arm now. 'I'm sorry, Aidan. I couldn't *not* tell you. Imagine you running into him in the street. Or being sat in Heeley's, and discovering the old fella enjoying a pint beside you is your father.'

'He's not my father, Bree.'

'I'm sorry. I know. You know what I mean.'

He gave her a tight smile as he rubbed the back of his neck.

'So, how long is he here for?'

Breeda hunched her shoulders. 'A few days. Maybe longer.'

Aidan looked down at the items in her basket.

'And I'm guessing the fancy dinner's in his honour?'

'Yeah, I figured I'd make him something nice this evening. Oona and Dougie are coming over too.'

Aidan nodded, then looked off distractedly towards the exit, his other sister still weighing on his mind.

'You look just like him.'

He looked back at her now.

'I do?'

'Yeah. You're the spit of him.'

He looked down at his feet again, a trace of confusion on his face. Breeda put her hand to his arm again, a need to fix whatever he was feeling.

'Listen, I know this might be clumsy of me, and way too rushed, but why don't you come over for dinner tonight?'

His eyes were on her again and he took a step backwards. Breeda dropped her hand from his arm.

'Dinner? With him?'

'And me, and Oona and Dougie. Nothing formal. He's looking forward to meeting you.' Breeda heard the words leave her mouth and wondered why she'd said them.

Aidan blew out through his cheeks. He rubbed the back of his neck again and shuffled about.

'Bree, I dunno. It's all a bit—'

'Just have a think about it. You can let me know this afternoon. No pressure, OK?'

He was biting his bottom lip and nodding silently.

'OK, I'll think about it.'

He'd looked back towards the street again.

'Listen, I have to go check on Big Sis.' He stopped as he turned, looking Breeda up and down. 'Nice coat, by the way. Were you a Sesame Street fan?'

She looked down and smoothed her free hand over the bright yellow wool.

'What do you mean?'

'You know, Big Bird!'

She reached over to slap him, but he jumped out of the way, the tiredness leaving his face for a moment.

'I'll call you later.' He waved over his shoulder and hotfooted it out the sliding doors.

Breeda placed some corn cobs and broccoli into her basket, pondering what Aidan had just told her about Dervil. But something else had begun to nag at her thoughts too, and as she sidled off towards the check-out area she realised for the first time that other people could be impacted by her father being here too. She didn't want to cause Aidan any upset, and as she picked up a second bottle of champagne, she tried to dismiss any concerns from her head. They were all adults, and if Aidan decided to come along then they would have a lovely evening. Unpacking her basket on the counter she attempted to revive the happy place her mind had enjoyed only ten minutes before.

'Breeda.'

A packet of shortbread fingers was now waiting its turn on the conveyor belt after her groceries. Breeda recognized the chubby hands drumming the packet, the left fingers covered in ink.

'Oh, hello Mister Sheridan!'

She waited for his 'Call me George!' comeback, the friendly quip as reliable as the sun rising in the East. But the moment passed, the silence only punctuated by the beep of the scanner and the swoosh of the sliding door. George Sheridan gave Breeda a tight smile, bereft of warmth, and returned his focus to his item on the counter.

Breeda looked down at her wrapped steaks on the conveyor belt, her cheeks suddenly burning. She had never seen that look in his eyes before – such a wariness, and a hurt. Was he miffed that she was buying champagne from here instead of from his wine shop? Surely the man wasn't that petty. Then the penny dropped. George Sheridan would have seen Nora out and about, parading her broken arm around the village. Nora wouldn't have blamed Breeda, of course – not in words, anyway. She was a paragon of subtlety when she wanted to be, practiced to perfection at throwing out a couple of dots and then handing someone a pen to join them. No, George Sheridan and Myra Finch and the whole damn place would be in no doubt as to whose fault it was.

'That'll be one-hundred and seventy-six euros and eighty cents please.' The young redhead on the checkout already had her acrylic-nailed claw out.

Breeda squinted into the depths of her handbag, then gave its jumble of contents a good shake.

Shit.

She could picture her denim jacket, draped over the banister at home, her purse still nestled snugly in the pocket.

Beside her George Sheridan's fingers were starting up an impatient tattoo on his packet of shortbreads. Breeda looked up at the unimpressed cashier.

'I'm really sorry, my purse is at home. I'll just nip back to get it. I'll be five minutes, max. Just leave all this here …'

Breeda abandoned her items at the end of the conveyor belt, then rushed for the sliding door. She clipped her shoulder on the door and felt the heat return to her face, imagining them watching her, Acrylic-Nails and Mr Sheridan, rolling their eyes and exchanging looks.

She struggled the car door open, then pulled it shut behind her, taking in a deep breath and forcing herself not to look in the rear-view mirror. It would all be fine. George Sheridan was just having a bad day. He'd be back to his normal chipper self tomorrow, and then they could share a pot of tea, and she could ask him about those extra shifts, and the empty flat upstairs for herself and Mal. She jabbed the key into the ignition and turned it, but the motor only churned and grasped, churned and grasped, then nothing. Gripping the steering wheel with both hands she closed her eyes tight against the world.

Not today. Please. Not today.

She would book the car in for a service tomorrow. But right at this moment she had the day to organize. Breeda turned the key once more, the motor churning and threatening to die for good. But it caught, and she exhaled into a soft relief. As she pulled out onto Main Street she couldn't help but think of how George Sheridan had looked at her like she was a piece of dirt. Breeda shifted in her seat and punched on the radio. To hell with him, she thought, as she drove up the hill towards home. To hell with them all. Breeda Looney was having her own fresh start. She had a welcome dinner to organize for her father, and nothing or no one was going to spoil it.

CHAPTER 38

Nora was in a foul humor. Her broken ribs had caused her the worst night's sleep and her arm had begun to throb in its itchy, clammy cast. She had woken up in a state of frustration and the morning had steadily gone downhill.

The flowers at Saint Colmcille's – always her pride and joy – had been a right royal pain that morning. She'd had to fiddle one-handedly at the altar display, the stems not cooperating, the arrangement looking like a dog's breakfast. She could only hope that Father McFadden wouldn't notice her substandard work. She'd sensed herself slide into a sulky mood and had abandoned the flowers in a strop. In a shadowy corner of the church she'd stopped to watch a couple of parishioners sitting silently on a pew, awaiting their turn at the confessional. She'd watched the curtained lattice, imagining Father McFadden in his muffled darkness, channeling God's forgiveness and doling out penances to his lowly flock.

And as Nora had stood observing, unable to snap out of her trance, a part of her suddenly became aware of a fissure ripping open in the murky depths of her memory. Something had echoed from below and was now coming to the surface, picking up speed on its way. Nora's fingers found the little crucifix at her neck, and she rubbed at it frantically. She closed her eyes to block out the memory, but it was coming, demanding and defiant. She turned her face to the cool stone of the church wall, but it was here now.

They were back in Dunry, in the hospital, twenty-six years ago. She could clearly remember Margaret slumped in the bed at the end of the dimly-lit ward, the evening rain pelting the window beside her. Margaret had looked drained and haggard after the overdose, her stomach freshly pumped, her wrist freshly tagged, and her body shrouded in that hideous, revealing gown. Nora had raised a cup of orange cordial to her sister's dry lips and had told her that of course she'd go over to the house and spend the night with eleven-year old Breeda. The worse-than-useless father had been back over in London on a building job for the past few weeks, so poor wee Breeda would be alone, no doubt scared witless at finding the house empty after school. Nora would hear not one word of apology from Margaret and had told her that her only concern was to focus on getting some rest. She had gently squeezed her sister's hand, and they'd sat for a moment, silently listening to the rain. When she'd glanced at Margaret, she'd noticed a twist of embarrassment hanging on her face. She felt dreadful for her, but she was keenly aware that she was angry with Margaret too. This was her second attempt. She had a daughter to live for, and a husband – if you could call him that.

As Nora had sat there, she wondered to herself if the rumors about her own brother-in-law were true; that he was an unfaithful bastard, willing to throw his leg over anything with a pulse. The gossip was doing the rounds in Dunry, and no doubt Margaret herself had heard it. Wouldn't that have driven anyone to the pills? Nora would choose her moment, but for now her sister's recovery was her priority. She leaned in and delicately kissed Margaret's cheek, then ran out of the hospital with her collar pulled up, skittering through the rain-slicked streets to the Looney house.

When she'd put the key in the Looney's front door she'd found Breeda looking less than traumatized. The fire was blazing, the TV was blaring, and the girl was happily licking her knife, a plate of beans on toast half-demolished in front of her. Nora stepped in with a look of puzzlement on her face. She shook the raindrops off her jacket and closed the door behind her. Then she realised – Breeda wasn't alone.

He was casually leaning against the kitchen door frame, watching her. His sleeves were rolled up and his shirt was open at the collar. He took a long sip from his tumbler. Over the rim of the glass she recognized the look on his face, the same expression she'd seen reflected back once from a gilt-edged mirror in a Soho pub many years before. Nora reached her fingers to her face and felt the ghost of his stubbled cheek once more.

'Hello, Nora.'

He swirled the dregs of his whiskey. She watched from the door as his glass caught the reflection of the firelight and the ice cubes gave up their tipsy echo. He came towards her.

'Let me take your coat …'

Nora's mobile chirruped loudly in her pocket and her heart jumped. A parishioner spun around on the pew and glared. Nora turned and hurried for the side door. It was just her alarm to remind her to call Myra for their midday chat. She exited into a blast of daylight, and walked quickly, keen to put distance between herself and the church. They needed a good storm. It was a muggy day, too humid for her navy tweed outfit, but she marched on nonetheless, trying to shake a feeling of being watched, of being chased through the streets of Carrickross by insistent memories.

By the time she arrived home she was hot and bothered, and Nora Cullen did not do hot and bothered. The air in the kitchen was lifeless and stale. She jiggled the key of the back door clumsily with her one good hand, and pulled the door wide open, desperate for some fresh air from the garden. As she turned back to the kitchen, she tugged impatiently at the top button of her white blouse. She flicked on the kettle and looked at the timer on the cooker hood – she had a couple of minutes. Myra Finch was a stickler for punctuality and could go into a sour mood if you didn't call when you said you would. Nora plonked the teapot down and slammed the cutlery drawer shut. What she really wanted was to knock back a sleeping pill and lie under a cool sheet. But instead here she was, rushing to make a pot of tea with one good hand. Perhaps her blood sugar was dropping, in which case she'd better have a biscuit. She stood on her tiptoes and rifled through the jars and boxes on the shelf, and suddenly remembered Myra scoffing the last of the Jaffa Cakes the other day upstairs. She reached back further, wincing at the pain in her broken ribs, and swept the herbal teas out of the way. There had to be some emergency biscuits somewhere.

As she peered into the cupboard, a barely perceptible change came to the air, a scent both familiar and forgotten. It pulled at the recesses of her unconscious, like the opening bars of an old song. She stood still for a moment, dazed and distracted. In the background the boiling kettle clicked itself off and the bubbling water settled. Nora blinked herself back into the room.

There wasn't one damn biscuit in the whole house.

The subtlest shifts in daylight moved over the kitchen floor – perhaps some rain was on its way after all. She stepped back and closed the cupboard door.

'Hello, Nora.'

She stumbled back hard into the table. Her favourite teacup slid and shattered behind her.

'Long time, no see.'

He was coming towards her, his knuckles tight, and she knew she could run no longer.

CHAPTER 39

Breeda begged her rusty Renault up the hill, and as she rounded the corner into Bayview Rise and came to a stop on her driveway, she felt her shoulders relax. Killing the engine, her smile froze, then slowly faded. The van was gone.

Above, a movement caught her eye and Breeda leaned forward to see Finbarr on the slope of his tiled roof like a surefooted mountain goat. He had a nail between his teeth and a hammer hanging from his belt. Breeda climbed out of the car and shielded her eyes against the glare.

'Hey Finbarr. I don't suppose you know where my Dad went off to, do you?'

Finbarr scratched the underside of his beard, removed the nail from between his lips and crouched down close to the guttering.

'Sure I always thought your father was long dead, Miss Looney?'

'Yeah, long story …' A momentary silence hung between them and Breeda shifted her weight from one foot to the other, a niggling little disquiet stirring in her belly. 'So, em, Finbarr …?'

'Oh, right, sorry. I'd say he drove off about twenty minutes ago. Not long after you left.'

Breeda looked back over her shoulder towards town.

'You alright? Can I help—'

'It's fine. Ignore me.' She turned back to him with a weak smile. 'I think I'm just tired after the long drive yesterday. Thanks Finbarr. Nothing to worry about.'

Breeda let herself in the front door. Her denim jacket was hanging over the banister where she'd left it, and she reminded herself why she'd come home. She pulled her wallet out of the jacket pocket and turned to leave, but as she did so she caught her reflection in the hallway mirror. A trace of uncertainty had crept into her face and she stood for a moment before turning and climbing the stairs, forcing herself not to rush. She tapped lightly on the bedroom door and pushed it open. The bed was still made – with a military precision she'd admired earlier – and she sat on the taut bedspread and bit her bottom lip.

Mal's mug still stood on the bedside table, drained of its tea. Breeda's gaze drifted over to the wardrobe, its door now closed. She walked slowly over to it and stared at the mahogany door. She knew his bag would still be in there. He'd just have gone to put a bet on the horses, that was all. She put her fingers on the handle.

Downstairs the front door opened. Breeda's fingers jolted back from the wardrobe. He was back. She turned quickly, instantly ashamed at doubting Mal, and headed for the stairs. It was the pointy black leather shoes she saw first – shined to within an inch of their toe-crushing lives. Above them, a skinny pinstriped suit gave way to a familiar over-bleached Hollywood grin. Breeda felt her own smile evaporate.

Johnny Nesbitt, from O'Donoghue's Real Estate, was stood in her front hall like lord of the manor, perusing his clipboard.

'Johnny. I didn't hear you knock.'

'Ah, Breeda…' He gave her the most cursory of glances, before squinting up the hallway. Out of his suit jacket he extracted a mini silver atomizer and sprayed a swift arc of apple-scented mist into the air.

'Cats. Owners get used to the smell. But boy oh boy do they stink!'

Breeda felt her hand tightening on the banister. His smile flashed her way once more.

'First viewing in a few minutes. You might want to …' He walked two fingers across the front of his clipboard, '… skedaddle. Also, that front lawn needs a good trim. You should get that sorted, pronto.'

He turned to fuss with his little wireless speaker he'd placed on the hallway side table and Breeda imagined how nice it would be to smack her hand across the back of his head. But she had more important things to worry about, including this evening's dinner for her guest of honour. Enya's 'Orinoco Flow' filled the hallway and Johnny Nesbitt jabbed at the volume button.

'I'm actually just on my way into town to pick up some groceries. So, I'll get out of your way.'

He was checking himself in the hallway mirror now, and Breeda watched his attempts at smoothing down an errant spike of gelled hair.

'I suppose I'm blocking you in?'

His branded car was straddling the driveway. Breeda regarded her own rust bucket for a moment, but knew that even if she could coax some life into it there would be zero chance of it making it back up the hill later.

'No – you're grand. I'll take my bike. Oh, and Johnny? Lock up when you're done.'

Breeda patted her coat pocket to make sure her wallet was in there, grabbed her bike from the side of the house, and set off up Bayview Rise. Finbarr's dog Pepper hooned up the road alongside her bike until Breeda reached the corner. As she rounded the bend a stiff breeze whipped up her mother's yellow coat into a flap behind her and she could feel the bite of the cold air on her cheeks. Down below on the harbor the kite surfer was long gone, and the waves had taken on a choppiness which hadn't been there earlier. Breeda's dark hair blew loose and wild as she freewheeled down towards the village, and she cast a glance at the bruised sky overhead, wondering if she'd make it home before the rain. She would just pay for the groceries and keep an eye out for his van. Then she could chuck the bike in the back and Mal could drive them both home for a pot of tea. As Breeda rounded the corner onto Main Street she kept her eyes peeled for any sign of the white *Looney & Sons* van.

Across the road from Flynn's supermarket she leaned her bicycle against a bollard and went into the bookies. A few flat screens dotted around the grubby walls were showing the same greyhound race. Two old fellas sat glued to the screens, but Breeda recognized neither of them. The place had a terrible air of desperation and wasted opportunities and she hated to think of Mal in here. Back outside she took in a deep breath and looked up Main Street in both directions. There was no sign of the van. She chewed distractedly at the inside of her left cheek and couldn't help but think of the wardrobe door back in her mother's room which now lay closed.

A rapping noise caught Breeda's attention, and she looked over to The Treasure Chest, where Myra Finch was beckoning like an eejit from the window. Breeda darted across the road between two cars and opened the door into the warmth of the gift shop. Myra had a crabby face on her. Nothing new there, thought Breeda. She bustled Breeda away from the door and flipped the *Closed* sign toward the street.

'Have you seen Nora?'

'No, why?'

Myra shook her head and walked back to the counter. She seemed more highly strung than normal, although it didn't take much to get Myra Finch in a tizzy. Breeda crossed to the counter now too.

'Myra, what's up?'

The old lady looked at her with eyes that brought a little tight knot of dread to Breeda's belly. Myra had picked up her mobile phone from the counter, but now she threw it back down impatiently.

'She's not answering. Every Wednesday, after she does the flowers, she calls me for a chat. At midday. Without fail.' Myra slapped the counter to make her point. 'I'm worried something's happened to her. A blood clot. Or another fall …'

Breeda felt the not-so-subtle dig and saw the harsh judgement flash in Myra's eyes.

'I'm sure it's nothing, Myra. She's probably just taking longer at the church due to her arm.' Breeda heard a flatness in her own voice and wondered at the lack of conviction in her words. She looked out the window. People on the street were pulling on raincoats and zipping up jackets. Across the road a mini whirlwind of crisp packets and lolly wrappers was being whipped into a frenzy.

She knew what Myra was waiting on. She was waiting on Breeda to say of course she'd cycle straight over to the church, and of course she'd check on Nora and report straight back like a good little girl. But Breeda held her tongue and kept her eye on the whirling dervish of litter across the street. Whatever mini drama Nora was caught up in now was of her own making. The apron strings were well and truly cut and Breeda wouldn't be reattaching them. Besides, she had her groceries to sort out next door.

'Tell you what – if I see her I'll text you, OK?'

Myra Finch opened her mouth, but Breeda didn't wait for whatever disappointment was about to leave her lips. She flipped the *Open* sign back towards the street and let herself out. When Breeda reached Flynn's, though, she stood on the far side of the automatic door, suddenly unable to go inside. She needed to think. A damp strand of hair had whipped across her forehead, and as she smoothed it back she tried to ignore the sense of apprehension, now clinging to her like a shadow.

'Twice in one day, Bree?'

The black Range Rover was parked with its hazard lights blinking and Aidan was hefting a bag of compost onto a flattened cardboard box in the back. He wiped his muddy hands down the front of his jeans and slammed the boot shut.

'So, I've been thinking – about this evening – if the invite still stands I'd love to come for dinner. Bree—'

But Breeda was looking beyond him, to a point a kilometer or so up the road, where the proud spire of

Saint Colmcille's pierced the dark and broody sky. The first fat drops of rain landed in splotches at their feet and Aidan popped up his jacket collar.

'Breeda? What's wrong?'

She focused back on Aidan's face and found the familiarity of the Looney eyes – the same eyes as her father's – suddenly jarring.

'It's probably nothing. I'm just being silly …'

He reached a hand to her arm.

'Tell me.'

Beside them the window of the car buzzed down.

'Aidan, we need to go.'

Breeda nodded a distracted smile to Dervil and got the slightest nod of the head in response. At the same moment the skies opened above them. Breeda heard a familiar whooping and turned to see Oona bounding down the pavement with a newspaper over her head.

Aidan grabbed the passenger door and ushered Breeda out of the downpour and into the car, then jumped in the back himself. Breeda slid onto the cushioned leather seat. Beside her, Dervil was checking her watch and drumming her manicured nails on the steering wheel. A few seconds later Oona reached the car, her wet jeans already clinging to her legs. Aidan slid over in the back seat to make room for her.

'Get in for a sec, Oona. It will blow over soon.'

'Thanks a mill, Aidan. Christ, where did that come from? Hi Dervil. Hiya Bree.'

The rain was drumming on the car roof now and Dervil flicked on the wipers. Through the windscreen Breeda could just about make out the spire of Saint Colmcille's against the churning gloom of the sky. She

265

turned to look over her shoulder at her bike, abandoned outside the bookies, and wondered how quickly she could cycle to the church.

'Bree, you OK?' Oona was blowing on her hands.

'Hmmm?'

In the rear-view mirror Oona's blonde hair was dark where it was wet. Breeda noticed the concern on her friend's face, no doubt mirroring her own.

'I was just asking is everything OK?'

Breeda turned to find both Oona and Aidan studying her, and she forced a smile their way. This was silly. It was just her paranoia, desperate to hook onto something and spoil a perfectly good day. She sensed Dervil turn to look at her now too and the color rose in Breeda's cheeks. The last thing she wanted to do was create a scene, and here she was with a captive audience. The car suddenly felt cramped and stifling, and Breeda felt a trickle of moisture – rain or sweat – run down the nape of her neck. Above them, the sky flashed brilliant and seconds later a low grumble rolled overhead. Breeda turned to Dervil.

'I'm sorry to ask, Dervil. But is there any chance you could drop me at Saint Colmcille's? It's on your way if you're heading home…'

Dervil said nothing, but she checked her side mirror and pulled smoothly out onto the road, the option of moving evidently preferable to the alternative of sitting there twiddling her thumbs.

'Thanks, Dervil.'

Breeda could imagine Oona and Aidan nudging each other behind her, but she busied herself with wiping the condensation from the screen of her phone. Nora's mobile rang through to voice mail. Breeda swiped to her home number, but that too went to the answering machine.

She would be at Saint Colmcille's, waiting out the rain. That was all.

Up ahead, a few tourists caught unawares by the downpour, dashed up the pavement, drenched, but laughing. One of them stepped out onto the road and Breeda leaned across and pounded on the horn. Dervil swerved and looked at Aidan in the rear-view mirror.

'Sorry, Dervil. I'm sorry.' Breeda slunk down in her seat and tried to slow her breathing. Oona leaned forward between the front seats.

'Bree, what's happening at Saint Colmcille's?'

'Oh, I'm just checking on Nora. Seeing if she's OK. You know, with her arm and all ...'

Breeda looked straight ahead at the church spire. The bloody thing looked no nearer than a moment ago. Her foot jabbed involuntarily at a phantom accelerator on the floor.

'Poor Nora. She's lucky you're still talking to her, though, after everything.' Oona rubbed her hand on Breeda's upper arm, then sat back.

Breeda made a noncommittal noise. In front of her eyes the wipers swooshed rhythmically, and she now thought of Nora's spare room – the springy mattress, the eerie crucifix above the bed, the sepia toned picture of Saint Brigid on the far wall. And her thoughts turned to what lay behind that picture of Saint Brigid. She remembered the concealed safe with its dark cavity full of bundles of bank notes and a framed seascape rumored to be worth something.

The Range Rover continued its journey up the soaked street towards the church. Breeda shifted in her seat. In the small space between her belly and her chest a slow and steady tugging apart was taking place. She turned her gaze to the drenched street and tried to push down the rising tide of panic. Her thoughts returned to the pub in London, two days before. She remembered sitting with her father in front of the fireplace, and how she'd experienced a sweet sense of release as she'd steadily fed the flames of her own pent-up anger. Her tongue could still taste the whiskey chasers that Mal had insisted on ordering for them both. And she could see them now, father and daughter, staggering back amongst the evening commuters towards Mrs Bennett's yellow front door. And somewhere in her muddy memory, Breeda could remember relishing the act of telling Mal all about the dodgy insurance policy, and Nora's hidden safe with its greedy little hoard of contents.

A crack of lightning flared around them and lit up Saint Colmcille's straight ahead.

'Dervil, turn right!'

Breeda grabbed at the wheel and the car bounced over the lip of the roundabout.

Oona screamed, and Aidan lunged into the space between the front seats.

'What the hell? Derv - pull over!'

'Dervil – please. Drive.'

Breeda glanced at Dervil and saw the shock of fright on her face. But in that split second Dervil also seemed to catch the desperation in the eyes looking back at her. She put her foot down and the tyres ploughed up a cascade of water.

When they rounded the corner a moment later the color drained from Breeda's face.

Outside Nora's house sat a familiar white van.

CHAPTER 40

Breeda stood on the top step and pushed her shoulder against the solid black of the front door. It didn't budge. Near the Range Rover, under a large golf umbrella, Aidan and Oona watched on. Breeda cast a glance at the white van, rain bouncing in bright sparks off its roof, then turned back to the front door and crouched down. Her wet hair lay plastered to her skull and she swept it back from the side of her head as she pressed her right ear tight to the letterbox.

Against the noise of the storm, from somewhere inside the house, came Nora's voice, muffled yet defiant.

'–got what you came for. Now get the hell out and don't ever come back here.'

A thunder of footsteps cascaded down the stairs. Breeda straightened up and took a step back.

'Shut up or I'll break the other one.'

The front door swung open. Mal Looney's face came to an abrupt stop inches from Breeda's. Behind him, in the hallway, Nora stood breathless and unkempt, holding the cast on her broken arm. Spotting Breeda, her face faltered briefly, then found a tight smile.

'Breeda!'

Breeda turned her attention back to her father. His eyes had softened, but a cool wariness now claimed his face. His backpack hung over one shoulder.

'Dad? What's going on? What are you doing here?'

A staccato of thunder cracked overhead. Breeda looked from her father, to her aunt, then back to him. His eyes seemed to have noticed her familiar yellow coat, and for a moment he stood entranced, lost in some old private memories. She lifted her hand towards his shoulder, but it stopped, suspended, unable to traverse the final few inches of air.

'Dad?'

He looked back at her face now but held his tongue.

'Your father and I were just having a quick catch-up. Weren't we, Mal?' Nora's voice was strained with a cheery chumminess, and when Breeda looked at her aunt she could see her rubbing at the little crucifix at her neck. The two top buttons of her blouse were undone. Her eyes were red and puffy.

Mal Looney cleared his throat and shuffled the backpack on his shoulder.

'Listen sweetheart, I'm sorry, but I just got a phone call. I need to get back to London.'

'But you just got here?'

'Yeah, I know. But it's Mrs B. She's had a fall.'

Mal looked over Breeda's shoulder and noticed the couple sheltering under the umbrella. Now Nora spotted them too.

'Breeda, let your father run along, and come inside for a nice cuppa. You're soaked through. Come on …'

Nora wafted her good hand towards Breeda, beckoning her in out of the rain and away from prying eyes. But Breeda didn't move. She closed her eyes and waited for it all to settle. It could all still be fine. They were telling her the truth, weren't they? Mal had just

271

popped over to see his long-lost sister-in-law and had just received an urgent phone call from London.

Breeda kept her eyes closed, then surprised herself, as the words came, slow and clear.

'Dad, what's in the backpack?'

She opened her eyes now. He was looking out beyond her, shifting on his heels, readying to leave.

'Listen, Love. I'll call you in a few days. Maybe arrange another visit, yeah?'

He had started down the steps now, and as Breeda turned she noticed the opening at the top of his backpack. A familiar edge was jutting out. She grabbed it firmly, and as he descended the middle step she pulled sharply upward. He spun quickly, but she had it aloft, her mother's painting, half-stuffed in one of Nora's old pillowcases.

He sprang up the steps and made a grab for it, but Breeda held it back behind her and kept him away with her other hand.

'Dad, what the hell?'

'That's mine! Give it to me, Breeda. Give it to me now.'

He had squared up to her with clenched fists, a determined fire in his eyes. Over his shoulder Aidan bolted up the path, closely followed by Oona.

Now Nora tugged at Breeda's sleeve, half-pleading, half-screaming.

'Just give it to him and he'll go. Please, Breeda. Good girl.'

'Dad, please tell me this isn't the real reason you came back ...'

He straightened up now.

272

'No sweetheart, I wanted to see you, honest.' He shot a withering look back at Nora. 'I'm only taking what I'm owed. And God knows this one has made enough money out of me, haven't you?'

Breeda glanced back at Nora and had to drop her gaze to the floor.

'I'm so sorry, Aunt Nora. This isn't what I wanted.' Breeda closed her eyes and whispered to herself, 'God, what have I done?'

She forced herself to look back at her aunt. Nora was attempting a forgiving smile, her eyes brimming with fresh tears as she clung to the banister with her one good hand. Breeda had never seen her look so wretched.

'No harm done, Breeda. It's fine. Let him go and you come in and get dry.'

Breeda shook her head, confused at Nora's lack of protest.

'No, it's not fine, Nora. It's anything but *fine*. Stupid, naive, clumsy Breeda. I just wanted … I just wanted answers. I wanted the truth and I had no one to give it to me.' At this she gave Nora a pointed look, then turned back to face Mal. 'And now …' She looked at the painting in her hands, saw him eyeing it, preparing to pounce '… And now I've got the truth right in front of my own eyes …'

Mal folded his arms across his chest, then winked towards Nora. 'Oh, I dare say you've got most of the truth, my girl. But I reckon old Nora could fill in a few gaps.'

Breeda frowned at her father. She placed the painting down carefully inside the front door, far enough from his reach, and waited for him to elaborate. Behind her

Breeda could hear Nora's breathing coming in short, sharp little gasps. She had turned her head away from them and was clinging with her failing strength to the banister.

'Nora, what does he mean?'

Mal sneered from the top step.

'Go on, Nora. Tell my girl the real reason you wanted me gone from Dunry. Tell my darlin' daughter why you made me disappear from her life …'

Nora was keening now, and Breeda watched on helplessly as the eerie sound echoed up the walls. She was suddenly terrified of where this was going. From outside came the sound of gravel crunching underfoot. Breeda and Mal turned. Oona and Aidan still stood under their umbrella, but now Myra Finch was scurrying up the path in a yellow plastic poncho, a face on her like a boiled beetroot. She went to push past the stranger on the doorstep, then stopped short when she saw the state of Nora. Her hand came to her mouth and she turned silently, her eyes searching theirs for explanation.

Mal seemed only too happy to have a larger audience.

'Shall I tell her for you, Nora? Well, Breeda, turns out there wasn't just one person in the family who disregarded the sanctity of marriage. Ain't that right, Nora?'

He had walked into the hallway now, his wet boots leaving brown smears across the black and white tiled floor. With his every approaching footstep, it was as if Nora's body was folding further in on itself. By the time he spoke again, she had shrunken into a curled-up ball at his feet.

'See, Nora paid us a visit one evening when your poor mother – God rest her soul – was in hospital getting her stomach pumped …'

Breeda could make out an urgent stream of whispers coming from the shape on the floor.

'Please stop. Please stop. Please make him stop.'

Breeda wanted to go to Nora. Her hand reached out, a desperate need to soothe her. But her feet were rooted to the floor, and she stood frozen, waiting. Whatever was coming, however painful, she had to know.

Mal continued. 'After you went up to bed that evening, Breeda, your aunt took another whiskey – to warm her up from getting caught in the rain – and before you know it, well, let's just say it's the devout ones that make the most noise.'

Beyond the front door the rain seemed to have suddenly stopped. Breeda reached a hand to the wall, the tiles below her feet stretching and warping in her vision. An image spasmed into Breeda's mind, a patchy memory of looking up from the telly to see Auntie Nora scuttling in from the dark street and shaking raindrops off her jacket. The memory had been a happy one. Breeda's Dad had come back early from London that day and as he'd entered the living room Breeda had remembered the lovely sound of the ice cubes clinking in his favourite tumbler.

'Stop lying, Dad. Just stop it!'

Nora's body was shaking on the floor, and now Breeda did rush to her side. She knelt on the tiles and gently smoothed the waves of grey hair, trying to ignore the faint flare of deja vu. From his standing point above them Mal's voice continued.

'After that she wanted me gone cos she couldn't bear to look at my face. Every time she saw me she was reminded of what she'd done.' Mal started to clear his throat and for a dreadful second Breeda expected a gob of spit to land on Nora. 'Not so holier than thou, after all, are you Nora Cullen?'

Breeda bent closer to her aunt.

'It's OK, Aunt Nora. He's a liar. Just breathe.'

But beneath Breeda's fingertips, Nora's face had turned slightly towards the tiled floor. Breeda's hand froze.

'Aunt Nora—' Breeda's heart pounded and her words came raspy. 'Aunt Nora ... is he telling the truth?'

Nora's wrinkles deepened as she squeezed her eyes shut. Breeda watched and witnessed a single tight nod. She pulled her hand back from the grey curls, the touch now too intimate. But she forced herself to lean in, and lowered her voice.

'Did he force himself on you? Aunt Nora, did he rape you?'

The words felt odd, coming from niece to aunt, and Breeda watched as something seemed to break within the woman on the floor, something deep and brittle and irreparable. A tiny patch of pale papery skin above the old woman's clavicle was pulsing wildly. Nora turned her head with effort, and the little rheumy blue-grey eyes cracked open and found Breeda's. Her words were almost spent before leaving her lips, the saddest whisper barely able to take flight.

'He didn't force me.'

The eyes closed again, the shame too much, and as hot tears escaped, Breeda watched a small series of tremors pass in waves through Nora's body, a valve released, a secret well tapped at last.

Breeda put her hand to Nora's hair once more and tried to quieten the hurried stream of apologies she gasped. She understood it all so clearly now: Nora's constant need for control and order, her church work and her tweed suits, her compulsion to be seen as a pillar of the community and her months of self-exile behind the high walls of the Dunry convent. It was all an ongoing attempt to put distance between that foolish woman from one night many years ago and this unblemished stoic version today. All of Nora's deceit and manipulation – burning the birthday card, faking the heart attack, putting the house on the market – all of it was powered by an abject terror that this day, this moment, might come into existence. The whole stinking lot of it had been driven by shame and guilt, and Breeda had been dragged along for the ride.

Breeda rose to her feet and turned towards the front door. Mal had stepped back to get a proper view of the scene unfolding before him. A vengeful smile flitted briefly across his face, and Breeda felt a twitch come to her fists. In her head a roaring noise had started up and she inwardly cursed it. She didn't want the blackness now. She needed to be present, to witness this scene through to its messy conclusion. She watched Mal's expression change, the smirk replaced by a look of unease. Myra had turned. And now Oona and Aidan were staring into the hallway. They stood watching her, and she realised the noise wasn't just in her head. It was coming up and out – primal and urgent – and now it carried her forward. Her hands smashed against his chest and face, and she battered and flailed and punched. Her eyes blurred – her own tears here now – and she watched his hands rise to protect his face. She thrashed and pushed and drove him backwards. And as he missed the top step and stumbled backward, she caught in his face a glimpse of surprise – something vital and candid – a flash of his younger self. He hit the ground in a messy backward sprawl, startled, impressed. Breeda watched him from the top step, her shoulders heaving, and raised a shaking hand to wipe her mouth.

Behind Mal on the wet gravel the backpack had given up its contents. Three thick rolls of fifty Euro notes had tumbled onto the path behind him and he remained blissfully unaware. Breeda readied herself to feel another sting of disappointment. But none came. He had used up all his credit and nothing he could do now could disappoint her further.

In the background Myra Finch was fussing over Nora on the floor. Aidan and Oona had moved to stand either side of Breeda. With their umbrella down Mal could see their faces for the first time. It took him a moment, and Breeda found herself savoring the etch of confusion on his face, as he clambered awkwardly to his feet for a closer look.

'Well, I'll be … You must be Adam.'

Mal's right hand, wet and grazed from the gravel, extended up towards his son as he reached the first step.

'It's Aidan.'

Aidan looked out beyond his father, his hand resolutely by his side. Breeda saw the apple rise and fall in his throat, and knew this moment would never be repeated; father, son, daughter, same place, same time.

Mal's hand hovered for an awkward moment, as he sized up the situation: Malachy Looney had no friends here. The same hand made a sudden move to reach in behind Breeda's ankles. She watched as it grabbed the painting.

'I'll just take what's rightfully mine.'

In one smooth motion Aidan's hand swung up and grabbed his father's throat. The painting toppled back to its resting place as Aidan lifted him up and launched him back down the steps. Mal was prepared this time, his feet keeping him upright, but when he came to a stop he noticed the banknotes on the path. He looked towards Aidan, then Breeda, a flash of embarrassment in his eyes, before he stooped and stuffed the rolls back into the backpack. He zipped it up and stood, then looked over his shoulder at the white van.

This is it, Breeda thought. Two weeks of crazy had led to this moment, and now here it was, approaching the dysfunctional finish line. Breeda felt Oona's arm link around hers. At the same time Aidan's arm rested on her shoulder. The three of them looked out, Breeda in the middle, ready now.

'You know what, Dad? Less than two weeks ago I thought you'd died when I was a girl. And finding that birthday card turned my world upside down. I fought to find you. I lost my home. I risked my sanity ...'

Oona's free hand rubbed at Breeda's forearm.

'I'd have gone to the edges of the earth for you—' She heard the crack in her voice and knew more tears weren't far off. 'I really would. And the thing I wanted more than anything in the world was for you to be alive, and to make things right between us. But this mess...'

Breeda glanced at Nora, then turned back to her father. '… this mess was never mine to fix in the first place.'

He was watching her, the rain soft in the atmosphere around him, a distant shaft of oystery light stark against the murky sky. The fight seemed to leave his body as Breeda's words seeped in. He suddenly looked miserable, standing in the drizzle, clothes soaked and backpack hanging, an abandoned boy on his first day at boarding school. Behind him, from the Range Rover, Dervil emerged. She closed the driver's door quietly and observed the scene from the pavement.

Mal jostled the backpack on his shoulder and rubbed the wetness from the back of his scalp.

'Well, it's been nice to see you, my girl. But I shouldn't have come. There's nothing for me here.'

Breeda bit her lip and nodded slowly, his words hitting their target perfectly. It did sting, after all. Mal suddenly seemed aware of the other people watching the drama unfold from the front hall, and he now looked impatient, his departure overdue.

'Just be careful not to turn out to be a looper, like your mother.' He raised his voice — a posturing fighter with one more round in him — then looked beyond Breeda into the shadows of the hallway, 'Or a whore, like your aunt!'

He turned his back on them, satisfied with his parting quip, and sauntered towards his van. As he reached the gate he noticed the blonde with the tight ponytail staring at him from the pavement. Through the soft rain Breeda could see a look of puzzlement hanging on his face as he drew closer to the stranger. He was struggling to recognize her, and she continued to stare boldly at him, as if daring him to look away. And as he got closer to her she said something. Breeda watched Dervil's lips move and a moment later saw Mal drop his gaze to the ground. He tugged his ear, then turned for his white van, and as he slammed his door shut Dervil walked up the path and stood with the others on the top step. She said nothing and stared determinedly ahead.

In the background, Myra had managed to get Nora onto her feet. The two women were now back in the kitchen and Breeda could hear Nora blubbering at the table as a bewildered Myra attempted to console her. Myra was calling for the others to come in out of the cold for tea, and Dervil, then Oona, headed back towards the kitchen.

Breeda and Aidan remained at the front door, looking out through the soft rain at the white van. The engine turned and a cough of black smoke belched from the exhaust. Breeda watched as her father's side profile seemed to consider something before he turned and looked at her one last time. Through the falling rain she could see something on his face now — regret or sorrow, she couldn't tell. Mal Looney held his daughter's eye and as his lips moved silently she wondered if he was praying to whatever God he believed in. Breeda watched as he brought his hand slowly to his mouth. And as he tossed the imaginary apple towards her she felt a searing ache echo in the depths of her heart as the years fell away and a million memories rushed to the surface. She buried her face in the warmth of Aidan's shoulder, the sad sight of her father suddenly too much. The engine revved and the tyres screeched and Breeda looked up just as the *Looney & Sons* van sped off around the corner and took Malachy Looney out of her life.

Aidan leaned in closer towards her and they stood quietly for a moment, side by side. Breeda closed her eyes and strained to hear the dying sound of the van's engine in the distance. But it was gone, swallowed by the wind and the rain. She pulled closer on Aidan's arm, freshly aware that out of the whole shambles at least one great thing had come into her life.

Myra's voice called out from the kitchen once more, and Aidan cleared his throat.

'Come on. We should go in. You're soaked through.'

He moved off but turned when Breeda didn't follow.

'What's up? Don't you fancy a restorative cup of tea? We can sit around the table and Oona can give us all post-traumatic stress therapy.'

Breeda smiled and shook her head. 'You go ahead, Aidan. I'll be there in a sec.'

She stood alone in the hallway and looked up from the painted seascape leaning against the wall. From the kitchen came the trace of their voices, attempting to make sense of what had just happened. She should go into them, she knew, try and calm them, and check on Nora. But still she stood there, hesitating. Breeda swept her damp hair back from her face and buttoned up her mother's yellow coat. Overhead the sky rumbled again, and she stepped outside onto Nora's front path. She tilted her face to the heavy curtain of rain, and let it wash over her. She would see this storm through.

CHAPTER 41

The day after Mal Looney drove out of Breeda's life she received a phone call from Oona.

'Bree, do you have a rucksack?'

'What?'

'And a good pair of walking boots.'

'Oona, what are you on about?'

There was a brief pause down the line.

'Bree, you need to get away for a while. I've spoken to Mister Sheridan. I've rescheduled my clients. It's all organized. You can't say no.'

'What? No.'

'And you'll need insect repellent too. Get packing.'

And so, the following Monday morning, Breeda and Oona landed in Spain in virgin walking boots to start a three-week trek along the Camino de Santiago.

Breeda found herself savoring the fresh air and the wide skies, welcoming the satisfying ache in her body each night which would bring instant sleep under a thin cotton sheet. Some days there were long stretches along wooded pathways and rural roads, when the two friends would amble in solitude for hours on end. And sometimes, in those quiet moments, Breeda's thoughts would turn to Mal Looney.

Breeda knew it would be too easy to lay the blame for the whole sorry episode at her father's feet. After all, the Nora Cullens and the Mona Sneddons of the world had played their parts too. But the sins of the father were now out in the open – something to be aware of as they sniffed around the periphery of her life – and they would be a burden that Breeda Looney would carry no longer.

One morning, as the path climbed gradually out of a verdant dell near a farmstead, Breeda decided to open up to Oona about the true extent of the blackness. Oona was shocked, and unable to hide her hurt at being kept in the dark. But she listened and helped Breeda begin the slow process of unpacking it all.

'You're like a coke bottle.' Oona had stopped to peel a hard-boiled egg, as Breeda wrestled a pebble out of her walking boot.

'Come again?'

'A coke bottle. Years of bumps and being shook up and you were never taught how to express your emotional needs. No wonder you sometimes feel like it's all too much, you know, that sense of overwhelm.'

Breeda flicked the stone away and applied some sunscreen to her nose. She knew not to interrupt Oona in mid flow.

'Therapy would be like a slow untwisting of the cap, a gentle release, not a messy explosion.'

Oona knew a woman – someone she'd been on a course with once – who was said to work wonders with anxiety disorders. She would give Breeda her details, but it would be up to Breeda to make contact. The thought of opening up to a stranger scared Breeda senseless, but she had to admit the time had come. It was time to release the handbrake on her life. Breeda made a promise to herself that she'd make her first appointment as soon as she got home.

And it wasn't long after she arrived back from Spain that Breeda spotted Aunt Nora in the village. Nora had blanched at the sight of her niece, turning on her heel and scuttering down a cobbled laneway into Madigan's cafe. So it came as a surprise, two weeks later, when a message from Nora flashed up on Breeda's phone. She invited Breeda to dinner in town one Thursday evening in the middle of July. It was a clunky dinner, the conversation stilted, with all-things-Malachy-Looney given a wide berth for now. As they'd perused their menus, Breeda discreetly raised her gaze for a moment and watched her aunt's expression of concentration, seeing faint flashes of her own mother sitting at her easel. Breeda could see the beginnings of a subtle transformation in her aunt: the crucifix still hung at her neck, but the buttoned-up tweed two-piece had been replaced with a blouse and cardigan and comfortable slacks. And it occurred to Breeda that the woman across from her might have finally begun to relax into her life a little, had maybe started to leave her shame behind.

Outside the restaurant, as the two women stood awkwardly, Nora looked off up Main Street.

'I've spoken to a solicitor.'

'Oh. OK …'

'About the house.'

'Right …' Breeda wondered where this was going.

'I still need to work out the tax implications for the transfer of deeds. But it's what your mother would have wanted.'

'Sorry, Aunt Nora. You've lost me.'

Nora turned to Breeda now, the old familiar flash of impatience quick to her face.

'Bayview Rise. It's yours.' Nora looked up the street again, her eyes darting to points in the distance, as she struggled with whatever she really wanted to say.

Breeda looked to the pavement. That house had been her home for twenty-five years. But deep down she couldn't shake the feeling that it was tainted goods now, financed by a falsified life insurance claim.

'Aunt Nora, I'm not—'

But Nora had turned to look at her now, a pained plea in her eyes.

'I've made a mess of things. We can both agree that much. I'm not saying this will make things right. But it's a start ...'

A lump came to Breeda's throat, and she too looked off up Main Street.

'OK, Aunt Nora. Let me think—'

But Nora had turned, already walking briskly in the direction of home. Breeda sighed, and set off slowly in the opposite direction, wondering what sort of relationship herself and her aunt might cobble together in the future. But as she walked further along the coast road, concerns about Nora fell away, and Breeda became aware of an insistent pull in her step, a quickening in her veins. She tried to hush the thoughts swirling in her head as they competed to be heard. She'd sleep on it, she told herself, try and temper the giddiness that was roiling inside her belly. But no sleep was to be found that night. About three a.m. she sat up in bed with a notepad and pencil. Breeda knew what she wanted to do and for once she wasn't going to stand in her own way.

With the remains of her savings Breeda started the transformation of the house. Dougie and Aidan were eager to lend their skills for free, and Finbarr joined in too, having finally finished the tinkering on his own roof. Over the course of two and a half weeks, work carried on until well after sunset. Bathrooms were reconfigured, walls were freshly painted, the kitchen was renovated, and additional lighting, signage and smoke alarms were installed. Breeda found a steely focus she never knew she possessed. She sought permits, uploaded a web page and placed her first ads. And on the fourteenth of August Breeda picked up the phone and accepted her first booking for a three-night stay at her modest guest house.

Ard na Mara — the Hill by the Sea — was open for business.

On the evening before her first guests were due, Breeda sat with Finbarr on his backstep, a daily ritual they'd fallen into over the past few weeks. They drank tea as they watched the shadows of the old stone walls slowly stretch across the patchwork fields down below. Pepper's face rested on Finbarr's thigh, Ginger had draped herself across Breeda's lap, and the companionable silence surrounding them was broken only by the cat's resonant purring. Down on the bay, the early evening sunlight glinted on the waves, and Breeda's eyes came to rest on the stone pier and the tied-up trawlers. It was all exactly the same, yet all so different. And Breeda realised that the elusive other version of her life – the one where she would feel content and complete – might just have been hiding here all along, waiting patiently for her to unearth it.

Later, after bidding Finbarr goodnight, Breeda stood quietly in the kitchen doorway. Six dining chairs which she'd sanded and painted, now sat expectantly around the long gnarly table, awaiting her first guests. Breeda nodded to no one in particular, flicked off the lights, then headed along the hallway with Ginger padding alongside her. As she turned for her bedroom, she noticed something outside, leaning against the frosted glass of the front door. It was a parcel, rectangular in shape, and neatly wrapped in brown paper and twine. Breeda looked up the driveway and beyond, but there was not a soul to be seen. The parcel had just a simple gift tag attached, one word in precise birdlike handwriting.

Breeda

Standing by her bedroom window, she carefully unwrapped it, letting the paper fall to her bare feet. She sat on the edge of her bed in the fading evening light and gazed at the painting in her hands. The familiar swimmer regarded her from his choppy Atlantic seascape. But this time, as her eyes settled on his face, Breeda noticed something for the first time: he wasn't looking at her, but at a point beyond, at something in the distance behind her.

And in that moment Breeda was no longer simply an observer.

She was with him in the sea.

She was the rise and the fall.

ACKNOWLEDGEMENTS

I would like to thank my editor, Bernadette Kearns, for holding my hand as I killed multiple darlings. A huge thank you also goes to Emma Finn, for providing invaluable feedback and sharing her considerable publishing nous.

My tireless team of 'beta readers' – Sally Harding, Deborah Wiseman, Deirdre Conway, Fiona McGrath, Ashley Casey, Elaine Fitzpatrick – your feedback was priceless and you're all amazeballs.

To the teachers and writing crew at The Writers' Studio in Bronte for providing guidance, imparting wisdom, and instilling the 'daily discipline' mantra. I got there in the end…

To Ged, for his unwavering support, and for making room on the path for me. You're the best and I love you!

To my family for their genuine interest, curiosity, support and faith. Thank you – it doesn't go unnoticed.

To the amazing independent writers and publishers out there who constantly strive to improve, challenge, learn and share. A rising tide lifts all boats, and I'm honored to be sailing alongside y'all. I'd particularly like to acknowledge Jane Friedman, Dave Gaughran, Michael Anderle, Craig Martelle, Kristen Lamb, Derek Murphy, Dave Chesson, Joanna Penn and Orna Ross (and the team at the Alliance of Independent Authors). I couldn't do it without your emails, FB groups, cheat-sheets, Q&As and knowledge sharing.

And finally, my heartfelt thanks to you, Dear Reader. Writing a book can often feel like walking a lonely road peppered with self-doubt and procrastination, so to know you've taken the time to read this story makes it all worthwhile. Thank you.

BONUS CHAPTERS AND A SHORT STORY

If you'd like a little more 'Breeda', sign up to the author's mailing list and you'll receive:

- A **free** and **exclusive** short story featuring Breeda Looney in her first fictional outing (not available anywhere else).
- **Bonus chapters** which didn't make the final cut of the novel.
- Updates on future books – you'll be the first to know about **new releases.**

Simply visit this hidden webpage:

https://oliversandsauthor.com/breedas-readers/

or zap the below QR code with your smartphone.

No spam ever. And you can unsubscribe at any time.

Printed in Great Britain
by Amazon

75694380R00177